KATE BACKFORD

THE
BLACKMAIL
ENIGMA

A NOVEL

The cataloging-in-publication data is on file with the Library of
Congress.

ISBN 9798798241194 Paperback
ISBN 9780578305295 eBook

The readers think The Blackmail Enigma is

A FABULOUS TALE IN A GLORIOUS SETTING!

"Wow, wow... So many twists and turns... What a story! I absolutely loved it! Had me second guessing every step of the way... The ending reveals a shocking event, you would never have suspected."

"What a treat! I highly recommend."

"I love the way the author weaves the different story lines together in a seamless manner and gathers them neatly in the end to solve the mystery, bit by bit."

"The dynamics of the storytelling makes one think... where is time gone by. The reader just flows through the book...At the end there is a logical, stylistic room, a window for continuation of the novel. It is also a great material for scenarios."

"In the world of 'entertaining' literature, the Mystery/Intrigue usually do not make the reader to experience that 'aftertaste,' that unenforced need and desire to think, digest of what was read... But not in the novel I just read... Bravo, Ms. Kate Backford!"

"A thoroughly enjoyable read with lots of suspense... The author beautifully describes places, sceneries, people and food ... which gives the reader an insight into the culture. A book you just don't want to put down!"

"I felt like I was immersed in the events' place and time, was spending time together with the book's characters, observed and participated in actions; looking forward for another novel from Kate Backford!"

Contents

CONTENTS

CONTENTS

Acknowledgements

First, I must thank my advance readers for their advice. They were an outstanding sounding board. In this regard, I want to acknowledge Lord Borwick, Samantha Carroll, Chamesou Toure, and Kenneth Shaw, who read the manuscript in its nascent form and provided extremely valuable input. I want to especially thank the acclaimed author Michael Dobbs for reading the manuscript and awarding me his encouraging words. I also want to thank Lord Borwick, from the House of Lords, for all the emails he answered relating to the UK Parliament. For four years, I was fortunate to live in Senegal, which helped me paint scenery essential to the African part of the book. I am grateful to one of my ancestors, who left me her 19th century diary on which I base some of the events in the novel. My editor, Bill Greenleaf, provided me with his excellent feedback, and helped me understand and address some of the issues I overlooked in the early manuscript. An enormous thanks to my husband, who cheered me on throughout this project. I could not have written *The Blackmail Enigma* without him. To everyone who contributed: Thank you!

Kate Backford

"And how shall you punish those whose remorse is already greater than their misdeeds?"

The Prophet: On Crime and Punishment

Khalil Gibran

Day 1

CHAPTER 1

The tall, gangly gentleman climbed into his black Bentley, smiling at his chauffeur, and settled in the plush seat. He was happy his business interests permitted him privileges such as this car. He leaned forward.

"Henry."

"Yes, My Lord," said Henry.

Henry's eyes were glued to the road. It wasn't a long drive to Westminster, but traffic was always a challenge. He was proud, driving this stately car and never forgot what he felt when he first saw it: Love at first sight.

"Did you see the article in The Times about my son?"

"No, My Lord."

At a red light, Henry said, "Lord Tensbury, you must be mighty proud of your son."

"Yes, I am, Henry. If Conservatives form the government, he would be the youngest prime minister in over two hundred years."

Tensbury had silver-grey hair with a high forehead, and he looked to be in his late 60's. Soft wrinkles around his mouth signified a cheerful nature. He considered himself a mindful and astute statesman. Sitting in the House of Lords for 12 years, ever since his dad died, had given him a keen sense of the political engine of the UK government. As a hereditary Lord his title could be traced back to the 19th century, and he took pride in that.

He pulled out his phone and opened the BBC app. The front page was about the election and talked about the Tory Platform. Further down, there was an article about his son Andrew's speech from yesterday.

His eyes scanned the page further. He found a quote from his son.

> *There is something I want to dispel right here and now. The newspapers write about what they call my 'aristocratic background.' They assume that this makes me somehow out of touch with the ordinary people of our country.*

> *I'm the youngest son of Lord Tensbury. My older brother, Samuel, will inherit the title, not I. I studied engineering and later worked in a solicitor's firm. My origins are similar to yours – those of a man who works hard at what he does and aspires to serve this nation at all times. If elected, I'll dedicate my every waking hour to fulfilling my responsibilities.*

> *I'm proud of my heritage. My ancestor, Alistair Tensbury, came from humble beginnings. He entered the military as a commissioned officer, and in 1839, distinguished himself during the First Afghan War. In the battle of Ghazni, he took command of his unit after his commanding officer fell. He held back the enemy until reinforcements arrived. He went on to fight many battles during ten distinguished years in the military.*

> *Later, his father-in-law left him some small investments in Africa, where he expanded the business. He built a thriving ship repair company*

in South Africa. He also became one of the largest exporters of Gum Arabic and other commodities from Senegal to Britain. As a result of his heroic exploits and business contributions, he was recommended for peerage, and Queen Victoria made him a Baron. Since that time, that title has been in my family.

"You know Henry, I never thought Andrew would end up in politics," said Tensbury, pride dripping off every syllable of his words. "Always good at math and sciences, that boy. I remember, when he was little, he tried to build a functioning helicopter using an erector set. Did you ever play with erector sets when you were a child, Henry?" He didn't wait for an answer. "I still do sometimes, I must confess. At home, I have a desk filled with empire state buildings, a couple of British castles, and even Westminster." He chuckled to himself. "But don't tell anyone."

"My lips are sealed, My Lord. And your older son. How is he doing?"

"Oh, Samuel? He's teaching law at Oxford and making babies. Can you understand how anyone would have three kids and still one on the way?"

Henry didn't answer.

They lumbered through the rush hour traffic, and finally, the car stopped. Henry got out and opened the door.

Tensbury rented space in a building on Cowley Street, which he had converted into an office. It suited him well because of its proximity to Westminster. Lords were assigned a desk in Westminster and received a pittance of public funds to employ a researcher or someone for administrative tasks. As a result, many of them, with their business interests, rented offices near the House and paid their own expenses. He had a flat on Maunsel St., not far from his office, so he could spend his working week in London and his weekends with his wife in his Kent ancestorial home.

Tensbury entered the anteroom where his office

administrator worked. It was sophisticated yet somewhat modern. His staff was always early, and he could hear voices emanating from the offices down the hallway.

The door to his research assistant, Jack Fernsby, was closed. A fresh tea aroma seeped out from the small eating area off the anteroom.

"Good morning, Sir," said his extremely efficient office administrator, who had worked here with him for a long time. "There's an envelope waiting for you in your office. A courier from a new service brought it."

"Good morning, Susie," said Tensbury cheerfully. Reading about his son's interview and the conversation with Henry had buoyed his spirits even higher than his usual upbeat nature.

"And how was your event last night?" a fresh cup of tea in Tensbury's hand, happily teasing her a bit. She was single, and he and the office knew she had attended the opera last night with a new beau. Miss Reed's series of gentlemen friends was legendary and a point of amusement in the office.

"Not my type," answered Miss Reed, blushing.

It was always the same answer, and they had stopped keeping count of her soirees.

One of the business development managers, Chuck, was standing beside her desk, having a cup of tea, listening to the exchange. Chuck and Tensbury gave each other a friendly look.

"Good morning, My Lord," said Chuck. "If your schedule permits, I would like us to take a look at that deal we are working on a little later today."

"Right. Let's do that."

"This morning I have an appointment with another potential client. I'm taking Oliver with me. He's good with numbers."

"So, a new potential client? Sounds promising. You'll tell me about it when we meet."

Tensbury tapped on Jack Fernsby's door and stepped in.

Jack was as much a trusted advisor as he was a parliamentary research assistant. For eight years, time and time again, Jack had proven himself essential with his quick wit and razor-sharp mind.

Jack met Lord Tensbury when Tensbury was visiting soldiers at Queen Elizabeth Hospital in Birmingham. Jack heard that Tensbury was a navy man and had seen some action in the Falklands conflict. For some reason, Jack and Tensbury had struck a bond.

"Soldier, what happened to you?" Tensbury asked, proffering his hand to the reclining dark-haired man with an angular face and somewhat blazing yellow-green eyes, laying on pillows with his leg in bandages.

"My Lord, I'm honored to meet you." Everyone knew Lord Tensbury would be visiting the ward this morning. "I took a bullet during a mission in Afghanistan and ended up with enough torn tendons and muscle that I'll probably never walk without a limp again."

"I'm sorry to hear that. Thank you for your service to our country. What will you do when you get better?"

"I've been pondering that, Sir. I can't return to SAS, so I'll have to use my other skills. I have a law degree, so I'll have to join a law firm." Jack tried to sit up taller in the bed.

Tensbury motioned to Jack and said, "don't sit up, I will sit down," and he sat on the chair at Jack's bed.

"I know that's an unlikely background for someone like me, Sir."

"It's a very interesting background. Know what, give me a call once you're released." Lord Tensbury handed Jack his card, "We will chat about it." The rest was history.

"Good morning, Jack," said Tensbury.

Jack had two large computer screens on his desk and was typing feverishly.

"Are you working on the coal bill?"

Jack turned from his computer screens. "Good morning, My Lord, I started on it, but I'm still finishing off the environmental control bill, which of course, links to the coal one."

"Let's take a look at what you have later this afternoon. I have a meeting with Chuck, but we'll fit it in."

With that, Tensbury carefully closed Jack's door.

Tensbury hated disturbing him. He knew Jack always kept his door closed when he worked. Casually dressed, contrary to others in the office, who always wore business clothes, he walked around in khakis and button-down shirts. He was conscientious and exacting, always addressing every little detail.

That's what impressed Tensbury the most when he first started working with Jack. Tensbury assigned him more and more responsibilities focused on House of Lords issues. This gave Tensbury added time to concentrate on his company, Arrowstood. It was a challenge keeping the parliamentary commitments on track while also running his business. Luckily, he had good business development people to support him.

A large mahogany desk dominated Tensbury's office. Behind it stood his comfortable, forest green, leather chair, armrests somewhat worn from the pressure of his long arms. His wife thought it was time to change the chair, but it had become part of him. Tall windows afforded ample light, even during dreary London spring mornings like today. He had had this office for over ten years, and he felt very comfortable there. It was large enough, and a group of his staff could congregate for an impromptu meeting around the small table in the corner. The company used the conference room mainly when they had clients over. He liked to keep his door open so his staff could easily join him when they needed to.

After entering his office, hanging up his coat, and putting his briefcase by his desk, he sat down and opened the envelope brought by the courier.

He pulled out the short note – his face blanched. He read the note again, put his elbows on his desk, head in his hands, and exhaled. Any previous enchantment expired.

"Jack, please come here," he said, after dialing Jack's extension.

Jack entered and closed the door.

Tensbury looked up and said, "I'm being blackmailed. I mean, blackmailed, without actually being blackmailed."

CHAPTER 2

Tensbury handed Jack the note. "A courier delivered it this morning."

Jack read it. Then, he read it one more time.

Dear Lord Tensbury,

Recently a person approached me, asking for details about my ancestor's friendship with Alistair Tensbury. She said she is working on a book on the English and American cotton trade in the mid-1800s. In particular, she asked if I have any documents or notes from that time. I'm assuming she is looking for some damaging information to change your son's chances in the upcoming election.

For some time now, I have notes, which I found among my ancestor's old things. It is about an unfortunate event both of our ancestors engaged in. In fact, "unfortunate" doesn't begin to describe this horrible event. It happened in West Africa in the late 1850s. I have no intention to disclose this information to those who want to tarnish your family reputation.

I have my own family challenges. My young daughter is very ill, and I'm scrambling to find a way to pay for her medical treatment. She has a rare cancer. Unfortunately, my insurance won't cover it. She is in Germany, where they have the experimental treatment for this cancer. The doctors believe the treatment will save her from becoming disabled for the rest of her life. I know you are a man of some means and may want to help my girl, if nothing else, then in memory of our ancestors' friendship. This treatment is around $250K. If you don't think my request is appropriate between people who don't even know each other, I'll understand.

If you can help, I need the funds next week. Sorry for the rush. We just found out the timing of the necessary treatment.

If you check your email now, you'll see a message from me. Please respond within a couple of days.

If your answer is Yes, I would like to meet at 1:30 PM on Wednesday, a week from tomorrow. A good place is the lounge of the DoubleTree by Hilton Hotel London – Westminster. Come alone. I'll recognize you.

I know this communication is rather sensitive. So, I arranged for a temporary email account, which I'll dispose of, together with all the messages. Please delete my message and your response on your side.

Please let me know whether you can help me. If you can, when we meet, it will be a good opportunity for me to give you the original papers related to the terrible affair. I'll be glad to get rid of these notes. I don't want them in my family. If anyone were to publish this story without the originals, one could easily claim it to be a fabrication.

Thank you.

Jack lifted his eyes.

"Bloody hell!"

Tensbury said nothing.

"So, what are you going to do about this, Sir?"

"No, what are WE going to do about this. I need your help on this one. I need your support thinking this through!" Tensbury's beseeching voice was unusual for him, different from his usually forceful modulation.

Tensbury felt a sense of desperation of the sort he hadn't remembered ever experiencing. If someone would release any significant negative information about his son prior to the election, it may sway the outcome. He knew the electorate was that fickle. He loved his son, but this was greater than that. It potentially impacted the future of British politics and thus the direction of the country. Tensbury was fiercely patriotic. The idea that some external force would affect the government of his country was abhorrent to him. Jack's cool head in times of stress had helped Tensbury out over and over again. There was no one else he could trust with this matter.

"Check your email, Sir. Did he send a message as the note says?"

Tensbury logged into his computer and pulled up his email application.

"I see it. 'Please answer Yes, or No' is all it says. Of course, I need to respond, 'Yes.' Nothing like this should jeopardize our Party's victory or Andrew's election."

Tensbury saw Jack looking at the email over his shoulder.

"Don't you think we should try to figure this out before you answer, Sir? We should take a couple of days to try to think this through."

Tensbury sensed blood draining out of his face, he felt shocked. His usual decisive personage – gone, but he took his hands off the computer keys.

Jack returned to his seat with his cup of tea in his hands. They both sat, each in turn, sipping his tea.

Tensbury's hand was shaking slightly. Usually, he was quick with prudent recognition of the right course of action. He always kept a clear mind, managing all the legislative bills and their consequences in his head. He thought that of all the years he worked with Jack, he had never been in such a state. He was almost sure Jack would do all he could to help him get out of this mess.

Jack held the note. "It's interesting how what's actually an extortion note can be interpreted as totally innocent. But, if you decide not to 'help,' this person may become more agreeable with the lady who 'is working on a book.' Who would be doing this, and why now?"

"I understand the 'why now.' He said so in his note, 'I'm assuming she's looking for some negative information to upset your son's chances in the upcoming election.' The note gives me till next Wednesday, a week from tomorrow. The election is the day after, on Thursday. But who, is another question. I'm not sure I buy this 'My young daughter is very ill' bit."

Tensbury pressed on his temples. He had a splitting headache.

Jack put down his tea and, surreptitiously, shifted his legs.

"Whoever this is, the person is making sure this note will be seen only by you and that there's no way to trace it. I'm also fairly sure this person uses one of those email services which doesn't require the owner's identity. Just in case, I'll send the email domain to my friend who knows this subject. The note's author also arranged that you wouldn't know the courier, right? It was someone we haven't seen before. Is that what Ms. Reed said?"

"Yes," Tensbury switched back to the primary matter of the note. "The time period the note refers to is my ancestor Alistair Tensbury's time. He's the one who was bestowed peerage by Queen Victoria in 1859. You know, Jack, I suggested to Andrew to talk about Alistair's achievements and his roots as an average man. In hindsight, it was a bad idea."

"Let's see. I'm sure Labor is looking for dirt on your son. They may know something about your ancestor, but not enough for a good story. With elections this close, I don't think this extortion event is a fluke. I tend to think Labor is behind this one. Fishing to see if you'll look into this professed debacle while they watch your moves. Trying to draw you out in some way. I don't know, Sir, but this game is getting dirtier every time. I wouldn't put it past Labor to do something like this. I think we need to find the source of this affair before it gets out of control. Just waiting till the specified date and paying out the money doesn't guarantee that this is the end of it. I suggest we put some effort into finding out what this is all about. Try to stop it, or at least prepare Andrew to address it before it gets out. Soften the blow."

Jack stopped, took a deep breath, and stared out the window.

Then he turned, his face red, "It makes me angry. The scope of the thing is daunting. If the implied information became known..." He stopped and added, "It's bad... Also, why is the letter addressed to you and not to Andrew?"

"Whoever wrote it knows that I have the money, and I'm passionate about my son winning. In fact, they might think I could believe that this is a frantic parent who has run out of options. Besides, my son's campaign is very public. A lot of people are around his headquarters. Someone else, such as his assistant, might see this message."

"Wait, I just remembered something which may relate to this."

Tensbury brightened a bit, picked up a note pad on his desk, and handed it to Jack. A note on the pad said 'Noah Arnol.' It also had a phone number and a URL.

"So, a couple of days ago, I received a call from a gentleman who has an oceanographic blog. He sounded Scandinavian. He said he had some interesting information about my ancestors. I meant to call him. I think we need to start with Mr. Arnol. Seems strange to receive a call like that out of the blue, before today's note, don't you think?"

Tensbury squinted. The sun was rising, and the light from the large window was bothering his eyes.

"Did you look him up online?"

"No. Frankly, yesterday I didn't think much about this. Now it's different. I don't believe in this type of coincidence."

"Sir, you don't mind if I check him out right now, do you?"

Tensbury knew that under ordinary circumstances, Jack would have gone to his own office to look into something, but not now. They needed to discuss whatever he could find.

Tensbury shook his head. "Go ahead."

Jack opened his laptop, which he always carried around in the office.

"Here's the blog," said Jack. "It seems to cover 19th century maritime history. And here's some information on Noah Arnol. He was a professor of Classical History at Stockholm University until he retired. He lives in Djursholm, and it says it's one of the more affluent suburbs in Stockholm. It looks like he co-wrote some of his research papers on Classical Rome with a man named Dr. Brock Tennyson. I see references going back for many years."

Tensbury had moved around his desk and was looking at Jack's screen.

"I know who Brock Tennyson is," said Tensbury. "He's part of the Cornelian Society. It's a group here in London that gives various levels of support to the Labor Party. I think he's the chair of the executive committee. Saw an article not long ago…"

He returned to his chair.

"Jack, that's the link," he said, emphatically, as he sat down. "If the Labor Party is somehow involved in this scheme, they would want to do it at arm's length. So, it would make sense to go through someone else. Plausible deniability, and so forth. They could be using Arnol as a vehicle to get to me. He calls me, says he has some information for me, tries to draw me out…"

"Not unreasonable, Sir," Jack said. "However, it might be a bit farfetched. Looks like the man is wealthy. Why would he engage in this sort of thing?"

"Precisely! He doesn't need the money. Perhaps he roots for the British Labor Party and wants them to stay in power. Sweden leans way left. Maybe he's helping his friend Tennyson. So, they come up with this idea, then they do some research and set up bait. They know my ancestor had the African business. They concoct this ransom thing just to unsettle me, hoping this, in turn, will put Andrew at a disadvantage."

"Come to think of it, Sir, I don't imagine a reputable man like Noah Arnol would get involved in a blackmail scheme. Why would he implicate himself like this? If there isn't any sick girl, then this is pure extortion. He would go to jail if caught. Doesn't make sense."

Tensbury digested what Jack said.

"You are right. Let's look at it from another angle. Perhaps he has been solicited by Labor to do the research work, but they haven't involved him directly?" Tensbury paused. "You know, this could also be initiated indirectly by one of the other groups that support Labor."

"Yes. There are quite a few of them." Jack nodded.

"That makes much more sense. Could be one of those. One of those groups could have started the political fishing all on their own, waiting to let Labor know if they find a real story. The long-time Labor affiliates will probably not engage in any out of the ordinary activities. But those who are new to the game could. It all depends on who finances one of them, and more importantly, who runs it. Someone inside such an affiliate may have concocted this blackmail scheme.

"Alternatively, if the blackmailer is who that person says he or she is, the 'she' who contacted the blackmailer may be from such an affiliate. And let me tell you, this type of entity won't stop. They'll keep trying."

"Sir, it might be a good idea to tell your son to tone down the ancestral narrative. At least while we are waiting for this to play out."

Tensbury nodded and picked up the phone. He dialed his son's number. It went to voice mail, and he left a message to return his call.

Tensbury picked up his teacup and put it right back down since it was empty.

He started picking non-existent lint off his trousers. A bad habit he had been trying to quell for years.

"Let's just sort out the possible scenarios," said Jack.

"On the one hand, it could be that this is just some poor sod with a sick daughter. He picked you because he has some information that shows something not quite honorable in both your and his ancestors' past. He knew you would be vulnerable right now before the election. At the same time, coincidentally, a rich man in Sweden, with a hobby in nautical history, finds some interesting data about your ancestors, which he's excited to share with you."

Jack got up and started a slow walk from side to side in front of Tensbury desk.

"Or, on the other hand, it's possible that the Labor Party is involved, fishing, trying to build a negative story about your ancestor. They want to release it right before the election. They need a story that will play against your son's narrative about Alistair Tensbury and may swing the outcome." Jack stopped.

"What information do you have about Alistair Tensbury during that period, Sir?"

"As I said earlier, Alistair started out as a military man and did some heroic acts while in the armed forces. Then he built quite a business empire in Africa. This is all public knowledge, you know. Anyone can look it up. But cooking up a story with some event as the note mentions – one needs facts."

"The Africa business may have gotten them started. Now they just hope that there's something dreadful during his time in Africa. I know it was a rough and tumble time back then." Jack took both of their cups, left Tensbury's office, and returned with fresh tea.

"Let's just say they have something. What might it be?" asked Jack.

He sat down.

Tensbury noticed that, for the first time in their relationship, Jack had sometimes begun omitting to say 'Sir' when addressing him.

It must be because they were now delving into his personal affairs rather than parliamentary things.

Tensbury, exacerbated, "I have no idea, Jack. No idea at all."

CHAPTER 3

Lillian Perry was in her cramped cubicle in the Labor HQ. She had a cheap office chair without armrests. *No budget for HQ comforts*, she thought. She was a light-skinned, small woman, upper 30s, and fiery. Freckles dusted her nose, and to most, her attitude made her seem taller. She had come a long way from getting an MA degree in communication from Kings and doing a year of studies in the US. She knew someone who knew a Member of Parliament, and that started her career. She was a permanent employee of the Labor Party organization.

During this general election campaign, she was thrilled to take on the role of Director of Research. One of her team's tasks was to research the Tories, especially their leader, Andrew Tensbury. She wanted her team to create a narrative of criticism with the data to back it up. Her team was good and came up with solid results, but she wanted something big. Her team fed research reports to the media group. They, in turn, passed the information out to the electorate using press releases, internet sites, or controlled 'leakage.'

The media group had an excellent relationship with an influential journalist in a major media outlet. Someone they had known for years. The journalist agreed to spill some material with a 'source close to the Labor Campaign' tag. That would allow for the release of more vital messages, potentially without second source confirmation. Since they were not allowed to advertise, except for a small number of party election broadcasts, it was a great way to keep the action going.

Lillian had told her team to look into everything surrounding Andrew Tensbury and leave no stone unturned. To examine his activities at Oxford and dig into his time at university in the US. Was there even a hint of an affair in his background? What groups or associations was he involved in? She wanted a report on his entire family. Did he have an illegal domestic worker in his house, for example? The whole family bit was important because of all the ruckus he made about his ancestry.

She thought about Alistair Tensbury. She had an inkling that 'something is rotten in the state of Denmark' to quote Shakespeare. And that's why she had sent Ethan to Senegal in West Africa.

Lillian picked up the phone and dialed a number.

"Hi, Ethan," she said. "How's it going?"

"Hi, Lillian. I'm in Dakar now. Just got back from St. Louis. These so-called taxi rides in Senegal are quite an experience."

She heard him take a pained breath.

"I'll have to tell you when I'm back. Now, about the project. People at the Gaston Berger, the St. Louis University, were very helpful. I went through a lot of old papers. I couldn't find anything useful, Lillian. Nothing tied to what we are looking for. Now I'm going to start looking here at the Dakar University library."

"Alright. Please call me as soon as you have something. There has to be something there, right?"

"Will do."

Lillian checked the time. Her team was in full swing, and she could also hear the din of volunteers making calls at the other corner of the floor.

She took a look at the email from Ethan from ten days ago. "It was all very promising when it started," she said, to no one in particular. "I hope it works out."

Ethan's email read,

> *Lillian Hi,*
>
> *I want to put my thoughts together in an email before I chat with you.*
>
> *I have a friend named Kevin. He and I are members of the local genealogy club. (I think I told you it's my hobby.) We usually help each other by looking through our families' documents and develop ideas from them. We then scan and catalog them.*
>
> *Kevin has a family history with a long line of clergymen. I was helping him scan different documents from the 1800s. It included notes from parishioners. Within the papers from Kevin's family, I saw a note from a parishioner to a vicar that was difficult to read. As I usually do, I enhanced it with Photoshop before logging and discussing it with Kevin. It got my attention since it said something to the effect that, 'I have perpetrated a <u>heinous deed</u> in Africa, which I can't describe here. I'll have to find some time alone with you. The weight of this event has burdened me for many years. I have told no one, but now, at this later stage in my life, I feel the need to do so.' Something like that. It wasn't signed. I cataloged it for further discussion with Kevin.*
>
> *Now, here comes the exciting part. Per your direction, our team has been spending time researching Alistair Tensbury. Andrew has kept*

bragging about him since he was the first Tensbury to become a Baron in the mid-1800s. Yesterday, during our meeting, to give us a flavor of Alistair's business dealings, you circulated one of his letters. I thought I recognized the handwriting. After work, on a hunch, I compared the script in that letter to the note addressed to the vicar. It was identical!

Ethan.

Lillian remembered jumping out of her chair and running to Ethan's cubicle. She told him to bring the documents he was talking about and meet her in the conference room. She then reviewed what he brought. Bingo! The 'vicar's letter,' as they started calling it, was addressed to a vicar near Kent, where the Tensburys had their ancestral home. Perhaps she found something she might use to tarnish Andrew's much-touted background. She hated the ridiculous notion of the aristocracy and its privileges, and all these Eton boys with their clubs and associations.

Lillian decided to have Ethan drop everything and focus on this 'deed' the note mentioned. Ethan had scoured the online sources and found nothing related, so Lillian had sent him to Senegal. As a result of her group's work, she knew a lot about the Tensburys. Alistair Tensbury had businesses in both South Africa's Cape and Senegal. Why did she send Ethan to Senegal and not South Africa? She just had a hunch that the 'deed' Alistair Tensbury referred to, most likely was perpetrated there. She assumed that, in those days, South Africa had a large European population living according to Western laws. Senegal did not.

Lillian knew Ethan would have a hard time finding anything. What a stroke of luck that he spoke French so well. Old documents in countries like that often were not digitized. She hoped Ethan could find something in one of the libraries or some other place. With the polls so tight, it was paramount he discovered something, anything. She hoped this lead wouldn't be like some of the others – take her down some rabbit hole.

There were only a few days left till the election. Lillian knew the electorate was fickle during the last days, and those who were undecided could be swayed easily.

Lillian left her cubicle for a cup of coffee. To augment her team's research, she was always on the lookout for any and all help from the Labor Party's associated groups. Back in her chair, she thought about the call she had with Dr. Tennyson almost two weeks ago. He was an Oxford professor of Classical History and sat on the board of the Cornelian Society. The society was a socialist organization, which supported Labor with ideas, research, and strategy in different policy areas.

Lillian's boss, James Miller, Chair of the Labor Party, suggested she give Tennyson a call since he knew him personally. She was able to reach Tennyson the same day. She introduced herself and conveyed the work of her group. He was very courteous and asked what he could do for her. She remembered not being sure how to proceed but then just launching into why she called. She said that he had probably read how Andrew Tensbury was spending much time lauding his family background. Specifically, he emphasized his ancestor Alistair Tensbury's simple beginnings and great achievements before peerage. Lillian mentioned her group's research of Alistair to ensure that Andrew Tensbury's reverence of this person was justified. She asked if Tennyson knew anyone who had researched Africa's business environment in the 19th century. Tennyson told her that he would ask around to see if anybody had any material or ideas.

Now, a week later, Lillian realized she hadn't heard from Tennyson, and she impatiently dialed his number.

"Hello, Professor Tennyson. How are you? This is Lillian from Labor HQ. I was wondering if you were able to give some thought to what we discussed last week."

"Yes, I was planning to call you. I checked into Alistair Tensbury's background but didn't find much."

Lillian's heart sank.

"However, I do have some thoughts. There was the issue about Andrew Tensbury's family owning shares in a French oil and gas company down in Africa. This came up while he was Business and Energy Secretary before he was elected leader. I haven't seen that in the news lately. That might be something you could research."

"Alright. That sounds precisely like the kind of thing I was looking for, Professor Tennyson," said Lillian. "Anything else you can think of?"

"No, I wish I could have been of more assistance."

"You have been a great help, Sir. Thank you for the suggestion. I'm going to see how I can use it."

"Glad to be of help."

Lillian got up with the notepad she had been using during the call and approached one of her team members.

"Hey, Mary," she said. "Can you break for a while and look into Andrew Tensbury's connection to a French oil and gas company in Africa? You should be able to find past articles from the time when he was Business and Energy Secretary. Write me a short report on how you think we can leverage it, please."

"Sure will."

CHAPTER 4

"So, what do we have? Two leads we can follow. The first one is the person who sent the note, and the second is this, Noah Arnol. We need to find out what Arnol's research for Labor turned up and what his role is."

"I agree, Sir, we need some more intelligence about Mr. Arnol. Most of the writing about him is in Swedish." He pointed at the screen. "We could get someone who knows the language to do some digging." He paused.

"Maybe we can have someone look this up in Stockholm. I have a buddy, George, from my SAS days who retired and now has a small PI firm. I believe he's still in touch with Jonas Erholm, who trained with us when we did joint military exercises. Jonas was in the Swedish Armed Forces – Försvarsmakten is their name, but, I think, he also retired. He might be able to help George with this. I'll call George." He got up, ready to leave.

"Jack, wait a minute. We have to be very careful. If the situation is what we think it is, they're watching my every move to see if I react."

"Yes, George will be discrete, that I'm sure of, and so will Jonas. I know them both well."

"Alright, call your friend. If he agrees, send him our

standard NDA with a clear stipulation that this is purely a research project using publicly available sources. You'll have to do the same with this Jonas person if he agrees to get involved."

Jack stepped out and dialed his friend. He answered right away.

"Hey, Jack," said George. Jack's name must have popped up on his phone. "Long time no hear. How's life up there in Westminster?"

Jack could 'see' George's happy-go-lucky face in front of him, pleased to hear his friend's voice.

"George, I should have been in touch sooner, but you know, the work here doesn't let up."

"Could have had a pint or two with your old pal, though."

Jack heard George chuckling. George paused for a bit, then continued. "So, what's up? You're not just calling to have that pint at the pub, are you?"

Jack explained what he needed.

"I'm working on a bill now regarding the environment. It appears that a gentleman named Noah Arnol may have worked on this subject in Sweden. The Cornelian Society, which helps formulate the Labor Party strategy, could have used his work. We need to research his efforts on this subject. We think there's more information about this in the Swedish sources. It would also be interesting to know of any other work he has done for the Cornelian society and/or the Labor Party. Do you think you can pick up this job and ask Jonas to support you in Sweden? It's kind of urgent."

"Of course, I'll do it. Give me a while, and I'll call Jonas to make sure he's available. I'll get right back with you."

George called after some time. "Jack, he can help. I'll leave right away. Should be able to get some time with Jonas at a couple of libraries in Stockholm today."

"George, go quietly, all right? This needs to be handled very delicately. The man can't notice we are interested in him."

Jack knew George well. George was let go from SAS because he got too aggressive during a terrorist interrogation. The powers that be had decided he was no longer SAS material. George was a hot potato, but this was a research project. Jack wanted someone effective, who he could trust to stay quiet about the whole affair. He was sure he could trust George in that way.

After George and Jonas returned the signed agreements via email, Jack gave George the info he had on Noah Arnol, and George promised to get on a plane right away. Jack returned to Tensbury's office.

"So?" asked Tensbury.

"He's on his way."

"Good."

"Now, we also need to find out who this blackmailer is as quickly as possible. If he truly has this type of information, we need to let your son know so he can prepare to address it in short order. It's better if he comes clean before the public hears about it from other sources, or at least knows how to respond. We need to look through whatever documents you have for that period, and then try to correlate it to what the blackmail note says. What additional information do you have about Alistair?" asked Jack.

"All my documents are in my ancestral home in Kent, near Canterbury. Takes an hour and a half to get there. I have a large archive of my family history. There are many binders full of documents. I believe I have everything my father had. The only other person that might have something is my Aunt Sally. She was always my grandfather's favorite child. The binders are organized by year, so we should be able to drill down easily." Tensbury got up.

Jack detected a determined note in his voice.

"Jack, can you join me for a drive to my home? You'll have to spend the night, so you might want to bring a change of clothes. We can stop by your place. I know it's a lot to ask, but, as I said earlier, I need help, and I have no one else to turn to."

There was nothing Jack could say. He didn't have a wife or children to go home to, and he was used to Tensbury keeping him in the office. Often late hours and sometimes weekends when Tensbury was deluged with work and didn't go home to Kent.

After picking up Jack's things, it was eleven in the morning by the time they left London.

Jack sank into the comfortable seat and stretched out his legs.

"Would you like a bottle of water?"

"Yes, please, Sir."

Tensbury opened the small fridge and withdrew two bottles of water and handed one to Jack.

Henry navigated out of London and then took the motorway heading south-east for Kent. Tensbury and Jack didn't talk much during the drive, each occupied by his own thoughts. An hour and a half later, they were close to Canterbury. Just outside of town, Henry turned off the road and then onto a long driveway. As the building came into view, Jack saw that Tensbury's home was actually a small castle. He realized he didn't have any idea about Lord Tensbury's wealth. Rippling hills of green surrounded the estate, and he saw several buildings close to the main house. It had been a comfortable ride in Tensbury's Bentley with Henry at the wheel.

"It's an ancient building, as you can see," said Tensbury. "It has been in my family over hundred-fifty years. Alistair Tensbury owned this home, and generations thereafter have lived here. I had to modernize it and put in new plumbing and power."

They entered the house through a towering portico, and a man met them at the door.

"Ah, John. Would you please take Mr. Fernsby's luggage to the corner guest room. Thank you, John. Also, please let my wife know I'm home. I'll be working late tonight.

"Tensbury kept his laptop case and handed over his bag to John.

Tensbury led the way down a long corridor. They passed a library and then entered a large room with several locked cabinets. As Jack came closer, he saw they all had date range labels. A large table dominated the middle of the room. There were also a couple of smaller desks of similar nature strewn around the room. The room was bright, and Jack saw several traditional bankers' lamps on the desks and the table. The lamps' green shades were casting a pleasant light.

"I haven't taken a look at these documents since I was young."

Tensbury went over to the cabinets and opened one of them. He pulled out several large binders and brought them to the table.

"The ransom note mentions that the purported event occurred in the last part of the 1850s. We should look at the binders for 1855 through 1860. But first, let's have something to eat. I'll be right back."

Jack caught a glimpse of himself in one of the floor-length mirrors adorning a wall. He smoothed down his hair which had become tousled from the car ride.

He sat down at the table and waited. He wasn't about to touch the documents without Tensbury in the room. The room had towering ceilings, with elaborate crown moldings. The windows extended from the floor to the ceiling, offering a spectacular view of a manicured garden with a large fountain in the center. In the corners of the spacious room were open fire hearths. They were covered in porcelain with hunting motifs. Firewood was stacked to the side, but the stoves were not lit. Large bookshelves lined the walls. Although it wasn't the actual library, it held a lot of large books.

Perhaps a reference room, thought Jack.

Tensbury came back, with what looked like a cook trailing him. She was carrying a tray of sandwiches, cups, and a pitcher of hot water for tea. After setting their lunch on one of the desks, the cook left. They were both hungry and ate quickly.

"Why don't we split these binders up," Tensbury said and pushed several of them towards Jack.

Tensbury took the rest, and they both started perusing the binders. The binders included documents from two companies. Alistair Tensbury had an interest in the Senegal Gum Arabic business, called IL&R, as well as in the South African ship repair company, called Tensbury Nautical Repair Company. Jack and Tensbury found bills of lading and trading agreements. They came across letters of all kinds, invoices, banking statements, and more. They also found correspondence from a lawyer in London.

Tensbury pulled out a letter that was in an envelope. Most other notes had been straightened out and fastened to the binder, but not this one. "It appears as if it was never sent. It is from 1857 from Alistair to a man named Garnier, and it's in French."

He handed the letter to Jack.

Neither Tensbury nor Jack was very proficient in French, but Jack could get by. "I remember, from looking at the other documents here, that M. Garnier was Tensbury's co-owner in IL&R. Let me read it to you, Sir. I'll do the best I can."

December 5, 1857

Dear M. Garnier,

As you know, I'm always pleased to work with you. In all these years of collaboration in IL&R, we have never had any disagreement. I thank you for that. As to my most recent transaction, I'm satisfied to own a larger share of the company. As one of the company's two primary owners, I look forward to continuing this most rewording relationship between you and me.

Jack said with mocked irritation, "The French always have

a way of wasting words and overdoing the pleasantries. I guess Alistair wanted to write a French-style note."

> *My last business transaction concerns me somewhat. As you know, I bought M. Philippe Fortin's part of the company. I'm sorry that our dear friend feels as though he should have had a better business arrangement. I believe I made an attractive offer, and he received a fair sum for his part of the company.*

"It ends there, Sir. This must have been a draft."

"Jack, do you remember seeing anything referring to a third co-owner of IL&R? Because I don't."

"No, I don't either. There was a lot of correspondence between Alistair and Garnier, but I didn't see any other owner mentioned."

"So, maybe Alistair didn't correspond directly with Fortin."

They pondered that for a minute.

"Well, it doesn't seem to have any relevance at this point, does it, Sir?"

"We reviewed the binders up until 1857 and only saw one document referring to this third co-owner. He probably didn't own a large part of the business at that time," said Tensbury.

"Still, we should pay attention to this Fortin guy and see if he's going to come up again."

Tensbury's phone rang. "Are you and Mum, alright?" Tensbury knew he was always concerned when he received a call from his dad unexpectedly.

"We are fine, Andrew. I have been thinking about your messaging now that we are so close to the election. I think it's better to refocus on your manifesto rather than speaking of our ancestry."

He could hear Andrew breathing on the other end of the line. He didn't say anything for a while.

"Dad, I thought we agreed that I should focus on our

ancestry in my messaging and dispel this narrative that I'm not one of the people. Talking about Alistair, and his life before he became a peer, has resounded positively with the electorate."

"We did, we did I just think that you have made the point and need to let the manifesto become more prominent at this time."

Again, Andrew took some time to answer.

"I'll trust your instincts, Dad," said Andrew.

"How's Mum?"

"Mum is fine. Proud of you, you know. And how are Jessica and the boys?"

"Tired of never seeing me home, they say. I'll be so glad when this is over. But I suppose that's when the real hard work begins." He gave a little laugh.

He had his dad's personality and was usually cheerful.

"You are doing great, son!"

CHAPTER 5

Harry MacDuff got up from his chair and stared out the window. He saw another dreary London day, even though was the month of May already.

Eleven years ago, Harry started his own company, Irina Consulting. Now, after days and sometimes nights of hard work, he was a veteran supporting election campaigns for MPs. Many had successfully run against solidly placed Conservatives. For this campaign, the Prime Minister's Office at 10 Downing Street hired him to support the Labor Party efforts. It included strategy formulation, opposition research, and communications.

Harry was a heavy-set man. He tried to find time for the gym but instead found excuses not to go, and his love of raspberry biscuits was well known around the office. His jet-black hair he attributed to his mother's Indian heritage and his ruddy face to his Scottish dad. It gave him an interesting, if a little disconcerting, look, but he compensated it with a friendly smile.

His phone rang.

"Hi, Harry. Did you guys find anything?"

"No. It's only been three days since we last talked, Otis."

"You're right, I am sorry."

"These things take time. I promise you, that the moment we get something, I'll call you. Meanwhile, please remember this is all confidential."

"I know, I'll be patient. Thanks. Talk to you soon."

Otis, a Ph.D. student in Cambridge, came up with some intriguing material while researching his thesis. It related to Alistair Tensbury and would seriously impact the Tory campaign.

Otis was a supporter of the Labor Party and took this information to his local MP. The MP realized it might be actionable, and this lead ended up at Harry's firm. It was a good lead, but a long shot. To work out, it required a lot of research and even more luck.

His phone rang again.

"Hi, Tim."

Tim assisted the PM, Mr. Nithercott, in mapping out strategy for the country and was also the liaison for Harry during the campaign.

"Harry, what can we do about the disinformation Tory supporters are spreading over social media?" Tim's voice was anxious.

"You mean about the National Health System, the NHS?"

"Yes. I'm not sure if you saw the pictures of those old folks on cots in the corridors of the London Bridge Hospital, but that shit has to be shut down."

"I saw it."

"We have not caused any shortage of personnel or hospital beds in London. We checked with the hospital and what they write is false. The pictures are definitely doctored."

"Right."

"We can't let the electorate assume that we have withheld funds from NHS. That's not our policy. Frankly, we are at a loss for how to counter this."

"I know. The disinformation campaigns on Twitter and Facebook are rampant. As you said, the Tories themselves are probably not the ones doing it. But some affiliate of theirs might. I wouldn't advise you to launch a similar campaign against the Tories. I'm just not a believer in that," said Harry.

"No, I don't want to, either. But what do we do?"

"You need to counter it in the PM press conference tomorrow. Head on. It would be best if you stressed that we're the Party of national healthcare. Don't go into details about what is in the media."

"Alright, but what if he gets a specific question about the content of the pictures? He's not good at that. You know how brutal the press is."

"Answer straight up. That we believe that these are doctored photos. That we checked the hospital and there has not, at any time, been a situation when patients are left in the hallways."

"Do you think he should use this time to talk about our plans for NHS?"

"No, I think you need to get this situation behind you first."

"Alright. Thanks, Harry. See you."

CHAPTER 6

It was late. Andrew Tensbury let the smoke slowly escape his nostrils. He had tried stopping, but under stress, he couldn't count on his willpower. He was standing on the right side of the Conservative Campaign Headquarters, or CCHQ as it was known, away from the entrance. He was making sure the staff couldn't see him smoking.

The CCHQ on Matthew Parker Street housed the national campaign organization, and it was buzzing. He was stressed at the moment and had often been in the last three weeks. Running as a leader of the Conservative Party, who might become the next Prime Minister of Britain, was a heady responsibility. He sometimes thought about what would happen after he won. He would meet the queen in Buckingham Palace... He had never met the old lady. At least, not at a private audience. He caught himself. He knew he had to stop thinking about it, otherwise he might jinx it. First, he needed to win this bloody thing.

Andrew was a tall man of forty-one, in good shape, although he had lost some weight during the campaign. His boyish look with unruly hair falling a little too low below his collar gave him an endearing look. He had an easygoing style and got along with almost everyone. His ability to talk to people while understanding their particular circumstances made him an effective politician. He also was very popular among conservative MPs.

A lot of what he had accomplished, he had done to shine in his father's eyes. Getting top grades at Eton, his computer engineering degree at Princeton, and matching his father's accomplishments by becoming a solicitor, and then entering parliament. Now he felt that he had reached a point where his father could genuinely be proud of him, which satisfied him immensely.

Andrew would think carefully about whom he would appoint to the Cabinet. He already had most of the team worked out. He only had several more spots to fill.

"Hey, Andrew," said Thomas Baldwin, also coming out to puff a little.

Thomas was his National Campaign Manager, and he was superb.

"Couldn't resist that cigarette, could you."

Thomas pulled out one himself and accepted a light from Andrew.

They shared a guilty look.

Thomas Baldwin was Andrew's old friend from Eton. He had a very successful marketing consulting firm and was always involved in Conservative causes. Like Andrew, he was tall, but that's where the similarities ended. His dark complexion stood in sharp contrast to Andrew's light looks. His muscular constitution revealed a physically strong build. At university, he was on several athletic teams. His dynamic and firm professionalism elicited respect from everyone who worked with him. Since starting his company, he had several campaigns under his belt.

Andrew convinced his friend to come on this operation and fight the battle together. Thomas reported to Ian Dilling, the Chairman of the Conservative Party. In fact, the Chairman and Thomas ran the campaign together. The Chairman was responsible for local programs, messaging, and canvassing.

He dealt with local data collection and especially feedback from individual constituencies. Thomas was responsible for the centralized effort of strategy, data mining, and central messaging. He also handled an extensive volunteer organization. He helped Andrew with his constituency events and almost daily press conferences.

Past campaign experience taught the Tories that both parts were equally important. Neglecting any one of the two could lead to losing an election. It happened before. While it was true that the centralized effort was paramount, general elections were actually contested in the trenches. Right from the beginning, Andrew made sure these two guys were more than compatible. No rivalry, only teamwork. Knowing past party elections' shortcomings, Andrew was leaving nothing to chance. This is where his innate organizational talent, and past training in large systems during his college time at Princeton, was genuinely handy.

"I see the concerned look on your face, Andrew. You are making the right decisions. It's a true conservative campaign as we always wanted, with true conservative values. We are not watering it down. Our manifesto is good and proper, and it resonates with people."

"Yes, I know. I need to control my nerves better. I'm lucky the jitters miraculously disappear when I talk to people."

"You're doing well, Andrew, and we will win this thing. Rest assured."

They stood quietly for a while, puffing on their cigarettes.

"By the way, are you prepared for the constituency stops tomorrow?

"I'm as ready as I'll ever be."

"The poll numbers are looking good. We are pulling away from Labor, although it's within the margin of error. But still… The Liberal Democrats will probably also add some seats this time," Thomas added as an afterthought.

"I worry about that. They might tilt the basket. We need a clear majority," said Andrew.

Andrew's daily constituency stops were important. The media, who followed every stop, reported directly to the electorate via traditional channels and social networks. Of course, the Party wasn't able to control their interpretation of Andrew's message. The majority of media outlets favored Labor. But Andrew was good at communicating, enjoyed the press conferences, and this shone through. He used this advantage in the last interview with BBC. Andrew repeated the main tenants of the manifesto while dodging many adversarial questions. Nithercott, on the other hand, had a difficult time delivering positive messaging through press conferences. Andrew's campaign had twice challenged the PM to debates, but they demurred both times. They knew Andrew was an excellent speaker and came out better on TV.

"It's incredible how polarized politics have become. The constant barrage of 'Fake News.' What we hear from the US doesn't sound so foreign anymore, heh, Thomas?"

Then remembering, "You changed the message for tomorrow from my ancestry to some other policy issue, right?"

"Yes, the speechwriters should have a new draft to you shortly."

"So then, I'll head home in a bit and work on the draft they send me. I'll nail down my opening remarks tonight and email them to you. We can discuss it tomorrow morning before show-time."

"Sounds good."

Tomas paused. "Oh, did you hear 10 Downing Street hired an independent research firm? It's called 'Irina Consulting,' I think. Labor is intent on digging up something on us to leak before the election."

"Let them dig. There's nothing to find," said Andrew emphatically. "Let them dig."

"By the way, another thing. I saw a report yesterday that indicates a foreign entity is trying to hack our systems. The report assumes it's the Russians. They would love for Labor to win again. They know we would increase defense spending."

"We have control over this, right? I mean, we can stop them?" asked Andrew.

"The systems guys are working on blocking them now. They haven't penetrated anything yet. Also, we aren't sure it's the Russians. Could be the Chinese. They don't like our stand on Hong Kong very much either."

"Either way, it's a damn situation."

"I'll let you know what the status is."

"Yes, please do that."

"Hey, I need to head back inside. Coming?" Thomas disposed of his cigarette butt.

Andrew followed Thomas back into the building and returned to the central 'hub' as they liked to call it. Thomas' desk stood in the middle of the floor, and he used it when everyone was working. Andrew went to his office, located right next to Thomas' office, in the back of the floor. He had his laptop before him, thinking about his statement tomorrow. From there, Andrew gazed at the animated looks on his young volunteers' faces. He had to win. He owed it to them and many other young people whose future would be affected by this election.

He checked his watch. It was time for him to leave. The team would continue working late into the night. He needed to sleep to be fresh for tomorrow's press conferences. Andrew packed up. He waved goodbye to Thomas, who was facing him, holding a cell phone in one ear, and a landline in the other. Thomas motioned for him to leave with his head.

He mouthed, "Good night."

Andrew left and was about to walk to his car, where he always parked it. Then he saw Richard, the chauffeur, standing with the hired car door open in front of the building. He looked at Richard and remembered that he was 'important' now. The Party hired a chauffeured car recently. If all went as planned, he would have to get used to it.

The fresh air felt good, and, for a change, it wasn't raining. It would have been good to take a walk. But…, the security decision was made – so, the car it had to be.

CHAPTER 7

Meanwhile in Kent, Tensbury and Jack continued their search late into the night. They were looking for any little nugget they could find – anything that would lead them to an understanding of any questionable business dealings.

Tensbury pointed to some pages clipped together. "So, here are the quarterly statements from IL&R in 1859. As we saw earlier, Alistair owned a substantial part of IL&R, with headquarters in St. Louis. At that time, it was the capital of Senegal. Now IL&R is an oil exploration company, and they moved its headquarters to Marseille. There's nothing remarkable in the 1859 binder about the African businesses, nor in the other binders. When Andrew was Business and Energy Secretary in the last year of the previous Tory administration, the Green Party gave him grief. They were unhappy because we still hold shares in this company."

"This is interesting, Sir." Jack appeared distracted. "What do you know about Alistair Tensbury's hunts? Because I have a letter here about one of them."

"I know he was an avid hunter when down in South Africa."

Jack pulled out a document from the binder labeled '1858.' "Here's a letter from someone called John Haddock. Let me read it to you."

South Africa, December 10th, 1858.

My Dear Mr. Tensbury,

On this last evening here in South Africa, I want to thank you for your gracious hospitality and commend you on this beautiful home here in Cape Town. I hope you agree we had a glorious time over these last couple of months. I can't thank you enough for leading me to Mr. Cugley and others so I could set up new trading relationships.

As you suggested, I will see about finding new Gum Arabic customers for your company in Senegal.

I feel fortunate that our mutual banker in London introduced us. I value our friendship that grew as we traveled down the coast of Africa on my ship. Our week of hunting was extraordinary. I never thought I would be hunting big game like that.

I know we'll hear from each other by the middle of next year. Our little agreement suggests so. I look forward to the outcome, no matter which way it goes. If you ever have your way over to Mobile in Alabama, I hope you'll allow me to extend the same hospitality you granted me.

Yours Sincerely,

John Haddock

PS. If you do come, I'm afraid we can mostly hunt deer and alligators. A far cry from the big game of South Africa!

Jack handed the letter to Tensbury. "Evidently, your ancestor met this man, John Haddock, and spent time with him hunting. Sounds like they became close. He must have been a trader of some kind. This was probably before Alistair became a peer because Haddock refers to him as Mr. Tensbury, not Lord Tensbury."

"Yes, it was. Alistair got his title in 1859."

Then, "What 'little agreement' could he be referring to, Jack."

"Could be anything."

"Do you think this is somehow connected to the blackmail note? Did the language of the note seem American to you?"

"I don't remember noticing that, Sir."

"The blackmailer wrote $250K. First, he writes 'dollars,' and second, he uses 'K,' which is very common in the States."

Jack took the note out of the envelope they had brought from Tensbury's office and reread it.

"I can't say. The dollar is ubiquitous, and many people in Britain now also use 'K' for thousands. It may just be someone who stumbled over correspondence between the two men. This person decided to blackmail you when the illness of the daughter came up. If there's such a daughter at all, that is."

Jack went over to the side table where the cook had placed a bottle of water, greedily drank a glass, and poured one for Tensbury.

Tensbury accepted the water. "We should count this letter as potentially supporting one of the leads."

"Yes, Sir, I agree." He paused.

"So, we already have someone dispatched to research Arnol. I think we should also contact a genealogist in America to look into what has become of John Haddock's progeny."

"Thought of that, but come to consider it further, there are potentially several hundred current descendants, so that would be a gargantuan task. It's certainly not possible within the few days that we have. It's a non-starter, Jack."

They continued their search. Nothing came up.

The same cook came in with supper. It was some delicious game pie and a cherry cake for dessert.

After the events of the day, at this late hour, Tensbury felt tired and old.

Jack's phone rang. "Good that you called. What have you got, man?" Jack walked out into the hall to take the call.

In a few minutes Jack was back.

"Sir, George and Jonas have been working since three this afternoon. They didn't come up with much, besides a few more details on Noah Arnol. He has been professor at Stockholm University for over thirty years and retired last year. He's sixty-six and is a professor emeritus now. He also spent two years as a visiting professor at Oxford. He wrote many papers, about two a year from what they could find. Many of them were co-written with Brock Tennyson, who also taught Classical History at Oxford and who, as you know, associated with the Cornelian society. Arnold's wife passed away quite a while ago, and they didn't have any children. He never remarried. The house he lives in has been in the Arnol family since the 1800s. It seems he's one of two brothers. The other one is deceased. Jonas thinks there might be some other sources they can look at, but he was tired, and they quit for the day. They will pick it back up tomorrow morning and will try to exhaust any additional sources. George will return tomorrow."

"So, they didn't come up with anything. Maybe tomorrow... It's been a hell of a day." Tensbury sighed deeply.

"Incidentally, I'm not sharing this with Elisabeth. My wife would be devastated. I'll tell her you are here to work on a bill, and we needed to get out of the office – a white lie. I'll introduce you to her tomorrow."

He got up. "I don't know how I'll be able to sleep."

Tensbury showed Jack to a large bedroom with an attached bathroom, and they parted for the night. Tensbury remembered how happy and cheerful he had been this morning.

It feels like a long, long time ago.

Day 2

CHAPTER 1

Hanna sighed. These transatlantic flights were always tiresome. They felt drawn-out, even though she was flying Business Class from San Francisco to London for the last couple of years. Her long legs still suffered.

She stopped working and pulled up the news on her laptop. After browsing WSJ, she checked the BBC. The front page covered next week's British elections. A voter was interviewed and quoted,

> *This Tensbury, he ain't a commoner like us, you see. He keeps talking about his humble beginnings. But we know! He comes from one of those aristocratic families. Besides, I never vote for the Tories anyway.*

She scanned the article further. It looked like the Tories might win. But then again, elections can be swayed by just some little tid-bit of information released in the last days. The 2016 US election could have turned out differently without the whole email server debacle.

It'll be interesting to see what will happen in the UK.

"Please put your computer away. We're landing soon." A flight attendant was bending towards Hanna's chair, a patient look on his face. Hanna complied. She pulled a brush from her purse and ran it through her light brown hair.

Last week Hanna and her Uncle Noah talked about his Nautical Blog. He was researching an 1800's ship repair company in South Africa. Alistair Tensbury owned it. Tensbury was also part owner of a company in Senegal, exporting Gum Arabic from Africa. What was the name of the company? Oh, yes, IL&R. At the time, Senegal was becoming a French colony, and the information was in French. Hanna's French was deeply ingrained from school, so her uncle asked her to look into IL&R.

It's fascinating that if the Tories win, Alistair Tensbury's descendant, Andrew Tensbury, will become the youngest Prime Minister of Britain in recent history. I should ask Uncle Noah in more detail why he was researching Alistair Tensbury's companies now.

Poor Uncle Noah. I had neglected him terribly during the past year. Always so busy being busy. I should never have let myself become so occupied and not have time to connect. I should have visited him more often. He is the most important person in my life – my only family.

The trip! He was so insistent. He said she must join him on this trip to Senegal to see what Signe described. Their ancestor Signe kept the family-famous diary. It had an exciting part about traveling down the coast of Africa in the 19th century. Hanna knew she had delayed this trip her uncle wanted to take for many years. He literally begged her this time - which wasn't in his nature.

"We have postponed it for so many years. I think it's time to do this finally," he had said, and she relented.

He had arranged their trip and sent her the itinerary. After her business meeting today, she would go to Stockholm and then both of them would head to Africa for a week.

She looked out the window, Heathrow came into view.

The airplane touched down. She checked voicemail. Nothing. Then she checked the numbers that had called her while she was flying and paused when she saw one with the country code 46. Sweden. The only person she spoke to in Sweden was her uncle, and this wasn't his number. She looked up. Her fellow passengers in her section were all gone.

"Please." The flight attendant motioned her to leave.

She scrambled to her feet and disembarked, dragging her roller board behind her. Exiting the gate, she hit "return call" to the unknown number.

A booming voice answered. Sounded Swedish. "Inspector Mans."

She hesitated. Inspector? The Swedish police?

"Hello, this is Hanna Arnol. Someone called me?"

Yes, Ms. Arnol, thank you for returning my call so soon. I wasn't comfortable leaving a message and hoped I would get you in person. I'm with the Stockholm Police and need to ask you some questions. Are you the niece of Mr. Noah Arnol?" The booming voice continued in accented, perfect English.

"Yes. He's my uncle."

"Ms. Arnol, can you go somewhere private right now and sit down, please."

Filled with dread, she shoved her way through a line of passengers ready to board the plane she had just disembarked. She found a chair. Her roller board fell over, and she made no attempt to pick it up.

"I'm sorry to have to tell you that Mr. Arnol is dead," he said. "The coroner is checking now, but it appears as if he fell down the stairs in his home and hit his head."

The booming voice was softer now.

"We found your name and number through the Richardsons, his neighbors." He stopped.

Her lungs felt like they had collapsed, and she gasped for air. Heavy seconds passed, and neither of them spoke.

"I believe you are in an airport, Ms. Arnol?"

Incessant sounds from flight announcements echoed around her.

"Yes. I'm in the UK. I'll call you…" she said and hit the

red button. She doubled over and stared at an old piece of chewing gum stuck to the worn, grey carpet. And then the tears came streaming down her face.

CHAPTER 2

After flying, bleary-eyed, to Stockholm, Hanna met Inspector Mans. He was waiting at the Medical Center in Danderyds Kommun, near her Uncle Noah's place. In a daze, she identified her uncle in the morgue. Earlier she called her office and asked to postpone her meeting till tomorrow.

She sat with Mans in the hospital cafeteria, a large cup of steaming, black coffee in front of her.

"Thank you."

"It's nothing," said Mans.

"I know this is part of your job, but thanks for being good at it."

She reached for the pitcher on the table. Her hand shook as she tried to pour more coffee into her cup. He seized the pitcher and poured it for her.

Inspector Mans. A typical Swede. Tall and thin. His face was sober.

"We are treating this as an accident, but we have to look at all possibilities. It's part of our procedure."

"This couldn't have been an accident," she mumbled.

"I'm sorry?"

"This couldn't have been an accident," she repeated resolutely.

She pulled her shoulders back and sat upright.

"He was a strong sportsman. He swam every morning. He ran up and down those stairs many times a day ever since he was a child."

"There was no sign of forced entry, and the house didn't look disturbed. We won't know until after the coroner takes a look. But based on my experience, Ms. Arnol, this was just a freak accident."

She tuned out. Again, she remembered her call with her uncle a week ago.

"Snuttan, you have to come now, Snuttan." He was the only one who called her 'Snuttan – little one' in Swedish. "You remember how we always talked about the missing pages from Signe's diary? They finally showed up, literally showed up. You'll be amazed when you read them. No, I can't tell you over the phone, you have to come here. Then onto Senegal for a week. It's important that we finally go. You always promised."

She cringed. They used to make interesting trips all over the world as she was growing up, but they never made it to Africa. As a Professor of Classical History, he had wanted Hanna to become as excited about history as he was. Because of his urgency, she had agreed to take that Africa trip finally.

Now he had passed. She felt as if it was her fault he fell. If she had only been here earlier...

Mans interrupted her thoughts. "Was there anything unusual going on lately?"

"No," said Hanna, feeling tense.

She didn't think her uncle's excitement about the pages he found was significant. And the research she was helping him with? No, that wasn't relevant either.

"Did he talk to you about any troubles or anything like that? Did he have any enemies?"

"No, he didn't have any enemies that I know of. He had some strong political views, but that doesn't get you killed, does it?"

"No, not in Sweden, it shouldn't." Mans gave a wry smile.

Hanna took a sip of coffee. "Inspector, my uncle was very important to me. He took care of me after my parents died when I was twelve years old."

"How did they die?"

"The gondola crashed during an avalanche in the Alps. A lot of people died." She paused.

"He was there for me when I came home from school."

She saw the question on his face.

"From Switzerland. I had been in a boarding school since I was eleven. It was hard at first, but after some time, I was happy there."

"Why Switzerland?"

"We lived in New York. My parents wanted me to get a good education. Their death came as a momentous blow. I'm the only child, and I felt rudderless. I didn't...," she stopped for a moment, "...have any close family except for my uncle in Sweden," she continued.

"My mother was American, but there was no one on her side of the family who was able, or wanted, to take care of me. On my dad's side, there was only my uncle, my father's brother. My uncle brought me into his home and cared for me as I was growing up. I loved him, and I know he loved me."

At that, tears began to flow, and she drank some coffee, furtively trying to hide them. "He was wonderful. He stepped in as a father, and I couldn't have imagined a better father than he was. I went to the Swiss school throughout high school, and every holiday or long weekend, he would bring me home to Stockholm."

At this, she looked at the Inspector. He was giving her his undivided attention. She wondered if this was part of his job. To listen to the bereaved. She decided to cut it short.

"He guided me through college."

She thought about all those trips they took and how she had learned to love history. But she chose business instead. While majoring in history at Cornell, she fell in love with an economics professor. When he transferred to Stanford in California, she followed him. She was accepted into the MBA program and got a business degree instead of pursuing a graduate degree in history. She never forgot how her uncle tried to hide his disappointment.

"I was on business in London when you called. I should have been here with him instead, and none of this would have happened," she blurted out. "I was supposed to come here after my London meeting. And I was to stay with him. Well, go to Africa with him," she explained. "He had always wanted us to visit Senegal. We used to take many trips together."

Mans looked like he wanted to ask questions but refrained from doing so, and she appreciated that.

"By the way, do you know his mobile phone password?" Mans asked.

Her uncle had an iPhone. She knew this because she had urged him to get one.

"No, I don't."

"Would just have been easier to get into the phone. We want to see if there are any calls, messages, or mail that might point to something related to the fall."

He withdrew a document from his folder.

"This is the Death Certificate the doctor issued this morning. The body is now going to the coroner."

"How long will that take?"

"The coroner's work could take as long as two days but probably less in this case. More like one."

"I need to set up the funeral. I don't know where to start," said Hanna, quietly.

"You will have to work with a funeral director to decide when and where you will bring your uncle from the morgue."

Hanna's face turned whiter than before. The idea of her uncle laying there alone made her ache to the core.

"How do I find a funeral director?"

"It's probably best if you discuss this with your uncle's lawyer. That is typically how people do it in Sweden."

"I don't know who the lawyer is," she said. Her anxiety built inside her. "I'll find out. I need to get into the house."

"You will be able to get in tomorrow."

But I have to leave for London tonight.

"So, how long do you think all of this will take before the funeral?"

"That's probably something you should let your lawyer take care of. I want to let you know though, that Sweden has one of the longest periods of death to funeral. You cannot expect to be able to book it less than two to three weeks out or longer."

I hope Uncle Noah has a good lawyer who will help me through all of this.

Panic burned in her stomach, and she felt very tired.

"I need somewhere to stay," she said.

"Do you know anybody in Stockholm?" Mans asked.

"I know the Richardsons. I suppose they already know what happened, but we are not close. I need a room to shower and rest."

"I'll take you to the Radisson in Solna. It's close."

"Thank you."

Before she got out of his car, she touched Inspector Mans's arm.

"Please find out what happened. I have lost a father for a second time."

Later in her hotel room, she stood in the shower for a long, long time. Thoughts spilled over her, along with the scorching water.

As a historian, her uncle had always had great stories to tell. Especially when she had one of her frequent nightmares, he would come to her bedside and hold her hand. During those little séances, he had taught her to love history.

There were few ambiguities in documented history. She felt that history was so tangible, so certain, so comforting. She couldn't say the same about business. Business was full of uncertainties – always.

Stumbling out of the tub, her skin burned as she dried herself. Hanna knew her friend was on a trip to India. She didn't even try to figure out the time difference between Sweden and Bangalore. She called Helen. Helen picked up immediately.

"Hi, honey. Are you okay?"

Hanna started crying again. Between sobs, she said. "No, nothing is okay. My uncle died."

"Oh, honey. I'm so sorry. Where are you?"

Her sobs subsided somewhat. Helen always had a calming effect on her. They didn't see each other often because of work but spent hours on the phone chatting about everything in their lives.

"Where are you, honey?" Helen repeated when she didn't hear Hanna speak.

"I'm in a hotel room now. It was terrible seeing him dead, Helen. It's strange. He looked so much younger than I remember, you know."

"What are you going to do now?" said Helen, sounding worried. She knew her friend could come up with some hair-brained ideas when she was stressed.

"I'm going out to his house to poke around. I have some things I want to look over before I fly to London tonight."

"Ok, honey, you have to promise me you'll call me from the house and let me know how you are. Promise!"

"I will."

CHAPTER 3

The next morning Tensbury and Jack had a quick breakfast. Tensbury introduced Jack to his wife. She had been pretty when she was younger, and she was still attractive. Perfectly put together in beige slacks and a white button-up blouse. She wore a navy sweater around her shoulders. Jack noticed how attentive Tensbury was to her. The terse manner he sometimes saw at the office, gone. Breakfast was served on a veranda with windows surrounding the room, and since it was May, it was beautiful. Now the rolling hills appeared brighter than they were yesterday when they arrived. Jack spotted a stable. He could see it was divided into two buildings and assumed they kept a lot of horses.

"My Lady, do you ride?"

"She's the best dressage horsewoman around," answered Tensbury for his wife, the familiar smile, creases on his cheeks.

"And you?" inquired Lady Tensbury.

"My parents didn't have the means to let me ride as much as I wanted. But later, I became a regular member at a stable in London. Now I'm too busy with work to have any time."

After breakfast, Jack and Tensbury returned to the room they were in the night before, each carrying a cup of tea. It was cold in the room, and Jack eyed Tensbury's thick sweater with envy. Despite it being springtime, Jack's thin pullover wasn't enough in this old castle. He cradled his cup for warmth. He soon forgot about the cold as they each dug into the binders, hoping to find additional information.

Jack got up after a while and stared out one of the large windows. From here, he could see the stables, and someone was washing down a horse. It was a fine-looking full breed. When he turned around, Tensbury was still immersed in the 1859 binder.

"So, nothing here." Tensbury sounded dejected. "But, speaking of other possibly lost avenues, something just came to me. Remember, I mentioned my old aunt? She might have more information about Alistair. She was closer to my grandfather than my father was. I haven't seen her for a while. She likes my children much more than she likes me. I'm not sure why. I know she's sick, and I should go see her," he murmured the last couple of sentences. "I'll give her a call and see if I can go pay her a visit."

Tensbury made a couple of calls and then recounted what he had heard.

"Talked to one of her staff members, Fred. She's in the hospital with the onset of emphysema. He doesn't expect her home for a while. I feel bad for her. He gave me the number to her doctor, and I left a message at the hospital. We'll see if the doctor returns my call."

Jack could see that Tensbury was getting more concerned and exacerbated by this affair as time went by.

"I have something else to show you. I have to fetch it from the other room."

Tensbury left. After a few minutes, he returned. He held up a slim book, worn by age, then opened it and fingered the pages.

"I owe much to this little book. Lord Arsot, a friend of Queen Victoria, wrote this small book where he mentioned Alistair. In it, the Queen read about Alistair's heroism in the

Afghan war. She asked Lord Arsot about him. He told the Queen that Alistair had two significant businesses. One was repairing ships from Asia and the other importing goods into Britain, providing industry with important raw material. As a result, she made him a peer." Tensbury looked tired, even though it was only late morning. He reverently handed it to Jack, who took a quick look at the book and handed it back.

"Too bad we can't have Andrew leveraging it anymore."

They returned to the binders. Yesterday they focused on IL&R. Now, they were spending a lot of time reviewing the Tensbury Nautical Repair Company.

"It was a perfect location for that business, Jack. Ships coming from the Indian Ocean, having rounded the Cape, often needed repairs after long trips. Take a look at this binder. Maybe I missed something."

After a while, Tensbury asked, "Are there any news clippings?"

"Let's see. Mostly invoices and receipts. Here is a list of personnel. Let me spend some time with this and see if I can come up with anything."

Jack pulled his chair closer and started examining the binder, page by page. Some were loose leaves, and he tried to make sure he returned them to their original place.

Half an hour later, Jack came up for air. There wasn't much else to look at, so they decided to leave. They were empty-handed and exhausted.

They drove back to London late morning.

In the car, Tensbury received a call from his son. He transferred the call to the car system.

"Hi, Dad. Everything alright?"

"Of course, everything is alright, son. How is it going on your side?"

"Wanted to know if you saw the press conference this morning. I changed strategies regarding the main topic, as you suggested."

"Didn't have a chance to, son. I've been busy working with

61

Jack. Was it well-received?"

"Press didn't notice anything. They just focused on what else I had to say. So, it was good." Andrew paused.

"Alright, Dad, just wanted to check-in."

"Glad you called me Andrew, my boy. I'm proud of you. You must be getting tired, though."

"I'm not. Thomas has it all under control, and the polls look good. I'm surprised, but there's so much adrenaline, I don't feel tired at all, even though the days are long. We lead Labor by a margin of error. But I know they're trying hard to find some leverage against us. Thomas told me that 10 Downing Street had hired a private consulting group to help them with their strategy. Irina Consulting. Have you heard of them?"

"No."

"They're really after us, Dad."

Tensbury didn't answer.

"Dad, are you there?"

"Yes, of course, I am. A little preoccupied, that's all."

"I'll leave you to it then. Talk to you soon."

Tensbury stared at Jack.

"Did you hear that?"

"About the consulting firm?"

"Yes. It does worry me."

"Me too, Sir."

Jack drank from his bottle of water.

Then determined, "The game is on, and we have to win."

They arrived in London early afternoon. Traffic had been heavier than usual.

Jack went to his office to check the messages. There wasn't anything of great urgency. He slumped in his chair and lamented his current situation. Yes, he wanted to help his boss out, but man, this was a lot of stress! His job was stressful enough under ordinary circumstances, but this was much, much worse. Sleeping at Lord Tensbury's place, although extremely comfortable, wasn't the same as sleeping at home.

He needed to pull himself together and help Tensbury make some decisions regarding the next steps. He walked through the anteroom to the other side of the office suite. He knocked on Tensbury's door and entered when he heard his deep voice.

Tensbury immediately blurted out. "Jack, I need to respond to that note. It's been almost two days since it came." He stopped as if waiting for Jack's approval.

"I think all I should say is, 'Yes.' The note says $250K. It's a lot of money, but it's just money. There are more critical things. I can't risk any damning information coming out before the election. What do you think?"

"I think that's right, Sir."

Tensbury hit 'send.'

"I feel better having done that." He sat back.

"What did I just agree to? I've reflected on that. You know what, Jack? I thought I would analyze my options using a systems course they taught us in business school. I used one of the tools I learned in the course, a 'decision tree,' and applied it to this situation. Let's see if it makes sense."

He carefully turned the screen on his desk towards Jack. "Here is what I have so far."

Jack studied the 'decision tree' on the screen.

> *First Outcome.*
>
> *At 1:30, the day before the election, the blackmailer comes to the hotel with the papers describing the African event. He is ready to relinquish them in exchange for $250K. As to why I was at the hotel at that time, my answer is: 'I am here in the hotel because I agreed to meet this person to help the parent in distress. Maybe assist with the sick child within the National Health System. It has nothing to do with the money he requested. The very thin briefcase I have with me is for legal papers. It can't possibly hold a lot of hush money. I,*

obviously, hear about the African event for the first time.'

If in addition, I become convinced that the blackmailer has no connection to Labor. He or she truly has a sick child, and the money this person desires will be the end of the ordeal. In this case, I take him to the office and exchange the money for the papers. I take the risk and don't prepare Andrew for a possible last-minute election bomb.

Second outcome.

A. At 1:30, nobody shows up, and it has all been a Labor ruse. The blackmail note and my answer show up in the media. As to why I was at the hotel at that time, my answer is the same as in the First Outcome, part A. Here is how I prepare Andrew in this case. Labor may or may not know about a terrible event in Africa. Most likely, it's a ruse. I tried to find any implied event in the family archive – nothing. Andrew's answer to any inquiries: 'I don't know of anything implied in the note.'

B. As in A., at 1:30, nobody shows up. Labor actually knows of some event relating to Alistair's business dealings. They bring it up through their surrogates and the media. Again, as to why I was at the hotel at that time, my answer is the same as in the First Outcome, part A. Plus, I did not know anything about the African event. Andrew's answer to any inquiries: 'I didn't know anything about this event. Would never have talked about Alistair Tensbury the way I did if I knew. But my Great Grandfather, Grandfather, and Father served this country honorably. I

intend to follow in their steps.'
If we find out about the African event before it
becomes public, we can prepare a more robust
answer depending on Alistair's business deal in
question.

"How is that, Jack? Did I learn anything in that course?" Tensbury's habitual cheerfulness peeked through.

"Very systems-like, Sir," Jack chuckled.

"So, Jack, you agree that this doesn't mean we cease our search. We still need to see if we can figure this out before the election."

"Agreed."

Jack's phone rang.

"It's George, I'll take it." He walked out to take the call.

CHAPTER 4

Thomas' phone rang.

"Hi, Thomas, this is Peter."

Peter's group provided some of the best resources for this campaign. Data Mining and Analysis has become one of the most important aspects of any election campaign over the years. Peter managed this effort flawlessly.

"Hi, Peter. What's cooking today?"

"I have something you should know about."

"Absolutely. Shoot."

"A couple of weeks ago, two young Tory sympathizers came here to volunteer for the campaign. They study computer science in college. One of them, Greg, was accepted, his friend wasn't. My people informed me, they thought the friend was too immature. Then the shit hit the fan."

'What do you mean?" Anticipating the worst, Thomas turned off the hands-free mode and picked up the phone.

"What happened next came in bits and pieces from Greg. His friend was upset at being rejected. He wanted to prove that he could be valuable to us. He tried to hack into the Labor HQ email but couldn't."

"Is that it?"

"Oh no, that wasn't enough to stop him. He got more imaginative and tried to hit some of the Labor affiliates. It seems that about a week ago, some stupid IT technician was doing maintenance on the Cornelian Society email server. For a short while, he accidentally took down an important part of their firewall. Greg's friend got lucky and got in."

"Oh shit! Do they know about this? Damn, this is awful."

"No, we don't think they know. But that's not all."

"You are getting me scared, Peter."

"Listen to this. Somewhere among the email messages, this hacker finds a note from a guy named Brock Tennyson asking a Noah Arnol in Sweden to do 'research' into Alistair Tensbury."

"Oh, oh."

"Exactly. I looked up Tennyson. He's on the Advisory Board over at the Cornelian Society. Then our reject hacker contacts his online Swedish friend and asks him about the local Swedish Internet provider. He wanted to know the type of modem/router in this Noah's neighborhood. The hacker says he met a girl online, and he wants to hack into her computer."

"They do that to each other now, don't they? Man, things have changed. Go on, Peter."

"Yes, it's sick. After getting the modem type, the hacker brings Noah's internet connection down in the afternoon."

"No!"

"Yes. But before he brings it down, he also finds a message from Noah to Tennyson. The message essentially says that he can't find anything on Alistair Tensbury from the 19th century. Noah also says something to the effect '… and what does it matter anyway – it's so far in the past, it can't affect today's outcomes.'"

"Did this Noah know who brought his connection down?"

"I don't think so. But he probably complained to the Internet provider about this. Because the next day the provider upgrades the firmware, and the hacker can't disrupt the connection anymore. Our hacker brags about his accomplishments to his friend Greg, whom we hired. Thankfully, Greg immediately told me about it. I was petrified. I told them to stop it immediately."

Tomas let out a deep breath. He felt like he had held it all through Peter's speech.

"Yes, stop it in every way! Make sure no one knows about it. Tell this hacker that if this becomes public, we'll report him to the Police. Remind him that people are locked up for long prison terms for lesser crimes than this."

Thomas moved his phone to his other ear. "By the way, don't let this get to Andrew, Peter. He has enough to worry about as it is."

"I won't."

As if some ether vibes reached Andrew, when he and Thomas grabbed a bite to eat later, they had a related conversation.

They were waiting for their order in a little cafe next door.

"You know, Thomas, I appreciate that we are running a clean campaign. The pundits say that we have something to do with the story about Labor not taking care of healthcare. It's, of course, bogus. I mean, why would we attack them with that? That's one of the major tenets of the Labor Manifesto. And, if we win, we won't touch the NHS."

Their order came, and they both stirred sugar in their coffee and took their first sip.

"I don't believe in the character assassinations and misrepresentation of a candidate's or Party's position. Facebook and Twitter, and all the other platforms, can be manipulated to spread false impressions and make truthful messaging difficult," said Andrew.

"You're right. But, on the other hand, just as quickly as the false information is pushed through, the target can refute it via the same platforms, rendering it useless."

"This requires a very sophisticated digital presence. Doesn't it? asked Andrew.

"It does, and we have it."

"I'm sure they do as well."

"They do."

Thomas drank his coffee. "I'm with you there, Andrew. I also believe in a clean fight."

"Yeah. Labor should restrict criticisms to relevant issues. That's also what I want from us, and I hope you are making sure we do."

"Of course. You have nothing to worry about. You know me."

"I know, but things might be going on that you are not aware of. I'm just asking you to watch out, that's all. I mean, opposition research is alright, but everything must be above board."

Thomas felt uneasy. He crossed his fingers that they had contained the whole hacking incident.

CHAPTER 5

After getting dressed in blue jeans, T-shirt and a form-fitting, green sweater under her coat, Hanna picked up her roller board and took a taxi down by the hotel reception. She wanted to get over to the house as soon as she could. She prayed the police had already left. She asked the taxi to drop her off at her uncle's house. As she got out, she stopped to look at the house before heading in. It was a stately house painted pale yellow with green shutters. This house has been in the family for over a hundred years. It was old but well cared for, and the way the sun shone, it almost gleamed. The gardening was perfect, with rose bushes along the driveway. In the summer, when the roses bloomed, the house looked palatial. Now, blue and white police tape circled it. It was late in the afternoon, and a bitter, spring Stockholm wind was making her eyes tear up.

Inspector Mans had told her not to enter the house yet.

But what the hell, the crime scene investigators have finished their job. It's my uncle's house, and it's probably mine now anyway.

She slunk under the police tape and saw the police lock on the entry door. She went around the back of the house. She always kept the key that she used when she was a child on her keychain. The door opened straight into the hallway. She entered now, carefully wiping her feet, just as she did when she was little.

The kitchen was to the left. It held particularly fond memories. Here is where they sat together over a cup of coffee, eating some of his delicious sandwiches. Here is where she told him everything that had happened at school since she was last home. He was as familiar with Andrea and Christina, the twins from the UK, as with Rebecca, the little redheaded girl from the States. They used to laugh till tears ran from their eyes as Hanna recounted all the crazy things that went on at school. Her throat constricted. She wiped her face with her sweater and resolved not to cry.

Hanna left the kitchen and passed through the long, wide hallway, reaching the foyer. She flung her coat on a coat-tree next to the entrance door. She turned around, as if she had entered from the front door. First, to the right was the library and then her uncle's office.

She had to find the lawyer's name before anything else. She entered her uncle's office. Neat manila folders were stacked on her uncle's desk. The leather pen holder with the gold Cross pen she had given him one Christmas stood to the right of the folders. She began to go through the folders but didn't find anything related to her uncle's lawyer. Then she opened the small file drawer in the right side of the desk and looked through the rack of pendaflex file folders. They were in alphabetical order with manila folders neatly placed inside. She got to a file named Bo Johannsson, Advokat. Good, a lawyer. She let out a deep breath. She opened the file. There were documents from Bo Johannsson on his stationary. She found the number and dialed. He answered on the first ring.

"Bo Johannsson."

"This is Hanna Arnol, Noah Arnol's niece. Are you my uncle's lawyer?"

"Yes, I am." His voice was smooth. He spoke good

English. "How may I help you?"

"My uncle died early this morning."

He didn't say anything for a long time.

"Right," said Johannsson, abruptly. "He was a good friend." Johansson paused.

Hanna could imagine him collecting his thoughts.

"There's a lot to take care of. How much do you need me to be involved?"

She welcomed his way of getting to the crux of the matter right away.

"I would appreciate it if you helped me with most things. I need help, Mr. Johansson." She quickly explained her situation.

"Right," he said. "I have a funeral director I work with. Your uncle was part of the Danderyd Church and his family is buried there. Including his wife and your parents. I think he reserved a place for himself in the same location."

"That's wonderful. I have been there many, many times and it's beautiful." Tears touched her eyes again, now thinking about her parents.

"I heard Sweden has a long time from death to funeral, but I would like it to happen as soon as possible. Can it be done in 10 days or so? Can you arrange that? I can take care of additional expenses."

"It'll take some prodding, but I'll make it happen. I'll also take care of the death announcement and will contact the University. I would need a list to get the announcement to friends and family," said Johansson.

"Of course," said Hanna. "I can send you my 'Christmas List' which I use to let people know how my uncle and I are doing."

"That will work. I'll take care of all other things. There are many documents to be filed with the state, and as executor of Noah's will, there's a great deal to prepare. I'll make sure we do the probate hearing after you return to Stockholm."

Hanna's heart slowed and she felt her anxiety ebb. It felt

good to have someone to rely on.

"I understand you are pressed for time, but there's something I need from you, Ms. Arnol. I need the text for the announcement. Would you write it, please? I'll send you a template right now. It shouldn't take you much time," said Johansson. "When I know the date and time of the funeral, I'll let you know."

They ended their call and Hanna set her computer on a side table next to the desk. She opened it and sent Johansson her Christmas List.

In a couple of minutes, she saw the email with the template attached. She started typing. The words flew out of her. She wanted everyone who would read it to understand how much he was loved. There was no mincing of words needed. Just her heartfelt feelings.

When she finished, she sent it back to Johansson.

Now, that's done.

She picked up her phone, found Patrick's number, and dialed it.

"Hey, Patrick." She didn't wait for his response and blurted out, "Uncle Noah is dead."

There was silence on the other side of the line. Patrick was the son of Brock Tennyson, her uncle's old friend in London. Hanna and her uncle often visited the Tennyson family in England. Although Patrick was older, they became friends, nonetheless.

Patrick finally spoke. "My God, what happened?"

"He fell down the stairs. The housekeeper found him this morning. They're doing an autopsy since we don't know exactly when he died. Or how."

"What do the police say? They should have some idea, right?"

"They're going through their process now, and I guess we'll find out." She sighed.

"How's your dad," she asked. She had always been fond of Patrick's dad.

"Dad's fine. He's been so busy with his work at the Cornelian Society lately, I hardly hear from him. He will be mortified when he hears this." Patrick stopped briefly.

"This is terrible, Hanna. I can't believe it. All those good times we had together."

She remembered the times they spent Christmas together at Patrick's house. They were so naughty running around the house, laughing even when they got caught.

"Dad and Uncle Noah were planning a trip to Italy next spring. Did you hear about that?"

Hanna sniffled. She didn't.

"Where are you?"

"In the house. I can't stand it now that he's not here." She choked.

"Do you want me to come? I can take off from here, you know."

Patrick worked in a law firm in London and was usually very busy.

"No, you don't have to. I'll be alright."

Hanna was quiet. She sat down on a chair in the hallway.

"Are you there?"

"I'm here. Do you have a few minutes?"

"Absolutely."

Hanna continued crying. So much for resolving not to.

Patrick just let her cry and didn't say anything.

"I feel so guilty. I haven't been to visit him since last year. We didn't even spend last Christmas together, can you imagine? I had a big deal going on and... you remember our Christmases in your house? They were wonderful," she sobbed.

"Yes, they were. We loved it when you came to visit. Remember how we used to run around hiding from Dad and Uncle Noah, who would sit there talking politics?"

Both she and Patrick grew up more conservative than his father and her uncle which was often a reason for mirth. She knew he was trying to calm her down.

She sighed, "Patrick, you know how important he was to me. I don't have anybody. Well, I have you and my friend Helen, but you know…"

Hanna knew that her relationships never lasted long. In the last couple of years, she even started thinking that she might never get married or settle down the way she worked.

"I don't know about getting married, but it would be nice to find someone I genuinely like. Someone to depend on in times like this. Someone like Uncle Noah. Smart. Adventurous. An outdoorsy kind of guy, you know?"

"You have your horses," said Patrick awkwardly.

"Yeah, right," said Hanna. "Good listeners, at least. And that's another quality I'd like in a guy. My uncle always paid total attention to whatever I was saying or doing. I should have followed his path and become a historian."

She knew Patrick had heard this story before.

"Can we meet tonight for a late dinner?

"Of course. Karen will understand. Text me when you get in."

"I've got to go. Love you."

"Wait, Hanna. Are you going to be alright? I don't like thinking of you there in the house, alone, with all the memories…"

"I'll talk to you tonight, Patrick."

She got up and stood there in the hallway. The wind picked up outside, and she heard some branches whip against the windows. She was familiar with the sound, yet it unsettled her.

CHAPTER 6

Despite what she had told Patrick, she wanted someone with her during her path through the house. It was eerie to be there by herself.

She called Helen on Skype. Helen answered, and Hanna saw her bright face displayed on her phone.

"Hi, Hanna," said Helen. "You look terrible, which I would expect. Are you at the house?"

"Yeah, do you have time to stay with me while I walk through the house? I can't bear it alone."

"I have time, honey. I'm done for the day and heading out to a late dinner next. But that can wait."

"Let me show you those damned stairs my uncle fell down."

She turned her phone around towards the stairs and then back again.

"You know, he could run up and down those stairs, two steps at a time carrying anything."

"Strange that he fell."

"Yeah. I just can't believe it. The police are looking into it. They call it an accident, but I think they're just plain wrong. Wrong," she repeated emphatically.

"What do you mean - wrong?"

"I don't know, just not right. Can't put my finger on it."

"OK ..."

"Let me take you to the library. There's something I want you to see."

Hanna turned left to enter the library. She looked around.

"Looks completely untouched," she said.

She turned the phone around to show the library.

"You know, I have such great memories of sitting up late at night here, reading. I read everything. From 'Serpico,' which took me away to New York City's dirty police officers, to Durant's Story of Civilization. I read every hefty tome about different periods of history."

"It looks like just a place to enjoy a book," said Helen.

"Let me show you his sports awards."

"Here are all the tennis trophies from when he was playing competitively. And here are some more recent ones. Like the second place in a swimming competition for seniors just last year. I mean, how could this have happened? He was so strong."

Hanna teared up again. She didn't expect an answer.

These damn tears won't stop.

"Remember I told you about my ancestor Signe?"

"The one who sailed around the world?" asked Helen.

"Well, only from Norway to South Africa. But still. She was only eighteen, and this was 1859. Can you imagine? Alone with all those sailors for months? You know, she was the only passenger. I don't think I told you, but I have her diaries."

She was walking in the library holding the phone up to her face.

"Here are her diaries. See?"

Hanna turned the phone around again.

"She wrote one each year until 1916 when she died. They look so small, don't they? Each of them looks different from another. Signe must have had a hard time finding the same type of notebook every year. Most are leather-bound with ridges on the back. See, like old books you might see at an antique bookstore. The year they were written is marked on each one of them."

"They're in Norwegian, right? Have you ever read them?"

"See here?" said Hanna. "Here are attached envelopes with English translations for each one. Remember I told you about my family? Uncle Noah translated them to English both for me and any other extended family member. The text is probably almost illegible even to someone who speaks the language. The ink is so faded."

"Great thing he did this for you."

"The 1859 diary is especially interesting to me," said Hanna. "This is the one where she writes about her trip to Africa. It covers the voyage to South Africa, including the detour to St. Louis in Senegal."

Hanna sat down in one of the large, leather chairs where she had spent so much time reading. She opened the translated diary pages.

"Listen to this, Helen. These pages are about the beginning of her trip. I used to be so proud of her leaving Norway all by herself. I'll read them to you. It's short."

"Go ahead, honey."

Dear Diary

Why will I travel to South Africa? To see my dear Lars. He is my fiancé, and I should be with him. I am tired of waiting for him to send for me. Also, to be truly honest, I want to get away from the newspaper office and all of Kristiansand. Get out and learn and take hold of something, where I can use my knowledge and desire to work, which I know is wasted at home.

Yesterday, people in the office talked about the trading ship Ingeborg, heading for South Africa. That's when I got the idea that this might be an opportunity for me to get out sooner. I got filled with a desire to leave now. I did not know then that my wish would come true. I mentioned this at home during dinner, and Pappa ground his teeth. Pappa, of course, thought I was out of my mind and going too far and at first, refused to even listen to me. But you know me, stubborn as I am, he relented. I spoke with the captain, and he said I could come and explained I would be the only passenger. So what? I can handle myself. Then I resigned from the office.

Dear Diary,

Today I said farewell to Pappa and everything dear in the city. I could never have imagined how sad it felt to leave. But you know me, I put on my happy face and dealt with the toll it took on my nerves. Poor, old, dear Pappa. I wish mother were here to support him. I know he thinks he will never see me again, but I'll be back in four-five years, and then we can all be together again. So, I told him to please be happy for me and that wish he could join me. Then I would never have to leave him. Everyone helped me prepare, each in their own way.

Dear Diary,

Finally, we left! I stood on deck as long as I could. Five years - it sounds so incredibly long, but keep your chin up now, Signe, I told myself! Then we passed Lund, and finally, Odderö disappeared. I left deck and went down to the Captain's salon to get a last glimpse of my dear Norway from the aft porthole. I suffered this afternoon a bit and got seasick.

"I'll stop there. Signe continues writing during the trip, but then some of the pages are gone. Torn out. I remember thinking that maybe something made Signe tear them out, or maybe someone else did it. Even someone from the family!"

"Interesting."

"Yeah, isn't? When I was young, I always tried to figure out what was in the missing pages. But neither my uncle nor I could come up with an idea that made sense of what that might be. It ends just as she arrives in St. Louis and picks back up as she arrives in South Africa."

She held the phone back up to her face.

"God, you look tired and red from crying. I wish I were there with you."

Hanna went on. "But about a week ago, my uncle called and asked me to come because he had found the missing pages. How I have no clue. I'm sure he didn't find them in this house because he had searched for them so thoroughly before."

"That's terrific," said Helen. "What's in them?"

"I don't even know where they are," said Hanna, despondently. "I don't know where he put them. That's one of the reasons why I'm here. To try to find them."

She scanned the library for anything that might give her a clue about their whereabouts, but no. Nothing.

"Do you have time?" asked Hanna. "I hope you can stay on the phone. You don't mind, do you? I just don't want to be alone."

"I don't mind one-bit, honey. Food can wait. I don't need it anyway."

Hanna knew Helen was always watching her waistline.

"Okay. I'm going to take a look at his office now for those pages." Hanna drew a breath and picked up the diary she had withdrawn. She returned to the office.

"I'll put you down for a minute and keep the speaker on. Hang on."

She placed her phone on her uncle's desk. Helen would only see the ceiling, but they could talk.

Hanna looked around. She couldn't see anything untoward here. Except her laptop on the side table, the room appeared utterly undisturbed.

"I just had an outlandish idea, Hanna. What if there were someone at the house looking for Signe's diary pages? The ones he just found? I mean, there must have been some reason she tore them out. I know this seems completely stupid."

"No, it's not stupid. Nothing is, at this point. Or maybe someone was looking for something else my uncle was working on? Someone could have made a quiet entry while my uncle was home and surprised him at the top of the stairs."

"Yes, and never intended for him to die. After the accident, they could have left quickly without searching further."

Hanna and Helen knew each other so well that they could predict what the other one would say.

Hanna switched on her uncle's computer, and both displays on his desk.

"I'm trying to log into his computer, but it's password protected."

She tried to guess his password. Didn't work. Hanna fingered the keys, hoping irrationally for some lingering warmth from her uncle. All she felt was cold plastic.

"Helen? Are you there?"

"I'm here."

"You know my uncle has a blog which he asked me to help him set up. The one I think he set up because of Signe's trip? That was about a year ago."

Hanna recalled their conversation. "He called me to help him because he said I was 'in the biz.'"

Helen laughed, and Hanna couldn't help smiling. It was the first time she did since finding out about Uncle Noah that morning. Hanna and Helen were both in the IT outsourcing business but had no idea about setting up blogs or websites.

"I just asked one of my solution architects for help. It didn't look like he minded. Gave him a break from what he was working on, you know. Plus, he probably thought helping an exec out would be good for his career. It didn't take him long."

She brought the phone up in front of her face.

"Sorry, this is taking so long. Thanks for being with me. I keep thinking that I'm keeping you from something."

"No, you're not. You know I'd tell you if you did. So, what's in the blog?"

Hanna put the phone back down.

"Give me a minute."

She turned to her laptop and typed the URL of her uncle's blog. Hanna looked through the posts, but nothing indicated anything about the missing pages.

"Now I'm going to check his files. Hold on."

She went through the folders on the desk again. Now looking for the missing pages. Nothing.

"Next, I'll look through the pentaplex folders inside the desk."

She found nothing there about the diary pages.

But something gave her pause. In the 'T' pentaplex was a manila folder named 'Tensbury.' Interesting. She pulled out the folder and opened it on the desk. It contained printouts about Alistair Tensbury and his South African company. One of the printouts had the name 'Leo' written at the bottom in her uncle's neat script. The folder also included sheets on the current UK election.

She also saw the notes on IL&R in Senegal she sent to him last week.

"Helen, I haven't told you about the research I did for my uncle last week." She recounted her work on Tensbury's IL&R.

"But the Andrew Tensbury in the news must be the descendant of that 1st Baron Tensbury. Isn't he?" blurt out Helen.

"He is."

"Do you think there's some connection between your uncle's research and this election?"

"Maybe."

Hanna closed her eyes and imagined her uncle working at this computer. Then she looked down on the desk.

"Wait, here is something stuck under the blotter. It's a slip of paper with a name on it. He has printed the name 'Professor Diallo' and a phone number. I don't recognize the prefix. It's 221."

"I just looked," said Helen. "It's for Senegal."

Hanna checked Senegal time on her phone. "Let me give him a call. You can stay on."

Hanna dialed the number. It rang for a long time.

"No one picked up. I'll have to wait and call later."

Hanna studied the note further. "It also says that a guide will be waiting at the airport when we arrive. That was my uncle's plan."

Hanna slipped the paper into her computer backpack, which she slung over her shoulder. She picked up the diary as well as the phone.

"Now, I'm going to head up those damn stairs."

The stairs had deep treads, and she remembered how difficult they had been to walk up and down when she was young. Before fourteen, when she had her growth spurt, she sometimes had to double up her steps.

Tenuously, she walked up, staying to one side, and holding on to the banister. She was uneasy. Had her uncle been alive for a while before he was discovered? Or did he fall and die instantly? She hoped the latter. The autopsy may tell.

Maybe Mans was right, and it was just an accident.

On the second floor, Hanna turned left and passed several rooms.

"Here is my old room. Look, he made my bed. He was waiting for me to come."

Now her tears returned in earnest. The combination of being in her own room, seeing her bed, lovingly made by her uncle, made her shake with tears. She stood there crying until she heard Helen calling.

"Hanna! Hanna! I know you are sad, so find someplace to sit and just cry this out. I'm here waiting for you."

Just as before, Helen's voice soothed Hanna, and she stopped heaving with grief. Soon Hanna was sniffling slightly and found a tissue box on her old desk.

"I'm okay now," she whispered. Looking around, Hanna said, "I worked so hard on that piano." She still sniffled.

"I guess it paid off, honey, because I love the way you play. Jazz, blues."

Although she didn't think she was very good at it and only played for close friends, Hanna loved playing.

Anemic Swedish afternoon sunshine swam in through the window. Hanna put her things down and sat in her chair at the desk. Her eyes landed on the heart-shaped mirror on the door of her wardrobe. This is where Uncle Noah would hide things during their games. One year, he had left her a ring from her grandmother, a ruby set in gold – her birthstone. But most of the time, it was just a little trinket or a bag of the Swedish candy she loved so much.

Hanna sobered up. "Hang on, Helen. I'm going to set you down again for a minute."

She opened the wardrobe where a few of her old things still hung. She savored the smell of the wood. So familiar. She climbed up on a ledge to reach the top shelf and groped around as she always had, anticipating some surprise. When she was small, she had to stand on the shoe rack to reach, but now she just stretched her arm towards the back. She saw something in the darkness and pulled it towards her. It felt like a large envelope.

"Helen, I think I found the pages!"

She opened the envelope and spread out the contents on her desk.

"Where?"

"In the old hiding place we used for fun when I was small, and even now as an adult. He knew I was coming, and I think he just wanted to play with me to discover this extraordinary find."

"So sweet of him."

"I'll tell you what I'm looking at here. There's a typewritten document on letterhead from 'Norra Banken Service AB' in Swedish."

"Do you still read some Swedish?"

"Not much. I lost a lot of it when I went to college. But I know enough to see this is in Swedish."

She put the letter to the side.

"Here are the pages, Helen." She placed the pages in the diary— they fit perfectly.

She picked up the phone and beamed at Helen. "Helen, I'm so excited. How I'm going to get it all translated is another question."

"How about Google Translate?"

Hanna looked down at her desk.

"The letter from the bank, maybe, but the diary pages will have to go to a translation service." The driven script her ancestor Signe had laid down on these old pages made it difficult even to discern separate words.

CHAPTER 7

"Helen, I'm okay now. I'm going to send these pages off to a translation service."

"Are you sure you are alright?" asked Helen. "Call me again if you feel low. Okay? Promise?" Hanna promised.

She went back down to her uncle's office to scan the pages. A printer stood on the table to the right of the desk. She plugged in her laptop and scanned every newly discovered diary page into a PDF document. Then she goggled translation services in Stockholm. She contacted three, and all said it would take some time to translate this type of paper. Handwritten documents over a hundred years old were afforded special attention, at a higher price, of course. None of them could tell her how long the translation would take. They estimated it to be several days. She asked them to keep the content confidential. They agreed to email the translations as soon as they finished each page. She decided to send every third page to each of the three translation services.

Who knows what is in there? These pages might hold all sorts of things given the suspicions Helen and I have.

Hanna needed to know who sent these pages to her uncle. She took the letter from the bank, scanned it, and ran the text through Google Translate.

Dear Mr. Arnol,

We have discovered a grave mistake our bank has made, and we apologize. We acquired the Norwegian bank, Nordvest Banken, from Kristiansand in 1951. It held several items that were placed in trust in Norway. Because of the acquisition, many items were misplaced. One such item is this package, which was put in trust in 1859 by Agnes Olsen.

In 1917 Agnes Olsen provided instructions for the parcel to be delivered in 1959 to a John Arnol at your address. The instructions indicated that if John Arnol was deceased, the package should go to the oldest descendant of this man. We believe this is you.

Hanna stopped. Olsen was Signe's maiden name. Agnes Olsen was Signe's younger sister. She recognized the name from the family tree she had studied growing up. Like the rest of the family, other than Signe, Agnes stayed in Norway her entire life. When Signe tore these pages from her 1859 diary, she must have decided to send them to her sister. Signe gave Agnes instructions to put them in a bank.

Why did she want them to be delivered after a hundred years? Wow, there could be something 'explosive' there.

The letter continued,

Mr. Arnol, we take full responsibility for this egregious mistake and apologize profoundly.

Johan Segmark,

Director, Norra Banken Service AB.

She saved the Google translation on her computer, put the original and the laptop in the backpack.

Hanna remembered something she wanted to take from her room. Negotiating the stairs again with care, she returned to her room. She fumbled in her desk drawers and extracted a picture she took from the library when she was a little girl. It was a faded black and white photo. She read the inscription on the back she knew so well, "Signe Arnol, Stockholm, 1910". It was written in the same driven script as the diaries.

In the photo, Signe had her head turned to one side, showing off high cheekbones in a rather gaunt face as she stared into the camera. Her thick hair was swept back from a high forehead and fell to the top of her shoulders. Several long necklaces tumbled over a flowing blouse or gown.

This was a woman who demanded attention and expected to receive it.

Hanna thought of her own features. Did she have some of these attributes? Would be nice to think so, but right now, she didn't feel very strong. Her uncle always said she looked a lot like Signe.

Maybe.

She had the same chin with a slight cleft, the long neck, and the strong nose she hated. The one her uncle called a 'Roman Nose.' She couldn't see the color of Signe's eyes since the photo was black and white. They were probably of a light hue. Maybe a mixture of blue and green like her own. She examined the image again. What did this regal woman look like when she was eighteen? Perhaps not beautiful in the traditional sense, yet attractive. And tall. Everyone in her family was tall. She wondered if the strengths of one's ancestors move down through many generations. She hoped she could be as strong and brave as Signe.

She sat there as the room turned darker. With the darkness, the sorrow engulfed her again. Searching for the pages had been a sort of quest. Short-lived but intense. Now the emptiness was back. Her ears strained, hoping in vain to hear her uncle's familiar 'Snuttan.' Perhaps calling her to dinner or an outing. As she told Helen, the fact that he decided to hide the pages in their old hiding place wasn't strange. They had continued that silly game into her adulthood. Even though it certainly seemed childish, the nostalgia of it satisfied them both. Especially since she visited so rarely.

She turned to the windowsill behind her and picked up a picture of Uncle Noah and her father when they were young. She used to carry it back and forth to school, and she wasn't sure when she began leaving it here or why. Perhaps when she went to college. Lately, with the selfie craze, she would snap selfies and send them to her uncle with a little text message. In turn, he would snap pictures of himself and of things he found interesting or beautiful.

That had become their primary method of communication over the last year. The messages were frequent. Hanna felt more connected than if they had spent an hour on the phone. At least that's how Hanna felt. She hoped he felt the same. Before the smartphone furor began, things were different. Maybe he had wanted those long calls, letters, or emails that she didn't send anymore. He certainly would have liked to see her more.

Hanna put the picture into her computer bag.

Memories tumbled over each other in her mind. The joy she felt when he picked her up from the airport when she came home from school. The pleasure of entering the house. Seeing the familiar things, and above all, savoring the familiar aromas in the air. Riding in his Volvo. Always the latest model, always gleaming red and smelling new. She got her driver's license in one of those cars, the instructor handpicked by her uncle.

Uncle Noah came over to the US for her college and her MBA graduation. She knew he had been proud of her Summa Cum Laude in college and her high rank among her fellow MBA graduates. He must have felt somber, even sad, to see her graduate with a degree in business rather than history. But he had kept up a cheerful face, and on the day of graduation, she knew he was genuinely happy for her.

Hanna leaned forward and rubbed her back. It had been a long day. She was back thinking about her uncle's death and its timing. An ominous sensation that something was terribly wrong fell over her.

Again, she picked up the phone and speed-dialed Helen.

"Helen, am I disturbing? Maybe you're eating?"

"Hanna! Of course not. I told you to call. I'm just having coffee. Wait, let me step away from the table."

Hanna could hear Helen excusing herself. Then she was back on the line.

"Alright. I'm in a quiet place now. Are you in bad shape? I expected it."

"No. I'm okay. Listen, I got to thinking about some things that I want to run by you."

"Want to Skype?"

"Nah."

"Okay. Shoot."

"Remember I told you how excited my uncle was when he found those pages we were talking about?"

"Yes."

"I got to thinking about how they might relate to my uncle's death. Remember what you said in the library?"

"Yeah, that someone might have caused his death accidentally."

"So, I'm thinking, did the pages cause this? Does someone other than my uncle know about them? If the answer to these questions is 'yes,' I have to find the 'who' in this riddle. I owe it to him. "

"Wait, I have to say goodnight to this guy."

Hanna detected Helen's muted voice, but she returned in no time.

"I'm back. So, what were you thinking?"

"Well, what is the possible sequence? About a week from now is the UK general election. Remember I saw the file about Tensbury and the Tory campaign in Uncle Noah's office?"

"Yes."

Hanna heard background noises again.

"Hey. I have to move to a table further away. Too many of

the guys I had dinner with are interrupting me. Hold on a second," said Helen.

Hanna waited.

"Okay. Sorry, continue."

"I'm not keeping you up, am I? It must be late over there."

"Hanna, you know what I said. You can bother me at any time. Besides, it's not my bedtime yet." Hanna could 'hear' Helen smile.

"Okay. So, just follow my train of thought here. I may be totally off the rocker, but I don't think so." Hanna took a breath.

"Let's say, British Labor, or its affiliates, are searching for negative information on Alistair, since Andrew Tensbury is always bragging about him. Specifically, looking into his business dealings on the coast of South Africa and Senegal in the 1800s. They know that my uncle is a historian who has a nautical blog covering the 19th century. It doesn't hurt that he has left-leaning views, either. They ask him to get some relevant info on Alistair to see if he had some questionable dealings at the time."

"Okay."

"But, if Labor is looking for negative information, then the Tories are also looking for the same information, to preempt the Labor disclosure."

"This was related to that research your uncle asked you to do, right?

"Right. And then, just by coincidence, Uncle Noah gets the lost diary pages. I'm thinking that he was astonished, because he found a reference to some really shameful event in Alistair's dealings in Senegal."

"What shameful event?"

"Well, he didn't know. He decided to go to Africa to find the description of this event. I think this is why Uncle Noah was so adamant about us going to Senegal this week, a week before the election!"

"Wow. Okay, and then?"

"Then, let's say, one of the Tory affiliates gets wind of the fact that the pages contain information that would seriously damage Andrew Tensbury's campaign, and by extension the Tory's. They want to get ahold of these pages to prepare Andrew for what could be coming. While searching for the pages in his home, they stumble upon my uncle, and inadvertently kill him."

"That's what I've been thinking all along, Hanna! So, what are you going to do?"

Hanna let out an exasperated sigh. "I don't know." She stopped. "But I'll let you go now. Just wanted to run my thoughts by you."

"That's okay. Glad you seem to be feeling a little better. Now, don't get me wrong, but I think our ideas sound a little farfetched. I know you! Don't get too hot headed and go do something stupid!"

"I'm not in any shape for that, so don't worry."

"You are going to London tonight, right? When do you leave?"

"Soon."

"Okay, call me again if you need to. I'm going to head up to my room and take a long shower, and then hop into bed. I have another grueling client meeting tomorrow."

After speaking with Helen, Hanna sat there, mentally going through the conversation.

It may be farfetched, but it may be right.

So, what am I to do now? I owe it to Uncle Noah to find whatever information he was looking for in Senegal. It might point to his killer. I don't care if Mans thinks this was an accident. I don't!

That's it! I am going to Senegal as Uncle Noah planned. I'll use the diary pages, as they come from the translation services, to guide me. Yes, by finding information that impacts the Tory campaign, I'll discover who killed Uncle Noah. When I find anything nefarious about his death, I'll immediately call Detective Mans.

Hanna picked up the diary and put it in her backpack. Then she heard her phone ring. A London number she didn't know. She almost let it go to voice mail. For some reason she picked up.

"Hello," she said, tentatively. She didn't really want to speak to anyone right now.

"Hanna, I just heard from Patrick about Noah. My dear, you must be heartbroken." She heard Brock Tennyson's deep baritone delivery on the other side.

"Patrick told me what happened. What a horrible demise for such a robust man! Falling down the stairs. I can't believe it!"

Tears came to her eyes again, and she tilted her head back so they wouldn't fall. She found herself unable to say anything.

Tennyson continued, "I know you are losing the only close family member you have. And that's also very tragic, Hanna. How are you holding up? What can I do, my dear?"

"Thank you for calling, Brock. I'm at my uncle's house and it feels terribly lonely. Patrick offered to come over, but I just need some time to absorb all this on my own for now."

Tennyson's deep voice shuddered. "I am losing a dear old friend. We have been working together for a very long time. It's hard for me to wrap my brain around this." Tennyson stopped. "He was a tremendous partner. We often argued, you know. He was stubborn."

A moment of silence ensued. Hanna pressed her phone against her ear, arm on her knee.

It was so comforting to hear his voice and to know this strong link that had existed between them.

"I recall all those times when you and Noah would come over to spend time with us in England. Oh, what devils you and Patrick were…"

"And I remember you and Uncle Noah discussing things, sitting in your library. Listening to you, built my interest in politics."

Visiting the Tennysons and running around with Patrick had been very important as she grew up. A thought entered her mind. This one pleasant, and she let it melt as if it was candy. The Tennysons had horses, and that's where she learned how to ride, Patrick ever the patient teacher.

"Brock, I'm going to make it through this. I really will." She knew she was trying to convince herself, as much as Brock.

"I'm seeing Patrick for a late dinner tonight."

"Good. Again, let me know if I can do anything, Hanna. I am incredulous. Such a giant of a man! His intellect and friendship will be sorely missed."

"I know how close you were."

Her head drooped further between her knees. She felt as if it was difficult to keep it on her neck.

"Let me know when the funeral is. Hanna, there are many in the Classical History community who would want to attend. How will they find out the facts about the funeral?"

"My uncle's lawyer is taking care of all the details and will send out the announcement as soon as we know the date. He has the list of our friends and relatives and the History Department at the Stockholm University. Would you please send me the list of the other people in the Classical History community he can add?"

After the call Hanna realized she needed to check into her flight to London for tonight and reschedule her flight to Dakar to leave from London tomorrow. Not from Stockholm, as they had planned. She pulled up her airline reservation. A flight was departing Heathrow tomorrow around noon. That would give her enough time to get to the flight after her meeting. She called the airline.

They charged a fee for changing the ticket.

Oh, well.

She checked the time.

Damn.

She had to rush to catch her plane to London. She called a

94

cab. She negotiated the stairs again and left the house the way she had come in – through the back. She felt good about having decided to go to Senegal. Could be just folly, but she needed to do something.

It was chilly outside, but just as she descended the driveway, the taxi drove up, and she jumped in. She turned around to stare at the house as they drove away. She would return soon.

CHAPTER 8

"Hey, George."

"Hey. Listen to this. Last night before hitting the hotel, I drove out to Arnol's house."

"Hold on! You were not supposed to do anything except research the man." Jack's stomach lurched. He prayed Labor didn't find out that Tensbury was pursuing this matter.

"I just wanted to see what kind of environment he lived in. It was dark and quiet. Maybe the guy was out. I don't know. That's what I was thinking. So, today, on my way to the airport, I swung by Arnol's house again."

"You shouldn't have done it."

"Yes, I know, but I figured that was research too."

"Alright, I'm listening." Jack tried to keep irritation and concern out of his voice.

"Wait till you hear what I found out. When I drove up to the house today, I saw blue and white police tape surrounding the property. I called Jonas, who still has connections with the police, and it turns out Noah Arnol died last night."

"What?" Jack's mind went blank. "What happened?"

He started sweating. His mind couldn't let go of the fact that Arnol was dead and the implications that brought. And whether this whole affair had morphed into killings and if someone else could be involved.

"Jonas' police contact said he fell down the stairs and that they don't suspect a crime."

"Yeah, they don't suspect a crime, but they put tape around the house!"

"Alright, let me go on. Maybe the police are just checking, but they didn't tell Jonas they suspect a crime. Anyway, an hour or so ago, while I'm talking to Jonas on the phone, I see this taxi stop at the gate of the house, and a woman gets out. She sneaks under the tape, walks up to the house, and stops in front of the door. Then she up and walks around to the back of the house."

"The police probably put a police lock on the door. So much for 'don't suspect a crime.'"

"I saw that she got into the house through the back door. I decided to wait. She spent quite some time there before she came out. Then, another taxi drives up. She gets in and takes off."

"You should have let me know before you decided to take a pass by the house."

"I know, but as I said, I wanted to see the neighborhood the man lived in. Besides, it's great we got a little more intelligence, even if we don't know who the woman is. I'm on my way to the airport now to catch my flight to London. I'll write up a report on the plane. Sorry, I don't have much."

"That's alright. Have a safe flight," said Jack, still not knowing how to react.

Jack stepped back into Tensbury's office.

"Major game-changer. George called and said Noah Arnol died last night."

Tensbury halfway rose from his chair but sank back down.

"Good God! Was he sick?"

"No, George said he fell down the stairs. From everything I've read, he was a sportsman, and photos I've seen show him as a very robust guy. He lived in that house for a long time, so I don't know how or why he could have fallen down the stairs in his own home."

"Lately, I have found myself having to watch my footing at the top of the stairs in my ancestral home. It's probably age, not the robustness," said Tensbury.

Then after pause, "Wait a minute. How did George find out about this?"

Jack recounted George's story.

"Why did he go there?"

"He said he was curious about the neighborhood Arnol lived in."

"Do you think he may have been so curious as to go in there and cause this to happen? Perhaps he got into the house thinking Arnol was out and surprised him at the top of the stairs."

In the back of Jack's mind, he remembered why George had been let go from SAS, and he felt queasy. He pushed the thoughts back.

Then calmly, "I can't imagine George doing such a thing, Sir. He's sometimes hot-headed, but not with something like this."

Jack pulled out the chair opposite his desk and sat down. They stared at each other.

"Does this change the game? Assuming Arnol was their man to poke at you, with him dead, Labor's project will go awry."

"Not necessarily. As we discussed, Arnol can't have been the guy who initiated the blackmail. He wouldn't want to go to prison. He just did the research. Now, if they are serious about it, they can pivot to another agent."

Tensbury had a thought. "What woman is George talking about?"

"I have to see if I can find out who she is. Since she had a key to get in, she obviously was someone close to the man," said Jack.

He opened his computer once more. "Let me look up Arnol again."

He pulled up Google and entered 'Arnol.' "There's a Jens Arnol." He clicked further. "Jens Arnol lived in New York and died many years ago. That's the brother George mentioned before."

Jack scrolled further down. "Here is an Anna Arnol. She also lived in New York and died the same year Jens did. Maybe an accident."

Jack continued scrolling and found a Hanna Arnol. "Another one here. The name is Hanna Arnol. And here is the link to her LinkedIn profile."

He logged in and pulled up her LinkedIn account. "Shows background and education etc., etc., but nothing about her family. Could be the woman George saw, right?"

"Could be," Tensbury gave an exhausted sigh. "Any other people there?"

"No, that's it. I'm going to take another look at Noah's blog. We don't have anything else to go on."

Jack pulled up Arnol's blog. "Let me browse through some of the posts. Here's the most recent one. It relates to how to locate captains' logs from the 1800s online."

"If there are a lot of posts, there may be a list of all of them," noted Tensbury. "Perhaps you can locate something that way. Amateurs with their blogs often have friends, and families populate their blogs. Especially in the beginning to get some traction."

Jack sat hunched over his computer, scrolling and stopping to read the posts now and then.

"Sir, you are right. I think I found out who this woman is. She has written one of the first posts. It's named 'Maritime from Norway to America in the 1800s.' She signs it as Hanna Arnol and says, 'Uncle Noah, so happy you can now focus on your interests in maritime.' How about that?" Jack was surprised at their luck.

"So, it's his niece! What else does it say?"

"Nothing else. But it includes a short bio and a photo. It's the same headshot we saw on LinkedIn. When George gets back this evening, I'm going to show him this picture. I hope this is the same woman he saw outside of Arnol's house."

"Right. Let's go back to LinkedIn. Let's get a better idea of who she is," said Tensbury.

Jack pulled up her profile again. "Works for an IT outsourcing company with offices in Palo Alto, California, and London. It says they have two delivery centers in Bangalore."

"Outsourcing," said Tensbury, somber look on his face. "That's where they take well-paying, technical and other jobs in the West and outsource them to India for a fraction of the cost."

"Not only India, Sir. Now they send those jobs to China, and even Russia as well. This is why you can't understand a word IT support says in any of the companies you deal with," said Jack, distracted.

Changing the subject back to Hanna, Tensbury asked, "What about her education?"

"She went to a high school named Montreux Lycée."

Jack quickly pulled up the site. "All girl's boarding school in Switzerland. Then Cornell for undergraduate studies majoring in history." He looked at Tensbury dramatically, then back at his screen again.

"An MBA from Stanford University. A pretty bright woman," he paused. "She lists her interests and hobbies as horses, history, and traveling. Under languages, she has German, Spanish, French, Italian and Russian."

"All those languages make sense since she went to a Swiss school. Russian is interesting, though. Why Russian? Then again, those schools always focus on languages. Notice she doesn't list Swedish, so I'm not sure how close she was to Noah Arnol."

"Based on the dates of her degrees, we can assume she's in her early to mid-thirties."

"I can't take any more of this right now," Tensbury uttered, exasperated.

They decided to take a break, and Jack returned to his office. They both needed to catch up on work they had missed since yesterday morning. Jack pulled up the bills he had been working on. He had a hard time concentrating. His mind kept returning to who could have initiated this whole scene. He wondered if Labor or some associated group could had been involved. Or, if, in fact, it was someone in the States they couldn't possibly track. And he wasn't sure, that it was of any use to try to find the culprit, anyway.

Then he reminded himself that, of course, they needed to find out if it was Labor behind it all. They needed whatever information existed. So that Andrew could build a story around it and preempt whatever they would release.

Jack saw George's number come up on his phone. He was sure George had already done enough for today.

"Hey, Jack."

"Hey. So, what are you up to now? Weren't you supposed to be back in London?"

"I'm calling from the airport. This day has been incredible! As you know, I was flying out of Stockholm this afternoon. Boarding the plane, I saw the same woman that I saw entering Arnol's house."

"Really?" asked Jack flabbergasted.

"Really! The plane wasn't completely full, and when we reached flying altitudes, I was able to grab the seat beside her. She was in a middle seat, and I told her I needed the aisle row for more legroom."

"Nice."

"Yes, it worked. She opened her laptop, and I grabbed one of the onboard magazines. Pretending to read, I was able to see what she was doing. We had Wi-Fi on board, so I saw her check email. Then she went to Air France's site reviewing an itinerary for a trip to Dakar, Senegal, leaving tomorrow."

"Senegal?"

"You know my good memory, right. So, when I went to the bathroom, I wrote down enough from her itinerary to complete it. I started with the two flight numbers and the names of two hotels. One hotel in Dakar and one in St. Louis. I also got the check-in date in St. Louis and the date of the flight back to London. The rest I finished by going to different websites. I'll send it now."

"This is fantastic work, George! What else?"

"Well, she took out an old, small notebook. Looked almost antique, like those they keep under glass in libraries, you know. She just sat there carefully rifling through the pages. It was handwritten. I don't think it was in English. Then she took a bunch of stapled pages. Those were typed and in English. The first page only had 1859 on it. She started browsing through the pages. I have a feeling they were the translation of the old book. I am guessing because every page started with 'Dear Diary.'"

"If you're right, then the old book is a diary."

"It must be. At that point, she stopped and read one of the pages. I only got a couple of sentences. It was something like 'We are on the way to St. Louis in Senegal. It's November, but we caught a storm.'"

"Were you able to see anything else?"

"No, that's about it. And just a while ago, I saw the woman grab a taxi at the curb."

Soon came the itinerary, and Jack read it through.

"Know what, George?" texted Jack. "Here is a picture of a woman I found on LinkedIn. Tell me if it's the same one you saw on the plane."

CHAPTER 9

"It's the same woman," came the message.

Jack got up and returned to Tensbury's office. The staff had left, and his door was open. He recounted the conversation with George, and they started talking at the same time. Tensbury's voice drowned out Jack's.

"Hell, now things are even more confusing," exclaimed Tensbury.

"Well, Sir, this whole affair regarding Arnol may be something completely innocuous. Like we discussed, let's say Arnol finds out something about your ancestor in Africa when he does his maritime research. Then he calls you to share the information. He dies before he can get it to you."

"Yeah, and I have a beautiful villa with a view of the icebergs on the North Pole to sell you," Tensbury smirked.

"Let's say you're right, then who made the ransom note?"

"I'm thinking. If it's not Arnol or someone else working for Labor, it might be a descendant of this Haddock fellow."

"Yeah, there's a queue out there taking turns to come after the Tories and Andrew," Tensbury said with disdain. "And what about Hanna?"

"This is getting more and more convoluted. Like Arnol dying. And all this about Africa. The ransom note is about something that happened in Africa. Or supposedly happened, that is. Then there's this American's letter from 1858. Remember Haddock? He writes about Africa. Now this woman is flying to Africa. And the old-looking book, maybe an old diary, she brings with her. The person who wrote the diary is in St. Louis in November of 1859. And there was a storm. Could that be the book leading Hanna to this event in Africa regarding your ancestor?"

"Africa, Africa, Africa. Hell, Jack!" Tensbury's voice was loud and angry.

"Sir, there's good news in this new twist. If Noah Arnol, and now his niece, are working with Labor, they may know something, but not enough to bring up. If they had known all about this event, they wouldn't need to go to Africa."

"You are right. If we pursue this and find out the whole story before Labor does, we may deflect it. Whether this is something innocuous or a Labor intrigue, I have a feeling it's not just smoke without fire. Something happened in Africa around 1858-59, and it likely involved Alistair. We need to follow this thread to find out what it is before it blows up in our face. We need to figure out what she's looking for when she's in Senegal. I mean, is she looking for certain documents, information, or is she going there to meet someone?"

Tensbury stared at Jack. "You probably know what I am going to say."

"Yes."

"You have to go, Jack."

"I know. But I need someone who does the job of following her around." Jack stopped. "And I have someone in mind who can help us arrange it."

"Let's not share too much information, though."

"Don't be concerned, Sir. I have an old acquaintance with a boutique travel agency. She focuses on Africa. She's very discreet. I bet she knows how to get someone at a good guide shop in Senegal. Then, for the right fee, I am almost sure I could find someone for this job. I would convince a guide to discretely follow and observe someone from a distance instead of guiding a tour. I'll set up the trip now." He got up and went to his office.

He booked the flight to Senegal for tomorrow and arranged for the hotel in Dakar. The itinerary George sent, placed him on the same flight as Hanna. The flights schedule left no way to get around it. He also wanted the hotel to be the same as Hanna's to manage the project of following her around.

Jack dialed his acquaintance's number. "Hi, Mary. It's Jack. Jack Fernsby." He paused. "I'm glad you remember me. Hey, something has come up, and I would like to take a little mini vacation to Dakar. Do you know a good guide shop there? Oh, you do. How long have you known this guy? Ten years! Alright. Sounds fantastic. I need someone who is a bit over and beyond your usual guide. Someone who speaks excellent English, and who would be able to take me to one of the other cities if needed. I mean, I'm going to need this guy glued to me, Mary. Yes, and I'm prepared to pay more than his regular fee if he can find the right man. Do you have my email? Great. Thanks, Mary. You are an angel! Cheers."

Fifteen minutes later, Jack's phone rang. The man introduced himself as being from the travel agency Mary mentioned.

"I'm the owner, and I happen to be in Senegal checking up on my group. Since Mary is such a good friend, I'll personally take you around."

"Thanks for your quick response. Mary told me that you guys are exceptional. I'm going to be in Dakar tomorrow night. If possible, I would like you to start the day after tomorrow in the morning."

"I just sent you a note."

"Yes, I see your email now. Thanks. This is excellent. I'll send you the name of my hotel shortly."

Jack was satisfied that he had accomplished the first step of this trip. He needed to go home and pack up his things. He quickly checked the Senegal Embassy website.

At least he didn't have to get a visa. He knew it was recommended to get Typhoid and Yellow Fever vaccinations, but he didn't have time. As he left, he stuck his head into Tensbury's office.

"I'm leaving now," he said.

"Good. I'm trying to work on some business things. Good luck and keep in touch."

"I will."

A bit later. Tensbury's phone rang. "Hello, this is Dr. Ahur calling. I'm returning your call."

"Yes, doctor. Thanks for getting back to me so soon. I was calling you concerning my aunt Ms. Tensbury. I understand she's in your care."

"Yes, she is."

"I'm wondering when I can visit her or at least give her a call. The nurse referred me to you. It's somewhat urgent."

"Your aunt has emphysema or chronic obstructive pulmonary disease. Combined with her diabetes, she's very sick and isn't in a position to communicate now. I do believe that things might improve in the next couple of days, though. At that time, you may call back and see when you can visit."

"So, you are expecting her to stay for a while?" asked Tensbury, discouraged.

"Yes, I am. We think our treatment may improve your aunt's condition, but it's going to take some time. Is there anything else I can help you with?"

"No, doctor. You have been most helpful. Thank you. I'll call her in a few days."

CHAPTER 10

Hanna saw Patrick weave his way through the line waiting to be seated at the restaurant in the hotel where she was staying. His light brown, slightly curly hair was somewhat disheveled, as always. He had a hard time keeping it in check and kept running his hand through it to try to tame it as he walked. He wore a pinstriped grey suit, the jacket draping his shoulders. A conservative blue and white striped tie on a white shirt completed the ensemble. When Hanna rose to greet him, he hugged her tight.

"Hanna, I'm so sorry! What an awful thing to have happened. You must be so heartbroken."

"Thanks for being there when I called earlier. And thanks for making it to a late dinner."

Patrick sat down and took a sip of water.

"So, what are you up to now? You have a meeting tomorrow, I think you said. Then back to Sweden to take care of your uncle's things?"

"No, I'm going to Senegal after the meeting."

Patrick's mouth dropped. "Senegal? What on earth are you going to do in Senegal at this time?"

Hanna explained her thinking in general. "I have to find out what happened."

The waiter came and took their order.

"I don't like this at all," said Patrick.

"You don't like what?"

"You'll be alone over there. I mean, it's Africa! There's social unrest left and right, and I'm not sure about crime, but I can imagine it's high."

"Actually, it's not. I spent time on the airplane reading up on Senegal. It has an interesting past."

"So what? What does that have to do with today, Hanna?"

"I just wanted to tell you that it's one of Africa's model democracies."

"Today, Hanna, today…!"

"Okay. It has a social-democratic government. Government-run medical care and all that. The economy grew by a whopping 6.8% last year, and they found some oil and gas, which they will be able to export. So, economically, they're doing pretty well."

"What does the US Embassy say about crime?

"Normal for any large city. Don't worry. Remember, I'm a veteran traveler," she said with a smile, touching his arm.

"How long are you planning on staying?"

"Just a few days," said Hanna.

"Hanna, I don't like you going there alone. As you were talking, telling me how wonderful life is in that third world country, I was thinking." Patrick looked at Hanna.

"Tell you what, a friend of mine, Eric Shaw, sometimes stays in Senegal for weeks on end. He works for UNESCO, and he's often working there on his projects. He's an American and used to be in the Marines. I'm going to give him a call right now and see if he's there and if he would be willing to tag along with you."

Hanna started to protest, "This is not needed. Uncle Noah has arranged for a guide, and he'll meet me at the airport."

Patrick held out his hand towards Hanna, palm facing her, in the universal sign for stop. He pulled out his phone, searched for Eric's number, then dialed it.

Hanna heard Patrick describe the situation. It appeared Eric was in Dakar now and could meet her at her hotel when she arrived. From the sound of it, Eric's work schedule was entirely his own, and he was very flexible.

"He's asking where you are staying and when you get in," said Patrick, holding his phone against his chest.

Hanna pulled up her itinerary on her phone.

She told him when she was getting in, pointed out that it would be late, and mentioned the hotel she was staying in.

Patrick relayed the information to Eric.

"Since you have a guide, he says he'll meet you at your hotel."

"Patrick, that was unnecessary." She was perturbed. "Frankly, I feel embarrassed about all this. I don't know how I should behave with him. What? Ask him to babysit me the whole time I'm there?"

"Don't be ridiculous. Eric is a good friend and knows Senegal well."

Begrudgingly Hanna glanced at Patrick. She understood his concern.

Always the big brother I never had. I do feel relieved someone will be there for me during my visit. How much do I tell this Eric about the trip? I don't know. I guess it depends on what kind of person he is.

"And one more thing," said Patrick. "You are going to be there in May, and I have to tell you, they mount a world-renowned jazz festival while you are there. I know how much you like jazz. You have to go. It might get a little rowdy, though, so be careful. As long as Eric is there, I'm not worried."

For the rest of the dinner, Patrick and Hanna reminisced about when they were young, and when Hanna and Uncle Noah came to visit the Tennyson family in London. They ended the dinner very late. Hanna felt exhausted, and she dragged herself to her room.

CHAPTER 11

Alain stepped into his apartment, and his cats scurried around him, anxious for food. He had left some dry food out for them, but they wanted the good stuff from the can.

"Hello, girls. Today is a day for special delicacies. The best gourmet meal, girls, because today is a special day."

Alain was the Assistant Comptroller of the Senegalese subsidiary of IL&R. He was single and enjoyed Dakar. It was African, yet metropolitan, with a large expatriate population from different countries. However, he was tired of it. Alain talked to his cats. He lived alone, and it was just a habit he had gotten into over the years. He put down his backpack with his laptop and quickly served his cats the food they so desperately wanted. When they were all standing there, tails in the air, he pulled out his laptop and placed it on the kitchen table. He didn't have a desk at home, but the kitchen table served just as well.

"Don't want to disturb your meals or anything, but you have to listen to this. Today I found two documents from the 1850s that show that IL&R engaged in some questionable behavior. Questionable? No, downright criminal, is what it was."

Alain went to his bedroom and changed into a t-shirt and

shorts and then returned to the kitchen.

"Have you finished your dinner, my angels?"

He picked up the three empty bowls, put them in the sink, and filled them with water. His cats were rubbing their bodies around his legs, now ready to be scratched. He went to the living room and flopped down on the couch. The cats followed. He started stroking and speaking to them as his hand touched their soft fur. Their purring commenced.

"Girls, lately, the name Tensbury has shown up all over the news because Andrew Tensbury will be the Prime Minister of Britain if the Tories win. He's the son of Lord Tensbury. Sometimes I see his representative here since the lord owns a part of IL&R.

"Remember I told you the attitude the company I work for displays towards me? I have been a good soldier, doing whatever I was told, and done it brilliantly, I must add. I kept the accounting of this subsidiary in excellent shape. I am always assisting and pointing to where we could improve our operations. But, girls, they don't value your daddy. Besides, I'm fifty-six now, and I don't believe I'll ever become the CFO. I'm tired of being relegated to the additional shit jobs with others taking credit for what I do. This last one, to supervise the company archives, tops them all.

"You know I've told you that I have been waiting for some tidbit to turn up. I could publish something that would embarrass IL&R. Today, I was doing the venerable job of sorting through archive boxes. I found something exciting. It was in the 1850's box. You see, in those days, Governor Faidherbe was fighting some of the native tribes for free passage on the Senegal river. The tribes' chieftains harassed Western Gum Arabic traders and extorted fees they called tolls. He was quite successful in some areas. But here comes the twist. Apparently, not every Western trader could be part of this beneficial deal.

"I found a note dated 1858 addressed to Governor Faidherbe. It asked the Governor to secure a deal to remove navigation tolls on a 'certain company.' For three years, Faidherbe wasn't supposed to extend a similar deal to any other trader.

"It wasn't signed. But since I found it among our documents, I had a hunch who the 'certain company' was, because I recognized the script. I compared the note to one of the documents signed by Alistair Tensbury in the mid-1800s. Lo and behold, it was the same handwriting. Mind you, girls, nothing in the archive points to the Governor agreeing to it, but still, Tensbury wrote it."

Alain couldn't help but feel gleeful satisfaction. He brushed a strand of hair up over his pate. He tried to hide the fact that he was going bald by slicking his hair over the top of his head. He knew it fooled no one, but still, it made him feel more comfortable.

"Very soon, I found another document, also dated 1859. This time Governor Faidherbe signed the note. He thanked Tensbury for his assistance in finding an excellent 'house repair company' to fix his house near Paris. He expressly referred to Tensbury's partner M. Garnier, as having made the arrangements.

"Girls, it seems like a quid pro quo to me. What do you think? You may ask, my little ones, if I continued looking for more damning documents tonight, but no. I figured I have enough to stir up some problems for IL&R. Also, the information will likely rock the Andrew Tensbury campaign. He has been referring to his heritage over and over. He specifically referred to Alistair Tensbury, who made this little agreement. Having an ancestor complicit in cheating competition and bribing the local government is rather ugly."

He extricated himself from the couch and his cats. They were now full and content, laying there with their eyes closed. On his laptop, he researched potential journalists at The Guardian. The Guardian wasn't a friend of the Tories, so they would have the most fun with this information. He looked at the time. He should find someone if he called now.

He reached the right man on the first try.

"Howard Reche here," came a gruff voice on the other end of the line.

"Hello, Mr. Reche. My name is Alain Boucher."

He let the journalist know who he was and where he worked.

"I have found some documents in IL&R's historical archive, and I believe you would be interested in seeing them. They involve Alistair Tensbury."

He chatted with the journalist for a while, describing what he had found. The journalist was cautiously excited.

"Please scan them and email them to me, Mr. Boucher. If we are to use the note, I'll have to come down to see the originals and bring a document verification expert with me. Otherwise, my editor won't let me print anything like this. I'll arrange a flight down tomorrow pending a review of the documents you'll email. This story is fascinating," said the journalist. "If written up correctly, that is."

"Great. I'll email the documents now and have the originals ready for your review. But one thing, Mr. Reche. I assume I can request that my name not be used or linked to this story. Can you assure me of that?"

"That isn't a problem, Mr. Boucher. We keep our sources confidential if requested."

They discussed how they would get in touch tomorrow. After ending the call, Alain happily pounded the table, which inadvertently woke up his cats.

"My dear little kittens. I know IL&R will eventually understand that I leaked the information. Who else has access to those documents? I don't care. My career here is over, and I'm happy about that. We'll all go back to France and onto my cottage near Monaco. What do you think about that?" His cats went back to sleep.

"Since I don't have a lot of expenses here, I was able to buy that little cottage. It's not much, but we'll be happy there until I figure out what to do. There must be plenty of work for someone like me around such a populated area. Now that will be a change from this god-forsaken country. I don't know why I stayed as long as I did."

He got the documents out of his backpack, placed them on his scanner, created PDFs, and then emailed them to the journalist. After only ten minutes, he received a call from Howard Reche telling him he would fly in tomorrow. He would bring a forensic document expert to verify the documents. Satisfied, Alain confirmed the meeting and went to bed. He dreamed of his cottage.

Day 3

CHAPTER 1

"Hello, Aunt Sallie? How are you?" Tensbury kept his voice in a lower, more calming timbre than usual.

"I think you know the answer to that." She coughed for what seemed like several minutes. "It's terrible, and they're mistreating me. I should be home by now." His aunt wheezed heavily.

"That bad?" asked Tensbury, not expecting an answer. "I won't take up much of your time. I want you to get better."

"Go on, then. Oh, wait, how are my favorite nephews? I wanted to call Andrew about something, but this hospital got in the way."

"The boys are doing well. They send their regards to their great aunt. You always spoiled them, you know."

"All right. What can I do for you, Simon?"

Tensbury was very uncomfortable. He was about to lie to his aunt. It was very rare and difficult for Tensbury to lie. As a child, he once told a lie to his father. Little Simon was jumping on and off a small fence around one of the stables. A bar broke. Tensbury told his dad that his large, golden retriever caused the damage. His father had a long conversation with his son, the dog sitting nearby, looking as if he was listening. At the end of the chat, it became clear that little Simon hadn't told the truth. Tensbury loved and looked up to his father, and he had never forgotten his dad's disappointment. Ever since that chat, Tensbury had a hard time lying.

Quickly Tensbury thought of a story to tell her. "I'm trying to put together the history of the Tensbury family going back to the 1850s when Alistair became a baron. I'm not finding a lot of background material in my records. Do you have any papers that relate to Alistair from that time?"

His heart was in his throat. He didn't want to sound too demanding. Yet, this was important. He had a hunch. She had something.

She wheezed and coughed for a long time. "I don't quite understand what you are doing. There isn't anything from that time worth having. You know, the good old days were not as good as people think. I don't have anything you would want. Why would you think I did? You should concentrate on your father and grandfather. They were good people with interesting lives." She coughed again.

"If that's all you are looking for, I have to say goodbye. I need to rest."

He heard a click, and the call was over.

Tensbury texted Jack. "Just talked to Aunt Sally. She says she doesn't have anything. But I think she does."

CHAPTER 2

There were fewer and fewer days left before the election. Lillian, exceedingly anxious, knew her group was running out of time. She called her team into the conference room. It was early afternoon, but people were fatigued working long days and evenings.

"Where is Ethan, Lillian?" asked one of her people.

"Ethan is off on a project. It's a long shot, but if it pans out, it'll show the rest of the campaign what this little research group is all about. We know we are great, right?"

She always pumped them up during these daily meetings. Now, she also needed to wake them up. There was still a lot of work to be done.

"We have a lot of projects that need attention. Let's start."

Almost everyone had sat down by now, and the last one in was closing the door.

"Let's go around the table. John, what's up in your neck of the woods?"

"I have something which might be good. During Andrew Tensbury's days at Oxford, he dated a woman, who converted to Islam and was later radicalized. She's friendly with a group of people who went to fight for ISIS. The Guardian did a piece on her a couple of weeks ago, but no one seems to have paid much attention. They didn't mention her old ties to Tensbury, but we can."

"That's good. Write it up please, I'll take it to the boss and see what he says. If we get the go-ahead, we'll pass it to our media group."

She perked up a little, hearing about John's find.

Lillian continued around the table, but the rest of her group hadn't produced anything juicy today.

"Alright. We covered most of the new things. Now let's talk about the Tories' weaknesses, which we can exploit. Not that you haven't heard this from me before but let me tell you again who the good guys are. We are!" She got up and started pacing. One of her fortes was public speaking. She enjoyed it and it got her energized.

"Our group is tasked with research to find material to emphasize popular Labor policies. We also conduct research to criticize unpopular Tory proposals. As the incumbent governing party, we are at a disadvantage. We have a long record of successes and, of course, mistakes. Our opposition, not being in government for a long time, only has their Manifesto. Tories can criticize our Manifesto, which tells the electorate what we plan. They also blast our record and disparage what we have done so far. We, on the other hand, only have their Manifesto to work from. So, we should work harder and smarter. And we do." She looked around the table.

"As you know, I studied in the States for a year. I had a chance to observe the difference between campaigns in two countries. The difference is between the well-educated electorate we have here in the UK and the somewhat naïve one in the US. Here everyone knows, to achieve any of our goals, we need a substantial redistribution of wealth. Those with greater wealth, accumulated this fortune because of the multitude of people who work hard every day. They contribute to our society and therefore enable the success of the few. For a long time in the US, progressives avoided discussion of this distribution. They always claimed that they would tax only very, very rich. They're coming around. There are now successful American politicians that finally call themselves Social-Democrats. We don't need to nationalize many parts of our economy – this isn't the 20th century. One can achieve equitable distribution by passing the right laws. The laws that regulate the business practices of companies and enacting appropriate taxation. We are not shy about our goals here, and we fight for a more and more fair society."

Lillian took a breather. She stopped pacing, picked up a bottle of water, and took a sip.

"Tories want to reduce taxes on the well-to-do. They keep telling us that the entrepreneurs and investors who risk their career and capital create new wealth. But we know that without the collective efforts, there will be no new companies. The joint efforts of the workers, the government, and the public at large are needed. Each contributes, and each must share equitably in the rewards." She wanted to make sure the group understood the dynamic of the wealth creation.

"They want to slow down our march towards net zero carbon emissions by 2030. They say it's too costly. Some even deny global warming exists. We say that it isn't too costly to build a clean economy for our children and grandchildren. Continuing on this path, we'll create new, high-skilled, high-paying jobs." Lillian looked at each member of her group to see if they were paying attention. They were.

"We'll continue reversing the worst excesses of privatization to lower the costs for the average Briton. We also hear the infamous 'tax cuts' once again. Also, Tories want to spend more money on defense instead of people's welfare. And to top it all off, they want to make sure there's no so-called 'illegal immigration.' We all know what illegal immigration means. It means that no one with the skin slightly darker than the lilies…, no reference to my name, can get in," she said, laughing.

There were laughs around the table. Now, everyone began to slump again. She needed to light a fire under their butts.

"We need to get something to the candidates out in the field." She slapped the table with the stack of papers in her hand.

"What we should do today, is first divide the Tory manifesto's weak spots among our group members. Each member will then tie his or her assigned Tory weak points to the statements from every Tory MP, which refers to these as position points. After that, each of us will write bullets on how these manifesto points will hurt the British people. Especially on how their immigration policy stand is prejudiced against people of color. We quickly need to get our candidates the talking points resulting from this exercise. We also need to provide the information to our social media group ASAP."

They parsed out the manifesto points between themselves.

"I know the pace is grueling, but we don't have much more time left."

Lillian stood up and held the door open for her small group as they filed out.

CHAPTER 3

Hanna's meeting was held in the morning at her company offices. Afterward, she changed out of her black business suit, pulled on her jeans, a white T-shirt, and left directly for the airport to take the flight to Senegal.

She had worked so hard on this deal, and she was very satisfied. Everything had progressed well. Most importantly, the investors were all on board to support the acquisition.

In the taxi, she typed out a quick email to her boss. She would send it when at the airport. He would be happy with the outcome.

Heathrow was a nightmare as always.

Later, after getting seated on the plane, she drew a deep breath. Her uncle bought business class seats, so it wasn't too bad. After the obligatory glass of champagne, she reclined her seat backward and considered her trip. She was happy she had decided to go. It felt right. She did worry a bit whether her guide would be there as promised. If not, she'd take a taxi. She had changed enough dollars into the local currency. Mentally she ran through what she needed to enter the country. She had gotten her vaccinations last week. She had started the malaria pills as well. She dozed off.

After a stop-over in Paris. Hanna arrived at Blaise Diagne

Airport.

As she came out of the arrivals gate, she saw a tall Senegalese man with a sign: 'Arnol.' She weaved her way over to him, ignoring men ready to grab her luggage.

"Bonsoir Madam," he said in accented French. "Je m'appelle Mustafa. Bien venue."

"Bonsoir."

"Where is the gentleman?"

"He isn't coming."

Mustafa seemed to accept that without a question. He grasped her bag and led her out of the arrival's terminal.

They exited, and she drew her first breath of African air. It was warm and very dry. She was relieved to see her guide deliberately negotiate his way around throngs of people, cars, buses, motorcycles, and mopeds. Here and there, a tour operator shouted and held up signs directing tourists to this or that bus.

Eventually, they reached Mustafa's car. It was a nice, clean, white, Saab. Mustafa opened the door for her, and she took a seat. It was hot inside but bearable. As soon as he got in and turned the engine on, the air blasted.

Thank God for Uncle Noah.

It seemed he had arranged for a good guide.

They reached Dakar. After driving through the center of the city, Mustafa chose a two-lane road. They drove for a little while longer. The car turned into a long driveway and deposited her in front of, what looked like, a mountain of stairs. Mustafa helped her pull her bag out while she clutched her backpack. They agreed he would pick her up at nine the next morning.

She looked up the stairs.

I don't feel like the Spanish Steps right now.

Exasperated, she looked around. Thankfully a porter appeared and accepted her bag with a wide smile.

"Bienvenu, Madam."

She mounted the stairs, grateful that she wasn't carrying

her bag.

The lobby of the hotel was expansive. Hanna saw a small man-made waterfall and palm trees growing in the middle of the reception area. Birds were chirping in the trees. To the left was a long reception desk with several clerks in attendance. They all looked immaculate in white shirts and maroon jackets.

In the middle of the desk stood a tall man. He wore khaki shorts with a tucked-in white t-shirt over broad shoulders and sneakers on his feet. He was trim, with the leg muscles of a swimmer or a sprinter. The rest of the reception was empty.

This must be Eric.

He was speaking with the receptionist. His hands were 'talking.' She liked that in a person. She had always sized people up before engaging them. A habit she developed in her work. Useful when going into meetings. He seemed to be an extroverted person. She preferred those. It was easier to communicate.

He turned around, and as she approached, he held out his hand.

"You must be Hanna Arnol." He was smiling broadly. "I'm Eric Shaw. Here, let me grab your bag while you check in."

"Sorry, it's so late."

"No problem. Patrick is a good friend, and I wanted to see you get off to a good start."

He kept up a steady conversation as she checked in. How was her flight? What about the ride from the airport? What did she think about her guide?

"You must be tired, but how about a nightcap before you go up to your room?"

She almost said no but was too tired to argue and let him lead her into a piano bar adjacent to the lobby.

A trio was playing 'Summertime', one of her favorite jazz tunes. They sat down on low chairs around a small table. She mellowed out almost immediately. Patrick was right. It was good to have someone she knew by proxy meet her. They both ordered a beer.

He was probably in his early forties, tanned with an open visage. His hair was almost buzz cut, giving him a boyish air. Hanna saw lines along his mouth and fans at the eyes, indicating a happy nature.

This is an upbeat person.

Patrick knew this man. He had readily recommended him to her, and she trusted Patrick implicitly. Eric made her feel comfortable.

"First, let me thank you again for being here."

"That's okay," said Eric. "Patrick is someone I have known for a long time. Tagging along with you, is a bright spot in my otherwise somewhat tedious days. Did Patrick tell you how we met?"

"No, he didn't."

"In my previous life, I was an attorney for a large firm with offices in London. I came over from the States to assist in an antitrust case in which Patrick was also involved. We hit it off. We were both bachelors and spent a lot of time together, playing tennis and bar hopping at night. Since then, we have kept in touch. Whenever I come to London, I call him up. He can't get away much anymore, though, because of his family. I'm happy for him. His wife seems like a great gal."

"I am glad Patrick called you. It's nice you will have some time to show me around. I'm a pretty independent person. But I admit the idea of having your company here in Senegal makes me more confident."

"Do you travel much?"

"With my job, quite a lot. Domestically mostly, and to Europe. I have also been on a couple of trips to our delivery centers in India."

"Do you like India?"

"We orchestrate those trips tightly to introduce potential clients to our services. I never get to see much. But I haven't been to Africa."

"What do you do, Hanna?" Eric settled in his chair.

"My title is VP of Sales and Business Development. The company I work for is an outsourcing company in California."

"What kind of outsourcing?"

"IT, mostly. When an American IT department is expanding, our staff in India takes on this work at a much lower cost than hiring new American employees. Except now, we have begun doing a lot of insourcing.

"What is insourcing?"

"Helping companies bring their IT back from outsourcing. Sounds weird, I know. My job is to present the proposal to company executives with a cost-benefit analysis. That's sales."

"Interesting."

"It is."

There were times when the Indian staff truly displaced Americans' jobs. Then the Americans found themselves with a pink slip. When that happened, she didn't like her job very much. The new goal to increase the insourcing part of the business made her much happier.

"I'm also responsible for business development. I am currently involved in a rather complex acquisition of an outfit in London."

"Sounds challenging." Eric stopped.

"How much did Patrick tell you about me?"

"Not much. Patrick did say you had worked together, you were with UNESCO, you had been a Marine, and that's about it."

"Let me give you a little background. In short, I grew up as a navy brat. My father was a Vice Admiral. I was expected to follow the same course, so I went to Annapolis and then joined the Marines."

"How long were you in the Marines?"

"Five years as an officer. Then I went to law school and after, to work for corporate America."

"That's a switch. From Marines into lawyering!"

"Drastic, huh?" he smiled.

"But that didn't last long either. At that time, my grandfather died. He left me enough money not to have to work for a living anymore. I turned some of that money into a small investment in the education of underprivileged kids. Now I work for UNESCO."

"You mentioned education of underprivileged kids. Why education?"

"I know that with proper education, these countries can flourish and contribute to the world economy. Not suck up support as so many of them do now. Good education is one of the many goals that are part of the UNESCO mission. I feel good dedicating my time to this. I'm now with the West African division in Dakar. I enjoy it."

The beer came. It was ice cold, and they both took a sip.

She was finally in Senegal. She was in the company of, what seemed to be, a nice man, and she had good plans in front of her.

Hanna knew he was waiting to hear why she came to Senegal. She wasn't sure how to begin.

"I have always wanted to visit Senegal. You see, in the mid-1800s, my ancestor, her name was Signe, when she was eighteen, traveled alone from Norway to South Africa. She made a stop in St. Louis."

"Wait a minute. Did you say eighteen?"

Hanna nodded.

"Young girls didn't do that in those days, right? I mean sail across half the world alone. That was pretty gutsy."

"Yes, it definitely was. I want to see if I can find out a little more about what Signe saw here. Also, I haven't taken a vacation for a while, and it was time to take a break."

Eric had an interested look on his face. Hanna let her eyes wander to the jazz trio. Now they were doing some Billie Holiday tune, which sounded great. The mug was 'crying' long rivulets of condensation running down the glass, and it was still cold. She didn't feel tired at all. She swept her hair out of her face.

Eric had been sitting quietly.

"So, Norway? That's your roots?"

"Well, both Norwegian and Swedish. My ancestor, the one who traveled here, married a Swede in South Africa. When they returned, they settled in Stockholm."

"Sounds like quite a voyage. I hope you'll tell me more later." He stopped.

"So, what about tomorrow?"

"Tomorrow, I'm going to see Professor Diallo out at the Université de Dakar. My uncle started a blog after his retirement, focused on Western maritime in the 19th century. I think our ancestor's voyage spurred his interest. I believe he connected with Professor Diallo because of his nautical blog. I'm hoping he can direct me to a local library or archive to find out more about my ancestor's visit to Senegal."

Hanna talked to Eric about the blog and how she had helped set it up.

"How come your uncle didn't join you?"

"It is a long story. I'll tell you about it tomorrow." Hanna knew it sounded strange.

Eric didn't comment

"How about I take you to the university tomorrow? You can let your guide know you don't need him for the day."

"What about your work?"

"My work gives me a lot of flexibility. We just turned in the monthly report. So, I'm at your service, dear lady." He mock-saluted her with a smile.

"Really? That would be great! How about ten? I need some sleep."

They agreed to meet in the morning. She pushed herself up to her room. Her heart lightened, knowing she wouldn't be alone tomorrow. The porter who helped her with her bag opened the door to her room. She walked over to the window, looked down, and gasped. It was beautiful. She was eight floors up, yet she could see the waves rolling in over a small beach below. Beach chairs were standing like soldiers waiting for tomorrow's onslaught of tourists. Lights lit up the grounds.

Happy, she gave the porter some change and put on her pajamas. This is a good start, she thought. As she shut her eyes, she saw the smiling face of Uncle Noah.

Day 4

CHAPTER 1

Andrew sat in the back of his chauffeured car. He pulled up the news on his phone and checked the BBC front page. An article, prominently laid out, said Andrew's girlfriend during his university times, was now a sympathizer of radical Islamist causes. The story implied that Andrew Tensbury was a lousy judge of people he associates with.

Andrew stared out the window where the early morning traffic was moving right along. The spread on this woman included her picture. In the photo, she retained her youthful smile. He wondered how they obtained this photo. Perhaps it was old, and she didn't look like that anymore. He remembered her well. She had always been a little crazy. A little on edge. That's part of what he had liked about her. She was so different from himself. He was always collected and on point. Theirs had been a passionate relationship, but it had been short-lived. It sorts of burned out.

Apparently, she had converted to the Muslim religion and frequented a mosque, which in the past had ties to people who went to fight for ISIS.

There were few days till the election. This article might have an impact on the electorate. The minute ISIS or terrorists were mentioned, everyone paid attention.

His car reached the CCHQ offices. He put his phone in his pocket as the car stopped and got out. He still had a hard time getting used to being driven. He entered the offices, and the sounds of all the volunteers making calls engulfed him pleasantly. Andrew placed his computer bag on his chair and went to see Thomas.

"Hey, Thomas." He needed to talk to him before the constituency stop and the press conference today.

"Did you see what Labor put out all over the media?

"Yeah, I saw it."

"Thinking they can get to me by bringing up some old relationship from school. ISIS sympathizer! What a crock of shit. How do you think we should respond? We have to counter with something."

"I know. You'll get a question today at the constituency stop. Thank God we have those every day. Otherwise, we would never get a chance to mitigate this type of crap."

"What do you think if I simply tell it like it is? That it's unfortunate that an intelligent woman like her would turn to this type of cause. I haven't had contact with her for many years. Not since Oxford."

"I think they'll accept it. We should go with that."

As expected, at the press conference, some journalists asked Andrew about the story. He answered as they had agreed. There was no movement in the polls.

CHAPTER 2

Jack nursed a cup of coffee in the restaurant of the oceanside hotel in Dakar. He had arrived on the same flight as Hanna last night, but he doubted she had taken any notice of him. Not that it mattered. He would make sure to look like any other tourist here.

At seven, promptly, a man walked towards him. Compared to the typically tall Senegalese, he was of average height. He was dressed casually in dark jeans and a light green shirt. Like most people Jack had met here so far, his skin was so black that it looked almost dark purple. The man flashed his sparkling teeth.

"Are you Jack Fernsby?" He held out his hand.

Jack half rose. "Yes, I am. I assume you are Malek Diouf?"

They shook hands, and Malek accepted a cup of coffee from the waitress, who magically showed up as soon as he sat down.

"Thanks for making yourself available on such short notice."

"Oh, I'll do anything for my friend Mary. Good thing you caught me while I'm in Dakar. When we spoke yesterday, I was already here, checking on my operation.

"Yes, great you are here. Mary spoke very highly of you."

"You made your project sound quite unusual. Although my guys are good, they're just used to handle customary tourist needs, to assist clients who want to tour the usual sights and to go here and there. It sounded like you needed something different." Malek stopped.

He spoke with a well-modulated voice.

"Thank you for agreeing to help me. It's my first time here in Senegal, and I am very curious about life here. Please tell me how you ended up with this business?"

"My parents came from Senegal to Britain when I was thirteen. They were both educated in Britain, and that's where they met. I went to school at University College London and got an engineering degree. Then I worked for a couple of telecommunications companies and realized that it wasn't what I wanted."

"That sounds like a good career," said Jack.

"It was a good, well-paying career, but it consumed a lot of my evenings and some weekends too. I decided I wanted my own company – more freedom for me and more time with my family. I built up a small group of twelve guides. We rent out our services, by the day, to visitors."

"How do you get your jobs?"

"My office in London focuses exclusively on the Senegalese market. Because of my relationships with Mary and other travel agents in Britain, I get a lot of referrals and I'm always busy."

"You said you only have twelve guides here. Are you planning to grow your business?"

"I want to, but it's tough. Finding reliable mid-level managers in Dakar is almost impossible. I found one great chap who helps me manage the group now and would like to find another. The good ones, the reliable ones, are all busy and make good money."

Jack watched Malek as he described his business. His face was animated and showed a pleasant disposition. From the few minutes he had been with him, it was clear that he had found the right man for the job. Now, Jack was concerned that they would miss Hanna when she would leave the hotel and lose sight of her. But first, he needed to see if Malek would agree to do the job.

Then Malek smiled and said, "So, what can I do for you, Jack?"

"I have a special project. I'm prepared to pay more than your usual fee. The job may entail traveling to towns outside of Dakar."

Malek took a sip of his coffee. Now Jack could see that the man wasn't as young as he seemed when he first walked in. Grey hair touched his temples.

"That's why I came myself. I'm looking forward to a 'special' kind of project. A lot of the time, I sit in a chair all day in London. Driving around Senegal will be entertaining."

Jack launched into the story he had spent some time engineering. "There's a woman, Hanna Arnol. She's staying here in this hotel. The company she works for back in the States is considering expanding its financial relationship with a British company that has investments here in Senegal, and Ms. Arnol has been sent here to research the company before the Americans commit to the deal. Well, the British company got wind of this, and now they wish to get a hold of anything Ms. Arnol might find in order to prepare their negotiations accordingly. And that's where I – and you – come in."

Malek narrowed his eyes. "Are you asking me to follow this woman?"

"Completely aboveboard, I assure you." Jack threw up a hand. "I'm a solicitor by training and have done plenty of investigative work on the company's behalf, but only in the UK. I can't do this job by myself, however, because I don't know the environment here. Also, if I follow her, I'm likely to stand out." He leaned back and exhaled. "So, here we are."

Jack watched Malek's face display a certain level of incredulity. He knew the story was far-fetched, but it was the best he had been able to come up with. On the one hand, he was glad that a Brit would be doing the job. On the other hand, a local guide wouldn't think twice about why he wanted Hanna followed. He knew Malek probably found it fishy.

Malek sat quietly for a minute, pondering, and sipping his coffee. Then he said abruptly. "Alright, I'm game."

Jack was relieved, a broad grin on his face, "I don't know yet how many days we are talking about. Should I pay upfront?"

Malek waved his hand in the universal sign of 'no.' "We'll take care of that after we are done. Do we start now?"

"Yes, we start now."

"Perfect," He stretched his hand across the table, and Jack seized it for a handshake.

Malek took another sip of his coffee and then used his napkin to wipe his lips.

"By the way, Malek, do you want anything to eat," Jack reluctantly offered. He wanted him to get started instead of eating.

"No, I'm fine with my coffee. So, let's get going. What's the job today?"

"This is what I would like you to do. Follow Hanna, find out what she's looking at, what she finds, whom she meets, and let me know. She mustn't know she's being followed. I'll stay here, and you can call me on the phone. I may want to join you later, but we'll keep that fluid. I have her itinerary. Here is a picture of her." Jack handed Malek his phone.

Malek studied Hanna's picture carefully.

"Send that to me, will you?" Malek paused. "You know, I'll engage one of my guides to help follow her. We need that. First, she would get suspicious if she saw the same car behind her often. Second, if I'm to find out what she's looking at after she leaves a place, I'll have to go in there. I would have to see what she saw or found. Meanwhile, my guy will follow her, and we'll repeat the cycle."

"That makes sense."

"Alright, I'll get moving now. I hope this woman hasn't

left yet. I'll keep in touch. And thanks for the job, man," Malek rose from the table.

"Don't thank me yet. I think it'll be difficult."

Malek didn't answer. Instead, he briskly walked through the restaurant and out the door.

CHAPTER 3

In the morning, they arrived at the Université de Dakar, also known as the Cheikh Anta Diop University. Eric drove up towards the main campus and parked in the packed parking lot.

"It's large," said Hanna, looking around.

"Yeah. It has a reputation as one of Africa's most well-known and prestigious institutions. Many Senegalese leaders graduated from here, and the alumni teach in universities around the world."

They asked some students for direction and found their way up to Professor Diallo's office and knocked. The door opened.

"Madam, I'm Professor Diallo," said the man in the doorway in broken English, offering his hand.

Hanna introduced herself.

"I received your message."

He seemed to be no more than forty, but he had to be close to fifty at a minimum and probably more, given his career. He was gaunt and wore kaki green slacks, a short-sleeved shirt, and what looked like sneakers.

He invited them to enter. The room had a very narrow doorway, yellow walls, a rickety-looking desk, and grey linoleum floor. As they entered, Hanna saw several framed diplomas hanging on the walls. The professor had a new looking computer screen on his desk and stacks of books and folders all over. The musty smell reminded her of her room at the boarding school in Switzerland. Never clean enough, always dusty and with the lingering scents of books. Despite the dismal surroundings, the room had the feel of academia, and it was welcoming.

After he waved them in, they took a seat in front of his desk on straight-backed chairs. He sat down facing them, hands placed easily on the desk, fingers touching. She instantly liked the man.

"Professor Diallo, this is my friend Eric Shaw. He works for UNESCO."

Diallo looked at Eric and nodded and said, "Pleased to meet you."

"I believe you were in contact with my uncle, Noah Arnol?"

"Yes, Mr. Arnol, the Scandinavian gentleman with the maritime blog. He was looking for information about ships at the St. Louis port. In 1859, I think it was. As a matter of fact, I arranged for a guide to pick you up last night at the airport. You must be his niece. He told me about you. Is he joining us later?"

"I'm afraid I have bad news. We were supposed to travel together, but he died unexpectedly right before our trip." Hanna stopped.

She was getting used to informing people of his death, and her despair had dissipated somewhat.

She saw the professor's face fall. "I'm so sorry for your loss. Your uncle appeared to be a nice man. The blog he created has many followers, and they often post interesting comments. I post as well."

"I plan to take over managing his blog," she found herself saying.

"I'm glad you'll keep his blog alive. So sorry..." he

repeated. Then sobered up. "So, how may I help you?"

"My uncle and I have always wanted to visit Senegal. You see, our ancestor arrived in St. Louis in 1859 on a ship that had broken its mast. I want to find out more about her time in St. Louis. I'm hoping you can point me to a place in the library that covers some of that information. I read French pretty well, and if you can recommend some sources, I can work on my own."

"No, you don't need to do that. I'll be honored to guide you personally. Being the head of the department for Senegalese History studies, I know my way around our large library." He smiled.

"Thanks, Professor Diallo. That's kind of you."

Energetically he stood and moved to the door. He kept it open for them to exit, then locked the door, and began walking down the hallway.

Hanna and Eric followed him down an open-air hallway that looked out over the main campus. Students were rushing around in every direction. Some wore western clothes, but most of the women were in beautiful local clothes, in all the colors of the rainbow. She heard them mostly speaking in French, but many in Wolof, the local language.

They turned towards the library building, Diallo leading. Hanna always wondered what drove people, and now she thought about how little she could imagine about this professor's life. She had questions she might have asked someone in America, but she kept to herself here. She thought of the lessons she learned the hard way. The American habit of asking rather personal questions of people you just met wasn't appreciated in other countries. So, she didn't ask him how long he had worked at the university, where he went to school, if he was married, if he had children, if he had dogs, etc.

Diallo opened the heavy, wooden door to the library. It was a cavernous room, filled with tables. Students were occupying all the space. They moved towards the back of the room. She could see a second floor with towering bookcases that looked like they were threatening to fall.

Diallo led them to some long tables where students were sitting, elbow to elbow.

"It's certainly different from Stanford," Hanna whispered to Eric.

"We can sit here. Let me go find some reference material." Diallo left in the direction of the wall of books.

With Hanna's backpack in her lap, they waited for his return.

Hanna looked around. She saw students, their noses in books, making quick notes on laptops. Hardly anyone spoke, and if they did, they whispered. Although the ceilings were very tall, and the room was quite large, it had a claustrophobic feel to it. Some students were on metal stairs on wheels looking for books on the upper shelves. She was used to libraries being less populated and having small chair arrangements here and there, for a break from the studies. Nothing like that here. Fluorescent lights gave the area a cold look.

"You see that guy over there," she whispered to Eric and discreetly pointed to a small man sitting a couple of chairs away from them. "I think he's the only other foreigner here."

Eric looked that way distractedly and didn't respond.

Diallo soon returned and dropped several volumes on the table. The students around them scooted away to make space. He sat down beside Hanna and opened one of the books.

"We are looking for the ships that visited St. Louis in 1859, is that correct?" asked Diallo. His entire demeanor had changed, and she felt like a schoolgirl with her professor.

"Yes, I'm trying to figure out what my ancestor did here in Senegal. She was in St. Louis on a ship named the *Ingeborg* in November of 1859."

Diallo said, "In 1859, St. Louis was the capital of Senegal, and it was the port city where many traders did their business on the African West Coast. This binder has some port logs for ships that docked at the harbor from 1858 to 1860. Many, but not all, books and other records were moved here from various places when this library was built. This is not a complete list, but it's all we have for those years." He rifled through the pages with a practiced hand.

"What I know is that *Ingeborg* was a barque ship," said Hanna.

Diallo was pointing at a rough drawing of a large ship with three towering masts and furled sails. "In that case, this is an example of the kind of ship she sailed on."

He was again running his finger along the lines of the text, reading and commenting as he went along.

"Here are the logs of ships that have stayed in port for some amount of time. There are many ships, flying flags from different countries, during the month of November 1859." He stopped. "And here is the *Ingeborg*, flying a Norwegian flag, and in port for several days. The log mentions that the ship was there for repairs."

Signe came on that ship! What will I see and hear in St. Louis? I needed the diary pages.

Diallo continued to study the pages in the book.

"There are trading ships from many countries around the world. Port record-keeping wasn't the strong point in those days."

Hanna drew a deep breath, disappointed. She wanted more information about Signe's ship.

"But the traders kept good logs of what they shipped. There's information here about a company named IL&R. They traded mainly in Gum Arabic in those days. They had several ships in port in November. By the way, IL&R had a major trading hub in St. Louis and still has operations with offices in Dakar," said Diallo.

This was the company her uncle asked her to research. The one where Alistair Tensbury was part owner. She found very little information about the 1800's IL&R online. She felt like she needed to follow up and visit their local office.

"Were there any noteworthy events in St. Louis at that time? Maybe some unusual trading deals," asked Hanna.

"I don't see anything unusual here, just mondain events." Diallo kept turning the pages.

Then he looked at Hanna, smiled and said, "I just told you that the traders kept good records, but there isn't much here about them either. I am sorry. I believe you can find some additional records at the university in St. Louis. It's called the Université Gaston Berger. They have a small but excellent library documenting the history of St. Louis. I have been there many times doing my research."

"It's on my itinerary," said Hanna. "I plan to go tomorrow."

"I'll take you there if you like," suggested Eric.

"I think we'll look through these books on our own now. We took a lot of your time already," said Hanna to Diallo.

"It was my pleasure to help. Sorry, we didn't find more." Diallo looked relieved.

"But before we part, let me again express my deep sorrow for your loss. I'm sure it isn't easy for you."

"Thank you, professor. I appreciate that."

"Now, I'll say goodbye, the Senegalese way." He gave Hanna a peck on each cheek.

After he left, Eric and Hanna continued to scan the books, but it seemed that, besides the comings and goings of the trading ships, they couldn't glean anything of importance.

After a while, Hanna said, "I don't think there's much more here. What do you think?"

"I agree. You'll have to wait till you get to Gaston Berger and hope for more information from there. I've never been there, but I've heard a lot about it. Small but nice, they say."

"Yeah. Thanks for offering to take me. I really appreciate it." She paused. "Are you sure you can take this much time off? I don't want to interfere with your work."

"You are not!"

"Thank you."

"Okay, let's go," said Eric.

On the way out, Hanna stopped by the librarian's desk. A young lady at the desk asked: "Oui, Madame?"

Hanna asked, "I just looked through some historical records about St. Louis. I wonder whether you get many foreigners looking for that city's history here."

"Not often, but this week a British gentleman was looking through 19th century St. Louis business records. In fact, he's in the library today."

CHAPTER 4

"Hi, Mary. Am I interrupting you?"

"Not at all, Lillian."

Mary pushed her chair away from her desk. Mary's cubicle was in the back of the floor, where the whole research gang was housed, and she had the advantage of having a window as a result. Lillian looked at a picture over Mary's shoulder, pinned to the wall. She saw a small boy, of perhaps three, sitting with a large teddy-bear.

"Is that your son?"

Lillian didn't feel like she had time for pleasantries, but it was something she had learned to do. It helped her get closer to her staff.

"Yes, that's him with a large teddy his daddy won for him at the fair last year."

Mary was a small, attractive woman with curly blonde hair. Her face was bright as she looked up at Lillian.

"Beautiful boy."

Lillian quickly changed the subject.

"The group is talking about a great piece of work on that conservative MP you dug out. So, what exactly did this 'Labor Assistant' say?" She chuckled.

Mary came up with that term. The 'Labor Assistant' was

none other than a conservative MP from a constituency in North England. His rhetoric played into the hands of Labor's message. It was almost a caricature of Tory's insensitivities on issues important to ordinary people. From his words, Mary created an excellent narrative for Labor.

"I wish all of their MPs would be so helpful," uttered Mary.

Lillian's phone rang. She saw it was Ethan.

"Hold that thought, Mary."

Lillian took a few steps out of Mary's cubicle and stood in the hallway.

"Yes, Ethan?"

"Hey. As I told you earlier, now I'm working at the Dakar University. There were two Americans here, a man and a woman. They just left. The woman looked like she's in her early thirties. She had a laptop and was taking notes. The guy with her was tall, kind of muscular. A Senegalese man was pulling down books and documents, but he left before they did."

"How do you know they were Americans?"

"I heard them talking on the way out. Definitely American accents. I'm going to check out what they were looking at. Call you later."

Lillian returned to Mary's cubicle.

"Mary, you were saying…?"

"That MP says that there's no need to push companies to promote women to executive positions in high-tech companies. He says this will happen naturally. That there will be more women in upper management when more women are going into engineering and science."

"How nice of him." Lillian scoffed. "I guess the rest of us should quietly wait around until then. This is precisely the sort of conservative crap the Tories are spitting out. Gender equality be damned in their minds. Get this sucker! Build some arguments to all these juicy quotes of his. We'll take a close look at them together. We should be able to push it out later today. Right?"

Lillian was enthusiastic, and her green eyes reflected her optimism in the afternoon light coming through Mary's window.

"It's something we should do with all targeted Tory MPs. Good work. Outstanding work. Write it up, please."

"Alright, Lillian. I will."

Back at her desk Lillian started the ball rolling with the MP angle.

About half an hour later, Ethan called again.

"Hi, again."

"Hi, Lillian. I took a look at the documents the Americans were reviewing. I couldn't find any direct reference to Alistair Tensbury, though. But I'll keep at it. Call you later."

John came up to her desk.

"Doesn't seem as if that girlfriend article moved the needle in the polls."

"Yeah, I saw that. Sometimes it takes a couple of days to sink in. Keep digging, John. Keep digging. Something will come up." She sounded surer than she felt.

She hoped he would find something substantial. Something that would create some turmoil. John and Mary were two of her best researchers. Neither of them had worked with her before, but they have both come up with different angles to run with. Mary with the MP idea, and John with the radicalized girlfriend. Then there was Ethan, of course. She still hoped he would come through.

Lillian searched in her bag for some ibuprofen. She had a pounding headache.

She wondered if she had taken on too much this time by accepting this job. She had always taken pride in her resourcefulness and achieved success as a result. Even as a little girl on the playground, she would challenge the boys to some game or another and make sure she beat them. Never the girls. Her dealings with men suffered because of this 'take no prisoner' attitude. In the past, she had a couple of relationships where she lived together with a man, but it never worked out. Usually, because work dominated her life. Winning was something that drove her day and night.

She wasn't sure if she could keep her winning streak this time. Or would she be beaten? Would she be unable to contribute enough of substance to make a difference? She believed that in the next few days, she must find something very powerful.

She swallowed two pills.

Lillian wasn't a person to give up. She would run this research group hard until the very day before the election. A moratorium on all election coverage was mandated on the day of the ballot. It worked, except for the social sites. It was difficult to enforce the rules on sites like Facebook and Twitter. Those usually ran stories even throughout election day.

She decided to get someone else on the letter to the vicar trail while Ethan was in Senegal. She picked up her phone and texted John. "Hey John, come on over again, please."

CHAPTER 5

Eric helped Hanna into the Jeep, went around the car, and hopped in himself.

Before he started the ignition, he turned around, "You didn't tell me your uncle died."

She sat quietly.

"No, I didn't, but I'll tell you more about it later." She stopped and stared straight ahead.

After a while, she asked, "Do you remember Diallo mentioned IL&R?"

"I heard that. Is that important to you?"

"Well, yeah, it is. My uncle asked me to do some research on IL&R because of my knowledge of French. He told me the research was for that oceanic blog I mentioned. He wanted a summary of what that company was like in the 19th century, what it traded in, who the principals were, and so on."

"As Diallo said, they still have offices here. I know they have a little library of sorts, documenting some of their history. How about I take you there after lunch?"

"That would be great," said Hanna. "What do you think we should do for lunch?"

"I'd like us to go to this restaurant called Chez Issa. It's out by the beach. You'll love it."

"By the beach. Must be good sea food."

"It is!"

"Again, thanks for offering to take me to St. Louis."

"No problem. I like that town. It's a UNESCO World Heritage location, so I go there often."

"I look forward to seeing it. I mean, that's the town Signe stayed in. All these years, I have wanted to visit and see what Signe saw in 1859. Going to St. Louis tomorrow will be great."

Then she remembered Mustafa.

"I need to let my guide know that I haven't forgotten about him."

She gave Mustafa a call about not needing him this afternoon or over the weekend. She assured him that she would still be paying him.

Soon they were on the road, and the loud engine hum of the Jeep made it challenging to talk.

"Hanna, prepare yourself. This trip will be rather hot, but it's not very long."

"Okay. I must say I'm ready to eat."

Eric expertly navigated through the city of Dakar.

"I'm taking you along the ocean towards Soumbédioune, south of us."

On her right-hand side, she saw beaches. They passed some tennis courts and a colorful playground. Unfortunately, many buildings obstructed the view.

It was the middle of the day and the sun was high. Hanna's hair was sticky with sweat. She tried to brush it with her fingers. Hopeless. The only thing that could untangle this mess was a long, cold shower and a lot of hair conditioner.

"Please tell me more about where we are going for lunch." Hanna leaned towards Eric and shouted over the noise.

"This restaurant is extremely popular with the upper crust in Dakar, despite being a bit out of the way.-It's out by a fishing district where the fishermen come in with fresh fish. Chez Issa always has the best, freshest fish." Eric turned to her and smiled. "You'll see."

She watched Eric as he drove with a hand on the manual shift stick and an easy hand on the steering wheel. His wraparound shades kept her from seeing his eyes. As they drove along the road, she held on to the rollbar of the Jeep, the cooling breeze against her hot skin. They passed a beach with many narrow, colorful fishing boats. Eric explained that they were called pirogues.

"Here we are." Eric swung the Jeep into a parking lot with a lot of high-end cars.

"Well, well, very fancy!" Hanna laughed.

"Oh, come on."

He took her hand as she jumped down. He led her through a portico with a sign that said 'Chez Issa.' As they entered, it felt like arriving in a new country. She saw low, wide buildings with fresh white paint. Tables and parasols in all colors, shielding patrons from the sun, filled a brick-covered courtyard. Several palm trees were planted in the area, providing welcome extra shade to all. The restaurant was busy, and virtually all tables were occupied.

Eric walked to one of the empty tables, pulled the chair out for Hanna, and then sat down in the opposite chair. There was a thin, white tablecloth on the table, kept in place by pins to not fly away, and a small vase with a Hibiscus bloom in red.

"We are close to the ocean, so it never gets too hot here."

Eric looked around with pleasure on his face. This restaurant was clearly a place he enjoyed very much.

"Have you had any Senegalese dishes yet?"

Then he laughed. "That was a stupid question. Of course, you haven't. You just came yesterday."

Eric leaned across the table and handed her a plastic-covered menu.

"There are many famously excellent dishes. There's a Senegalese dish called Maafe. It's chicken, fish or lamb cooked in a peanut sauce and it's very popular. There's also Yassa, which is either chicken or fish marinated in spices and lemon juice. It's excellent. Especially if you like a somewhat sour taste. And then there's the national dish, Thieboudienne, which is rice with fish. Too complicated to describe, but I prefer it. It has a lot of vegetables in addition to the fish. Very spicy. It's terrific here since they get fresh fish from the village every day. It's all delicious."

A young man came up with a bottle of water and glasses and asked what they wanted to drink. They chose to stay with water, and both ordered Thieboudienne. The aromas coming from the kitchen were heavenly, and Hanna could feel her stomach rumbling.

"Eric, you wanted to know about my uncle?"

"Yes, I am sorry to hear that he died."

"I was on my way to meet him right after a business meeting in the UK. The morning I flew into London, he fell down a flight of stairs in his home. He was my family. When my parents died in an accident, I was only twelve. He took care of me throughout my childhood. There wasn't anyone else, nor would I have wanted anyone. He was wonderful to me." She felt the grip of grief encircle her heart again. "He supported me throughout college and my MBA, although I knew he wanted for me to become a historian like he was."

"What sort of historian was he?"

"Classical History. But my uncle was knowledgeable about history in general, especially Western history. He taught at Stockholm University for many years and did a lot of research. Published many papers. As I mentioned, when he retired, he started the nautical blog."

"Yeah, IL&R, the company here, you have researched."

The food came.

"This is so delicious, Eric."

Hanna was savoring the bold taste. "Do you know how it's prepared?"

"I'm not a good cook, so I can't tell you exactly. But I've seen it prepared. It takes about two hours to cook. I hear the key is the stuffed fish and the local vegetables simmered in the tomato sauce."

"Well, I've never tasted anything like it." Hanna took another bite of the cracked rice with fish and closed her eyes, enjoying the texture and the taste.

"I'm glad to see you like it. Everybody doesn't."

Having finished, they asked for coffee. Most people were now on their feet, leaving. A man in his fifties was circulating among the tables. He was clearly the owner saying goodbye to his patrons.

"Issa," called Eric. "I want to introduce you to someone."

The man he called Issa extricated himself from a couple he saw off and came over to their table.

"My friend, please join us." Eric pointed Issa to the chair at the table.

"Bien sûr," said Issa and sat down.

"Coffee, please," he asked one of the waiters that were passing by.

"Issa is the owner of this excellent restaurant. The best place in all of Dakar." Eric was slapping Issa on the back and laughing. "Issa, this is Hanna Arnol, a new friend of mine. She'll be staying here for a couple of days. Or maybe more," he added, playfully winking.

Issa was a man of average height. He was wearing the traditional Senegalese attire called a boubou – a wide, long robe. It was light blue and embroidered in a deep yellow color.

"Enchanté." Issa kissed Hanna's hand. "Eric is an old friend. What brings you to Senegal, Hanna?"

"I'm pleased to meet you as well. I have always wanted to visit Senegal." She briefly told him about Signe visiting St. Louis and how she wanted to find out more about her stay there.

"Issa, how long have you been in the restaurant business? The food is delicious here."

"Well, that's a long story. I'm not sure if you two have time to hear it."

"We love stories, don't we, Hanna." Eric looked over at

Hanna with a gleam in his eye.

"The story about my restaurant begins back in 1859. Eric, I don't believe you ever heard this either."

Hanna turned her chair toward Issa as he began speaking.

1859 again. What else might have happened that year?

"My ancestor, also named Issa, and his wife Astou, left St. Louis for Marseille in 1859, we believe. By that time, those Senegalese who could afford the voyage were welcome in France. Evidently, Issa had earned money from a project in St. Louis." He stopped as his coffee was served.

"What I'm telling you are just tales that have been handed down from generation to generation in my family. The story goes like this, my ancestor Issa had enough money to open a restaurant in Marseille. I'm sure it was just a small place. The French were interested in African things then, and I imagine trying out Senegalese food was one of them.

"After a couple of years, his business really took off, and apparently, he then began putting his money behind halfway houses. According to the narrative, he wanted to help others who immigrated to France from Africa and who were not as fortunate as he was. Meanwhile, his restaurant business became more and more successful. As his resources grew and the flow of Africans coming to Europe increased, he kept opening halfway houses."

Issa was undeniably proud of his ancestry.

"Now here is something interesting, which we never figured out. Upon his deathbed my ancestor kept repeating how guilty he felt about something that occurred before he left Senegal. He kept repeating that he had gotten himself mixed up in some horrific deed perpetrated by some Englishman he called the 'Red-Headed Devil.' As the story goes, my ancestor would not let it go, but the family never found out what he was mumbling about, and that part of the tale died with him."

"Good story, Issa. By the way, I never asked you. Why did you decide to open this restaurant?"

"I didn't tell you, Eric?"

Issa looked from Eric to Hanna and back.

"Well, I've been lucky. I inherited one-fifth of the fortune my family amassed over the years. The rest belongs to my sister and brothers, who still live in France. Although I was born and raised in France, I thought it would be fun to come to Senegal at this point in my life. My children are grown, I'm divorced, so I have no real obligations in France. I opened this restaurant, and it's not only fun but gratifying. I had no idea it would become so successful.

"For now, I'm happy here, and if I get bored, I'll go back to France, I suppose. Or come up with something else," he grinned from ear to ear.

"Alright, you two. I have to say goodbye to some lingering guests. I'm very pleased to have met you, Hanna. Eric, I'm sure I'll see you around?"

Issa got up and approached a couple that was getting up from their table.

Eric and Hanna walked out of the restaurant and hopped back in the Jeep.

After the drive back to Dakar, Eric dropped her off at the IL&R office building. "Let's talk about our trip to St. Louis tonight," said Eric.

"Yes, you have my cell number."

Hanna opened the doors to IL&R.

CHAPTER 6

Hanna entered the IL&R building. It was cold inside. Ever since she came to Senegal, it had either been too hot or pleasantly warm, but never cold. The lobby had high ceilings and was brightly lit. On the right-hand side as she walked in, was a seating area with green, leather-upholstered chairs. Together with a matching green sofa, they surrounded a glass-topped table with magazines. On the left-hand side ran some steps up to the next floor. There was no one around. She stood there, trying to figure out where the 'little library,' Eric mentioned, was.

After a few minutes, a middle-aged, Caucasian man in a greyish, poorly styled suit walked down the stairs, speaking to her as he descended. "Welcome to IL&R. How may I help you?" he said to her in French.

"Good afternoon. I'm hoping to speak with someone who knows IL&R history."

"Then, I would be the right person to help you. Let me introduce myself. My name is Alain Boucher. I'm the assistant controller here. I'm also the IL&R archive custodian."

"I'm Hanna Arnol. I appreciate you taking time to talk to me."

They shook hands. Alain Boucher was a short, unassuming man in his forties. He had pasty, white skin and was thin as a rail.

"Is there a fee?"

"Oh, no. We are very proud of our company. Our archives reflect our history from the 1800s when M. Garnier founded the company. Let me take you to our little exhibition room. Please follow me."

He opened a door under the stairwell and held the door open for her. She followed him down a corridor, took a left, and stepped into a small room. Alain flipped a switch. This room was nice, with light walls and well-placed lighting. It was furnished with wooden furniture. Several off-white armchairs with small tables stood along one of the walls.

"Here is the public archive." Alain pulled out two huge, heavy binders and placed them on a table in the seating area. The binders looked more like tall boxes. "They contain various selected documents and correspondence representing the major events in the company's life over the years. The document arrangement is chronological, from the opening of the company in 1823 until today. And over here, we have some artifacts and mementos that may interest you." She followed him over to the displays along one wall. He flipped a switch, which lit the exhibit.

"This is lovely, thank you."

She saw old newspaper clippings and pieces of what she thought was Gum Arabic. Newer pictures of their oil and gas rigs were off to the side. She felt uncomfortable. Silly, but it was as if she was examining someone's private belongings in their presence.

"I'll leave you to it." He gave her room. "You can give me a ring on the phone over there when you finish, and I'll see you out." He indicated a black phone mounted on the wall by the door. "You are welcome to take any notes you would like, but please don't dislodge any of the documents in the archive."

He gave her a feeble smile.

"Of course. I understand."

"See you later then." He left, closing the door carefully.

Hanna took a closer look at the clipping describing Gum Arabic. The clipping said that the gum went by Gum Arabic, Senegal Gum, and Indian Gum. It was a natural substance of the hardened sap from various species of the acacia tree. The gum was soluble in water, edible, and primarily used in the food industry as a stabilizer. Additionally, manufacturers used it as a key ingredient in various industrial applications. The clipping about oil and gas described the location of the offshore rigs.

She dropped her backpack on one of the chairs and sat down on another in front of the archive.

God, it's cold in here.

She opened the large binder. The first document was a copy of a faded newspaper cutout of the IL&R opening ceremony. The founder, M. Garnier, was from the Bordeaux area of France. He had built it into a significant exporter of Gum Arabic. Later his son took over.

Hanna slowly perused the binder. It had a slew of documents. She was looking for anything related to Tensbury around November 1859. That is when Signe was in St. Louis.

The first letter she found that was interesting was Alistair's letter to Garnier. It was about the new American market for IL&R.

March 7, 1859

Dear M. Garnier,

I am pleased to inform you that we may have a new market opportunity in America. Last autumn, I had the pleasure of meeting Mr. John Haddock. He is a cotton trader from America. We spent a few weeks together in England and then in South Africa. He was interested in the opportunity to supply American companies with our Gum

Arabic product. He wasn't sure when he can begin shipments, as it depends on his customers in America. He indicated that he might have his first ship in St. Louis in the October-December time of this year. Mr. Smith will be in St. Louis to meet Mr. Haddock's ship.

I would appreciate it if you would direct the operations to have our usual first shipment ready in mid-October. I am working on a financial arrangement with Mr. Haddock. If this relationship doesn't work out for some reason, I will assume losses related to this first shipment.

Yours Respectfully,

Alistair Tensbury.

She brought out her phone and took several pictures of the letter. Then another letter caught her eye. It was a letter from Alistair Tensbury to Governor Faidherbe, penned in 1860.

In it, he mentioned that Western traders were paying navigation tolls to the native tribes for the usage of the Senegal River. These tolls increased the cost of gum products in the West. He wrote that the French authorities should make an effort to force the tribes' chieftains to stop this practice. He also strongly suggested that all traders should enjoy toll-free commerce.

As a postscript, he indicated that he would continue to lead Western traders in supporting many charities in Senegal. In particular, he mentioned the school for mixed-race orphans in St. Louis.

Hanna took a picture of this letter too.

She had all kinds of questions. Why did Alistair Tensbury send such a note to the governor? What did he mean by 'all traders should enjoy the toll-free commerce?' What was that all about? Did some of the traders have special arrangements? Why did he have to boast about his philanthropic activities?

And why did I find this letter in IL&R's archive? She thought it was probably because of the philanthropy.

Hanna knew that Faidherbe was the Governor of Senegal during that time. That meant he would have been the governor while Signe was in St. Louis.

She remembered a few things from the research her uncle asked her to do. During Faidherbe's governance, the French built trading posts and forts up and down the Senegal River. They needed to curtail tribal control of the river.

She went back to reviewing articles and letters in the archive. She was hoping to find something involving a trade deal that went bad. Or some other negative information involving Alistair Tensbury that Labor might want to get their hands on.

After an hour or so, without success, she gave up.

She called Alain and said she was ready to leave. He entered within a few minutes and saw her to the door. She thanked him profusely and hailed a taxi.

While riding back to her hotel, Eric called.

"So, how was IL&R?"

"Not much, except a couple of letters, one rather puzzling. I'll show you later."

"Are you tired?"

"I am. No offense, but we had a late-night chatting yesterday. By the way, I really appreciate you hanging out with me today."

"My pleasure. Are you up for a trip to Gorée in the morning before we head up to St. Louis?"

"Yes, I would love to. I read about it. It's the island off Dakar, right?"

"Yes. It lies about one mile from the main harbor of Dakar. It's a gorgeous little island with a dark past. Gorée has seen many Western colonialization periods. It was known as a trading port through the 19th century. Apart from Gum Arabic, they also traded in slaves. Gorée is a UNESCO World Heritage Site. It's a must-see if you visit Dakar."

"So, what time do you want to leave?"

"I figure if we leave the hotel at nine, we can take the ten o'clock ferry and be back by mid-day. Then we can have lunch and head out to St. Louis."

"How long is the drive to St. Louis?"

Hanna again realized how lucky she was that Eric would join her to St. Louis.

"On a good day, it's three to four hours. On a bad one, it can be five to six. It's a narrow double-lane road. If there's an accident or goats crossing the street, everything gets choked up. I usually use a UNESCO Toyota for trips to St. Louis. It's air-conditioned. You will be comfortable."

"Great, because my butt isn't hard enough for that long of a drive in your jeep. It still hurts from the drive to Chez Issa," said Hanna.

"Oh, it looks hard enough to me."

Neither one of them spoke for a couple of seconds.

"How about we have breakfast together at your hotel? We can meet at eight in the restaurant. What do you think?"

"Sounds good. Talk to you tomorrow."

For the remainder of the ride in the taxi, Hanna thought about Eric. She hadn't known him for long, but he seemed to be a great guy. A marine that became a lawyer and then went to work for a non-profit like UNESCO. He must have stories to tell!

She reminded herself that she would be visiting for only a couple of days, and he stays in Dakar. He surely had a home in Paris too, where UNESCO had its headquarters. She shouldn't get attached.

This is not a dating visit.

She got back to the hotel, and it was time for dinner. With the huge lunch at Chez Issa's, she knew she wouldn't be hungry again that night.

She took a long shower and untangled her hair using lots of hair conditioner.

Then she fired up her laptop and checked email. There was

a slew of work-related messages. She scanned them. Nothing she needed to attend to.

Where are the emails from the translation services?

Looking in her 'junk' box, her heartbeat quickened. There was a message from each of the three translation services. Excited, she opened the first one, from 'Aktiv Translations.' They said they had only translated Page 1. They noted that the page was double-sided and long. More would be coming soon. She opened the email from 'Swedish Translation.' They had attached Page 3. They also said they would send more within the next couple of days. The third service said a page should be coming within a day or so.

Hanna took her computer bag and removed the translation of the old diary. She looked at the last pages before the torn-out section. Although she had read them so many times growing up, she wanted to remind herself now of what came before the pages she had just received. She had glanced at these pages on the plane from Stockholm, but still …

Dear Diary,

We are now on our way to St. Louis, Senegal. I'll see Africa sooner than I thought! We have deviated from our path to South Africa because we caught part of a dangerous large storm. I asked Captain Taraldson about storms when we began the voyage. He said, "It will be November when get to Africa. The storms run between June and October. We should be safe this late in the season. But you never know. That is what makes my job so interesting."

I can tell you; it certainly wasn't interesting to be part of it yesterday! The storm was frightening. Ingeborg heaved and heaved. It was the first time during the trip that I have been scared for my life. I prayed to Neptune then, and I guess he heard me since we were safe. I learned that these storms move at different speeds, and this one moved pretty quickly. We caught the very bottom end of it as it moved westwards. Our ship reached the storm remnants when most of the high winds were gone, but a strong gust managed to crack the mast. If we had been just a little bit further west, we would end up in the middle of the storm. Then I don't know what would happen. But all is well and calm now.

I have been up on deck, and the weather is clear – calm after the storm, as they say. Captain Taraldson estimates we'll reach St. Louis in one day. There, the repairs will take place. I'm so much looking forward to seeing the 'Dark Continent.'

That's it for now. Tomorrow I'll be able to write about St. Louis.

She placed the old, translated page to the side. Now she was going to start reading the previously lost pages. She clicked on the first PDF. This was the first page she had received. There were two entries on what must have been a two-sided page.

Page 1 – First side

Dear Diary,

Can you believe it? I'm in Africa, and I'm staying in the Governor's house close to the port. Having spent almost a day moving closer to West Africa's coast, it was delightful to see land.

We entered the Senegal River delta, and there it was, St. Louis, above the dunes, a small city with palm trees here and there.

St. Louis is on an island in the middle of the river. Speaking with Captain Taraldson, who has been here before, there is a church, a mosque, a tower, and Moorish houses on the island. All seems to sleep under the blazing sun.

To the west of the island-city, we saw a town of very small huts. The captain says that the town has an entirely African population and separates St. Louis island from the ocean.

We arrived at the port, which isn't large but has long piers from which the merchants load their wares.

A while after we docked, a Senegalese girl in a dazzling, colorful outfit came with a message from the Governor's office that I was welcome to stay at his home. Her French was pretty good. I placed some of my dresses and garments in a valise, with her help, and joined her for the short walk to the house.

The house looks like a palace. A large, beautiful building with many rooms. I was able to clean myself properly for the first time in many weeks. Now I'm in my nightgown, ready for bed. The air feels pretty warm, after the ship where there is always a cool wind blowing, but I welcome it anyway.

More tomorrow.

Page 1 – Second side

Dear Diary,

Today was my first full day here in St. Louis, and I slept in. Such a joy to be in a real bed. Sleeping on the Ingeborg, a big ship, is fine, but this is like a dream. Servants had come and removed my dirty clothes and laid out some clean ones that I had brought from the ship.

I spent the day reading the French newspapers even though they were dated.

I spoke for a long time with Governor Faidherbe's Senegalese housekeeper, Madam Ngai. She speaks perfect French. She is in charge of all the servants and manages the house for the Governor. She told me that St. Louis was founded in 1659 and that it is the oldest colonial city on the West African coast. The narrow island is just over 2 km long and about 400 m wide.

She says about a thousand people live on the island itself, not counting all the traders that come and go regularly. She confirmed that to the west of the island is where the African population lives. They have an inadequate water supply, and the people often suffer maladies as a result. I was happy to hear that Governor Faidherbe is directing public works to bring fresh running water to people's houses there, just as on this island. She said he is also building a bridge to connect that part to St. Louis Island. Right now, all the traffic is via boats.

In the evening, Governor Faidherbe held a dinner party in honor of an Englishman. I did not meet him until dinner. His name is Mr. Tensbury.

Hanna stopped.

She met Tensbury! Wow.

Here was the first connection between Alistair Tensbury and Signe's diary.

Hanna was excited.

Madam Ngai told me he lives in South Africa, where he has a business that repairs ships on their way to and from Asia. He is also part owner of IL&R, a company here in St. Louis. It exports

Gum Arabic. Madam Ngai explained that Gum Arabic is a highly desirable product in the West. If I was interested, I should ask Governor Faidherbe, she said.

Well, you know me, I'm always interested in everything. I'll have to see if I can find a moment when he isn't occupied. Which will be difficult. All sorts of people always surround him.

It seems Mr. Tensbury works closely with Governor Faidherbe and has helped him set up trading posts up and down the river. He approached me before dinner. Mr. Tensbury has a handsome face, and his smile is gentle and warm. I suppose he is my father's age. He introduced himself and asked all sorts of questions about my family, the ship, and where I was going. He seemed genuinely interested. He had just come in from South Africa on board the vessel called Adelia. Because he came from the South, he missed the storm as it moved west. He told me that many ships perish in these sorts of storms. He said he had business interests here in St. Louis but was on his way to London.

Madam Ngai's staff served an excellent dinner with a very spicy Senegalese dish made up of a delicious fish, cracked rice, and different sorts of vegetables, some of which I have never tasted before.

Interesting that Signe ate the national dish as well and liked it.

Once more, she felt the tug of family strings on her heart, and for a change, it was a rewarding feeling, not a sad one. Now she was getting to know more about Signe in St. Louis. Some of what she was finding out from the diary corresponded to her own feelings here, and she hadn't even visited St. Louis yet! The translation went on.

At the table, we discussed many topics. Everyone was surprised to hear a woman knowledgeable in subjects, especially the sciences. I was proud of myself, I must admit. All those years studying with Mr. Nilsen paid off.

After dinner, we retired to the living room for dessert and coffee. I was very self-conscious. People looked at me, and I thought, maybe my clothes were not properly pressed. Looking around and comparing them, I don't think they were in style. But no worries about such trivialities.

Oh, I almost forgot. Another gentleman joined us for dinner. His name is something like Garnier (not sure of the spelling). He is the other owner of IL&R. He, Mr. Tensbury, and Governor Faidherbe spent a lot of time speaking. That's it for tonight.

She kept thinking, what could have prompted Alistair Tensbury to write the letter she found at IL&R?

Hanna opened the next PDF. It was another diary page. She reminded herself that this was Page 3 and that she was still waiting on Page 2.

Page 3

Dear Diary,

Today I had a most exciting day. I told Madam Ngai that I needed a few things and asked if there were any stores where I might purchase them.

I wanted to buy some coffee for the trip to South Africa. Captain Taraldson loves his coffee, and I wanted to bring him some. She told me that here everything is sold in a market. There is nothing I might want that I could not find there. She loaned me her 'girl,' as they call their female house servants, to lead me to the market and translate for me. It was the same girl who had fetched me in the port when we came in. She said many vendors spoke French but not all.

We did not have to walk far to get to the market. Everything is centralized around the Governor's palace. Madam Ngai was right. Everything was available. Stall upon stall sold everything from ostrich feathers to pearls. They even sold cages with small birds that sang so pretty. I found the coffee I needed.

The girl, whose name is Astou, helped me negotiate the price of the item. She said it was customary to negotiate, and the sellers expected the buyers to haggle over the price. I'm sure she is right, but it still made me feel uncomfortable. I'm not sure if it's the right kind of coffee, though. They claimed it was Arabic and it is much more finely ground than our Norwegian coffee. It smells delightful, and I think the captain will be happy.

On the way back, Astou insisted on carrying the package and told me about herself. She said her fiancé Issa would bring her to France to get married and start their life there. It seems the French government has extended the rights of full French citizenship to the inhabitants of St. Louis. Astou said her fiancé has just completed a big business project which would allow them to set themselves up in France. She said she did not know what this project was, but it had paid him a lot of money. I could tell she was very proud of him.

More tomorrow.

She now had more questions. How popular was the name Issa here? She just met an Issa whose heritage went back to an Issa in the 1800s. And that ancestor Issa also made money from a project just before leaving St. Louis for France.

Hanna stood by the window and watched the waves. It was still early in the evening, and tourists that had stayed late on the beach were meandering back, towels under their arms. She didn't see any children and wondered if this hotel marketed itself that way.

Before going to bed, she checked the news on her laptop and read about the British election. What a fight it had turned out to be.

After reading, Hanna stretched out on the bed and stared at the ceiling. It had been a long day, but she was satisfied. Finally, she was beginning to follow what had been hidden in those pages for so long. As she fell asleep, the question 'why' kept swirling in her mind. Why did Signe remove these pages?

CHAPTER 7

"Hey, Jack. It's Malek."

"How's it going?"

"She left this morning with a man driving a Jeep. I decided to find out who he was. I have some friends in the police who helped me out. I did some favors in the past to one in particular, and he owed me. So, using the license plate, I got the information. He's an American, Eric Shaw, and he works for UNESCO here in Dakar."

"What more do you know about him?"

"Nothing, really. He's been here for some time."

"I wonder how she knows him."

"I followed them to Dakar University. First, they visited someone on the second floor, which is where the professors have their offices. Unfortunately, I couldn't follow them there without being seen. They came down with a Senegalese man, who I think was a professor."

"Go on." Jack was impatient.

"Then they went to the library, and I followed. I sat as close to them as I thought safe. The Senegalese man brought over several binders to their table. They studied them with him to great length. She had her computer out, but I don't think she ended up taking many notes from what I saw. Then the

Senegalese man left, and she and Eric spent some more time with the binders. After they went out, I checked what they had been looking at, and it was St. Louis port logs from November 1859. I snapped some pictures of the pages. I'll send them to you right away.

"Where are they now?"

"They're on their way out of town. My guy, Moussa, is following them. I'll wait to hear from him and then decide if I should pursue them at this time or wait for them to come back. I'll let you know."

After the call, Jack settled back in his chair in his hotel room, thinking. Then, as he often did to analyze the problem, he opened his computer and wrote his thoughts in a document.

Jack couldn't wrap his mind around it. He knew he needed more information.

A while later, Malek called back. "Moussa told me they stopped at a rather prominent restaurant called Chez Issa. The owner's family is very well known in Senegal, but I can't imagine this has much to do with your work. They have a successful business in France, which goes way back to the 1800s. I'll wait here in town till they return."

Malek signed off without any pleasantries.

Jack called Tensbury and recounted this morning's activities, as well as his analysis.

"Thanks, Jack. Keep me posted."

"I will, Sir."

Later, Malek called again.

"They returned to the city after lunch, and now Eric dropped her off at a company named IL&R. Moussa said she went in. I caught up with him, and he and I are both sitting outside the building, waiting for her to come out. It's a French company with offices here and a long history in Senegal."

"I know about the company, Malek. Now we might be getting somewhere."

"Glad you think so. I don't know if she's meeting somebody at the company or just interested in something related to the logs she saw at the university. IL&R has a company history room where they keep a public archive... Wait, Jack. She's coming out now. She's hailing a taxi. Moussa is going to follow her."

"Malek, I just remembered something I wanted to see at IL&R. Would you visit this 'company history room,' you mentioned, and take a look at what happened in 1859. In particular, I'd be interested in anything referring to one of the owners of the company, Alistair Tensbury. Also, if you find something about him, see if it looks like she was looking at the same papers."

"Would you like me to do it now?"

"Yes, please."

"It'll be difficult for me to find out what she was looking at in there. I'll do my best."

"Thanks. Talk to you later."

Approximately an hour later, "Jack, I saw one document that might be relevant. An 1859 letter from Tensbury to a man named Garnier. From the other information there, I know that Garnier was also an owner of the company. The letter is about a new market in America. I just sent you the picture. I tried to determine if she looked at this letter. I can't be sure, sorry."

"Thank you, Malek, this is very interesting. Great job." Jack looked at the letter Malek had texted him and forwarded it to Tensbury.

Tensbury called. "Jack, interesting letter. Where did you get it?

Jack described Hanna's and Malek's IL&R visits.

"Remember, Sir, the diary she looked at on the plane? It refers to November 1859. I think she saw it, alright. Anyway, here is a potential link between the blackmailer note – if it's from America – John Haddock's South African letter, and a possible business deal between Haddock and Alistair."

"I think you are right."

"Sir, I know that many what-ifs, maybes, and how-abouts, are running through our heads, but let's wait until we get a bit more data. We may be able to nail something down. We'll have to wait and see what else Malek can come up with."

"I agree."

"I must say, Sir, that I'm delighted with Malek's performance so far. He's the right man for the job. We got lucky."

"Great. Let's see what Hanna is going to do. Keep me posted, please."

Tensbury sat at his desk. He could hear the people in his office leaving for the day. It was difficult for him to get his thoughts together. He hoped Jack would continue making progress. He seemed to be gaining some traction.

Traction on what?

Tensbury hoped for more relevant information soon. Perhaps Hanna was on a discovery path that might lead to something.

Outside the window, dusk was falling. Tensbury's thoughts moved back to the blackmail note.

'... this horrible event. It happened in West Africa in the late 1850s.'

He got up and stood by the window. Tensbury saw people saying goodbye to each other outside the building.

Is Labor just blowing hot air to see if I'll rattle? Is Hanna finding information that will augment Labor's knowledge of this 'event?' The event, they will use to contradict Andrew's earlier story about Alistair. They will then place him into the 'Bad Aristocrats' bucket and run with it.

What don't I know about Alistair? Or was this a legitimate situation, where someone has a sick child and has resorted to this type of behavior to save his daughter?

A draft found him, and he shivered.

Maybe it will be best if I pay the guy off and be done with it. If he shows up that it is. What are we gaining from going

KATE BACKFORD

after the Arnol link? Will it really help if Andrew knows what is coming from the Labor machine?... Yes, it will!

He turned around and sank back down in his comfortable chair. He looked at the framed photographs on the wall. Some of them he considered important. Himself in Parliamentary robes. Must have been some ceremonial occasion in the House. A photo with the Queen, taken at some official meeting. It was just a handshake, but still worthy of celebration. His diplomas took up the most space. A large frame of his law degree was prominently displayed over his head as he sat. In a corner was his MBA diploma. He had done both at Oxford. He took his MBA before he started his company, which helped him sort out marketing, sales, and advertising.

In fact, he couldn't have navigated the ins and outs of running a company without it. Now the company was a successful going concern. Engrossed in thoughts, he looked with love at photos of his wife and two sons.

His reverie was interrupted. He saw one of his business development managers standing at the door of his office.

"Come in, come in." Tensbury remembered his scheduled meeting. It was relatively short. They worked through the issues holding up the deal. Afterward, Tensbury wanted to get ahold of his son. He had been thinking of him all afternoon.

He tried to reach him on his cell but got voice mail. Rather than leaving a message, he called CCHQ.

"Yes, I'm looking for Mr. Tensbury," he told the person who answered. It sounded like a very young girl.

"Whom may I say is calling?"

"Tell him it's his father."

"Oh, yes Sir, just a minute."

"Hello." Tensbury heard a man's voice on the line.

"Who is this?"

"This is Thomas Taylor, Sir. I understand you are trying to get ahold of your son."

"Hi, Thomas. I can't reach him on his phone, so I thought

I'd find him at this number."

"Sir, he's here, but he's tied up in discussions to prep for the upcoming debate. Would you like me to call him over?"

"So, they finally agreed to a debate. That's splendid! Alright, I won't disturb him in that case. Tell him I called. It's nothing urgent. He can give me a call when he has a minute. By the way, when are you holding the mock debate? You are going to hold it, right?"

"We are focusing on strategy now and plan the mock three days from now."

"Thanks. I'll try to be there."

"I'll let him know you called, Sir."

CHAPTER 8

Thomas hung up and drew a deep breath. It didn't sound like it was important. He needed Andrew's full attention to the tasks that were in front of him. His constituency stops, and now this debate prep. Today they concentrated on the debate strategy all day. They were making good progress. Andrew was a quick study and was very familiar with the platform.

They just needed to prepare him with clear answers to questions they knew could come up and help him not to waver from his message. Never. Not once. Just repeat the answer differently and move on. Moving on was the trickiest part. Andrew had to remember which arguments to pivot to when presented with a topic he wanted to get away from.

As discussions moved along, it dawned on Thomas – not that he didn't expect it to happen, he did, but still – his old friend would very likely be the next UK Prime Minister. They were close. He remembered the last time he and Andrew had their little annual "Boys Only Ski" weekend in Austria. They had missed it this year due to the election. Thomas always hit the Black or even Orange Hills. Andrew stayed on the Red. On the slopes, sitting with a cup of hot chocolate, they discussed everything in their lives. At night they played pool in the bars. He hoped that next year they would not miss it, and that, even with Andrew as PM, their tradition wasn't over.

Eventually, it was time for Andrew to take a break.

As had become their regular habit, they stepped outside for a cigarette. The air was cool but refreshing after the stressful day inside.

"We have known each other for a long time. Have I ever told you how I became, what we call, a 'conservative'?" asked Thomas.

"No, but I'm sure I'll hear it now," Andrew laughed.

"Yes, indulge me for a few minutes. I'll never forget the first time I heard the Greek-sounding word 'Anacyclosis' in Eton."

"Oh, yes, Mr. Brosley? Let's see if I remember it correctly. It was the cyclical theory of political evolution. The one from monarchy to kingship, then tyranny, aristocracy, oligarchy, democracy, and then to another state. The Greeks call that state 'ochlocracy' or mob-rule. Then, finally back to monarchy again. Do I remember correctly?" Smiling like a good pupil, Andrew was proud that he knew the correct answer.

"Yes, you are right! Good memory. Mr. Brosley wasn't that good at explaining the differences between Plato, Aristotle, and Polybius' interpretation of this theory. Being the curious kid that I was, I had to read more about it and figure it out for myself. In a way, my political philosophy developed by thinking of the best way to prevent one of the links in this cycle. The link of degeneration of democracy into mob-rule. The ancients tell us, and history has seen many examples, how this degeneration starts. People develop a sense of entitlement and accept the pandering of demagogues."

Suddenly Andrew started laughing. "You know what I remember? I remember Mr. Brosley's fable. He told us he read it somewhere, but I think it was his creation. Remember about a building with a basement?"

"Yes, I most definitely do. Since you remember so well the

Anacyclosis, I'll try to resurrect the fable. He repeated that one so many times, I must remember it. Here it goes. A Fable by Mr. Brosley. Performed by Thomas Baldwin."

There is a large multi-story building. Many different people work there. They have different ideas and aspirations. They come from different backgrounds and cultures. Beyond the goals and tasks of their jobs, they don't agree on much.

The people know the environment on every floor of the building well. But very few of them ever venture into the basement. So, they haven't seen the walls of the basement, the building's foundation.

Ever since they were at school, their teachers and professors taught them a lot about the upper floors. The teachers especially dwelled on the life of the less fortunate there. But since the teachers also didn't know about the foundation, they paid scant attention to that part of the building.

The foundation and the basement were built and taken care of by the generations which came before the people on the upper floors. But life being what it is, there came a day when the people had to hire a new manager of the foundation.

They had a choice. They could hire a gentile manager who shared their taught views of life on the upper floors. He even said that 'we can bring many things up to the floors for the less fortunate among us. It will not be too heavy. Our firm foundation will hold.' There was one problem with this manager – he was not that good in foundations.

The other manager they could hire was rough and

*not well educated in the upper floors' life. He
wasn't known for his nice personality. However,
when he was substituting as a manager last year,
he improved and strengthened the foundation
significantly – he proved to be good in
foundations.*

*The majority, however, being true to their
education, felt passionate about the upper floors
they wanted. They prevailed and hired the genteel
manager.*

*For a couple of years, the building held. The
cracks that appeared were patched and patched
again. But one day, the weight was just too much.
The building crumbled and took the upper floors'
people down with it.*

"Thomas, this is great. What a memory!"

Thomas took two bows.

He was fired up. He went on, "Now, Labor socialist's desire for excessive wealth distribution is a step in overloading the building in the fable. The evil of removing the ability of a person to enjoy the fruits of his or her labor, so beautifully described by Ayn Rand, is unnatural. It corrupts individuals and whole societies." Thomas took a deep drag off his cigarette and exhaled.

"I know, I'm preaching to the converted, but bear with me here. American 'progressives' often talk about happy people living in socialism in Scandinavian countries. The Chinese talk about their benevolent one-party dictatorship. The one that leads to great economic development. The Russians talk about their special, one-party, one ruler 'democracy.'

"What they're not talking about is that those countries can pursue these political variations for one reason only. The reason is somebody else has been the source of the majority of the new wealth creation in the second part of the 20th century. From the transistor to the internet, and everything in between, it all came from the highly individualistic, capitalist America.

"Once there's no more truly capitalist America, there will be little new wealth to distribute. Socialist Europe will slowly degenerate into some kind of totalitarian rule. This is why I want to kick the socialists out before they do further damage to our country."

"Wow, Thomas, that was some speech! Of course, you know, I share this sentiment. But a more pragmatic goal drives my desire for our party to get back at the helm of the UK. This is probably my engineering training talking, but I want to see our growth match America or even some Asian countries. I want us to be one of the driving forces of this century, and most of all, a force in technology and biosciences. In succeeding in this goal, we'll lift the fortunes of everyone in this country."

"That last statement is great! We should consider including it in the debate. Let's discuss it with the group." Thomas shivered.

"We need to head back. It's getting too cold out here anyway."

Day 5

CHAPTER 1

Alain sat in his small office, staring at the newspaper article published in today's Guardian. His company subscribed to most major newspapers with large circulations in the West. He knew others in the company had seen the article as well. In fact, he was sure his boss had read it. He was also aware that it was too late to think about that now. He had made his bed and had to lie in it. He understood he would get fired.

His phone rang.

"Alain, please come to my office." His boss sounded gruff.

"I'll be right there." Alain got up and put his jacket on. He straightened his tie and walked out the door, towards what he knew would settle his path.

He knocked on his boss' door.

"Come."

He stepped in the door, and before he had a chance to sit in one of the chairs facing the desk, his boss started talking.

"Did you see The Guardian today?"

"No, I didn't."

Of course, I did.

"They published a story about our company. The information must have come from our archives. You are responsible for them. Do you have any idea what happened? We'll need to get hold of The Guardian to see if they can publish a retraction. You need to get me the name of the editor-in-chief."

His boss's words and sentences were tumbling over one another.

"I'll have to see the article, Sir. Let me look and see if I can find that editor. If there isn't anything else…"

His boss shook his head.

Alain left.

He would get fired as soon as the first shock passed. He was sure he did the right thing.

A retraction, ha, the look on my boss' face was priceless.

CHAPTER 2

"Hey, Ethan," Lillian spoke on the phone while walking down the hallway.

"Hi, Lillian."

"I don't know if you have seen it, but The Guardian came out with an article slamming Tensbury. Did you? No? The article describes how Tensbury, in 1858, played some games with the tolls on goods passing through the Senegal River. He worked out a deal with the governor at that time and got the tolls removed for only his company, IL&R. They also reported that he did some quid pro quo with the governor to get that executed. Take a close look at IL&R," said Lillian.

"Well, that's a happy turn for us, isn't it? I wonder who has it in for Tensbury? What was their source?"

"Just states 'our sources.' We sure didn't dig this one up."

"IL&R had an office in St. Louis, and it moved when Dakar became the capital. The headquarters is now in Marseille, but they have a sizable office here in Dakar. I did visit IL&R. They have a small exhibit with a historical archive available to the public. I didn't find anything crooked relating to Alistair Tensbury."

"Nothing?"

"Definitely nothing hinting to any big crime like what

Tensbury alluded to in the note to the Vicar. As I mentioned, I've been checking libraries in St. Louis and Dakar and found nothing. Frankly, Lillian, I don't really have any more places to turn to. I'm going to take another look in the university library here, but I don't hold my hopes up very high."

"See what you can do." Lillian was discouraged. That sinking feeling of potentially being beaten, returned.

As she ended the call with Ethan, she thought about the debate. She knew the strategy team had what they needed from her group. She still hoped she could come up with some damning information on Andrew Tensbury, or on the Party, or find some other angle to stick it to them. She wanted to have it before the debate.

CHAPTER 3

Andrew called his dad.

"Hi, Dad. Did you know what was coming out in the news before you said to change the messaging about our family?"

"You mean that article on Alistair's issues with the tolls? No, I didn't know. I'm as surprised as you are."

"It's good that I stopped, though. It was timely. Now I need to find a way to diffuse that article. Any ideas?"

"I checked the web on Senegal to see what else happened around that time. I think here is how you might handle it. First, you say that this inappropriate business behavior shouldn't be condoned in any way. Next, you state that the business practices in 1858 in Africa were not up to our current standards. Historically, we know that the French removed all navigation tolls several years after this letter to the governor. Then I would say that, of course, this should be looked at together with all 1st Baron Tensbury's philanthropic work in Africa. He was the main contributor to a school of mixed-race orphans in Senegal. The first such school in West Africa."

"Yes, from what I remember, he was also a large contributor to causes related to the African community in England."

"Right, I'll send you the documents and articles I found.

Maybe your researchers can dig a little further and come up with more."

"Thanks, Dad. Those are good points. Please forward the docs ASAP."

Then Andrew walked into Thomas' office. "As we agreed, we need to put something together to counter that article we saw this morning. My dad gave me some ideas. He'll send us docs to support them. We need to do it fast."

"Good. I'll look at those, and we'll act today. Also, I'm working with our chairman since the focus now is more and more on the constituencies. I know you and I have a fairly good grip on that, but he's my boss, you know?"

"Yeah. We are doing the constituency stops every day. They're important, but, God, I'm tired of them!"

"It's not just our constituency stops. We're ramping up the door-to-door canvassing as well as phone work. We also made sure that the data for our lists, which drives all these efforts, is aggregated appropriately. Andrew, I think you should take a breather for the rest of the day. See your family for a while. It's only going to get worse."

"Alright." Andrew left.

Thomas had a moment to pull his thoughts together. Something had been on the back of his mind for the last couple of days. He couldn't forget the conversation with Peter about the hacker and what he uncovered. It was great that they stopped the hacker before it got out of hand. But now that he knew the Swedish man's name, he wanted to find out more about the type of people Labor and its surrogates engaged in researching Alistair Tensbury.

Thomas started googling Noah Arnol. Stockholm University professor emeritus of Classical History. What he saw told him that Labor had good 'assistants.' He viewed his list of publications, some with Tennyson from the Cornelian society, who was also a professor of Classical History at Oxford.

Suddenly, Thomas' hand froze on the computer keyboard.

"What's going on? What is this?" he said out loud. He spotted Arnol's obituary from the university. An 'untimely death,' it said. Just a couple of days after the hacker got his email. He brushed the stupid thoughts out of his mind. He was sure this was just a coincidence. He didn't believe in conspiracy crap at this level. He told himself that the older gentleman just died.

Thomas considered it further. He was concerned that Labor researching Alistair Tensbury may be one of the soft spots of Andrew's campaign. He resolved to pay special attention to anything about Alistair – that's where the danger could come from. There are a few days before the debate. He hoped Labor isn't going to spring anymore 'old news' about Alistair's business dealings at the last moment, or, worse yet, at the debate!

He decided to take an action that could potentially change things. Maybe he could soften the blow of these damaging stories somewhat or even change the narration. He walked down an aisle, a couple of desks from his office.

"Hi Seth. How are you today? If you have a few minutes, I would like to run something by you. To see what you think." Seth was one of the guys in the media group.

"Absolutely, go ahead."

"This article about Alistair Tensbury today made me think of some of the good old days. The days when a newspaper would call and ask your comment on the subject, before publishing anything negative."

"Some of them still do."

"Yes, but not in the case of this article. So, what do you think about asking your contacts in the major outlets to do just that? To contact us for a comment before they publish an article related to this campaign? Be it negative or positive. I know it may be naïve, but you could tell them that we'll try to add some precision and color to whatever they uncover. Then they can decide to include our material or not."

"I think it's a good idea. Maybe some of them will be receptive. Of course, they will immediately ask for something in return about our campaign. No problem with that. I have plenty of soft stuff to give them."

"Great, let me know how it goes. Thanks, Seth."

CHAPTER 4

Hanna was sitting in the restaurant of her hotel with a cup of coffee. She had been sitting there for a while. She came early, and now Eric was late. Bored, she looked around.

At the table next to her, she heard a couple with British accents. They were talking about the upcoming British election. They said they should make sure to be home to vote. Hanna listened with half an ear but perked up as soon as she heard Tensbury's name. They referred to The Guardian article that came out today. They discussed if anyone, usually voting with the Conservatives, would vote Labor because of this article.

She saw Eric enter the restaurant and find his way over to her. He bent down and kissed her on the cheek. "That's how we say 'Hi' here in Senegal." He sat down.

"How are you this morning?"

Her cheek felt hot where he had kissed her.

"I'm good. Slept really well. I was tired."

"Glad to hear that."

Eric was pouring some coffee from the carafe on the table into his cup. He looked calm and well-rested.

Hanna updated him on the letters she had found at IL&R yesterday.

"So, Tensbury asked for equal treatment for all traders. This was in 1860, right?"

"Correct."

"This is an ancestor of the Andrew Tensbury who is going to be PM if the Tories win, right?"

"Same."

"This is interesting, because today The Guardian published an article connected to this. Have you read it?"

"No."

Eric conveyed the gist of the article.

"Let me think a minute." Hanna wrinkled her brow and took a breath. "Tensbury decided to reverse himself two years after he had requested the special three-year treatment."

"Right. The letter you found at IL&R, Tensbury wrote one year before his special deal was to expire. The Guardian article didn't say that there was a record of the governor acting on Alistair's request for exclusivity. However, it did say that Tensbury, through his partner in IL&R, was somehow helping the governor fix his house outside of Paris. Looks like a clean quid pro quo. The Guardian is a paper with a large circulation. They must have made sure all this information was bona fide before publishing. I wonder where they found that info?"

"You know, just before you came this morning, I heard a British couple refer to some article that might help Labor."

She looked around. "They're gone now. They said they wanted to get back in time to vote. That must have been the article that drove that conversation."

Hanna paused and thought about something.

"I think I know why Alistair Tensbury, in 1860, was trying to extricate himself from the shady arrangement mentioned in the article."

"Why?"

"Based on what I read when researching IL&R at home, Tensbury got peerage late in 1859. The 1860 letter I photographed yesterday, he wrote when he was already a Baron. Now, you can probably guess what prompted him to write such a letter."

"Yeah. He wanted to come clean because of his new status," said Eric.

The waiter came and topped up their coffee cups.

"Eric, I need to fill you in on another reason why I'm here."

He was stirring milk and sugar into his coffee. "Yeah, what's that?"

"I told you my uncle and I always wanted to visit Senegal because my ancestor Signe stopped here on her way to South Africa."

Eric nodded.

"Signe wrote a diary throughout her life. My uncle had them all. In the diary of the year 1859, the one that covers the trip, she writes there was a storm, a mast cracked, and they had to stop in St. Louis to fix it. Curiously, all the pages for the days in St. Louis and her trip to South Africa were missing." Hanna opened her laptop and found the two translated pages.

"Missing, because she didn't write anything?" asked Eric.

"No, really missing. Torn out. My uncle was the oldest member of the family, and the diaries belonged to him. We looked at the 1859 book in the library often and discussed it many times. We didn't know who might have torn out the pages from that diary as it passed from generation to generation, or if it was Signe herself who removed them. Then, recently, my uncle called and told me he had them."

"Interesting. How did your uncle get them?"

"He didn't say how he got them, but he said he would read them to me when I came for our Senegalese trip. I remember how poor her handwriting was. These were old, old books. I assumed it would take him some time to translate those pages from Norwegian into English. But he was excited, that's for sure. I was happy to hear how cheerful he was."

She continued, somber. "Then he died, and I had no idea where the pages were. Finally, I found them in his house.

There wasn't any translation that I could find. Which means he didn't get around to it. There was one letter in Swedish, which accompanied these pages. I ran it through Google Translate."

Eric raised an eyebrow.

"It's pretty accurate, you know," Hanna smiled. "The letter was from a Swedish bank, saying that the package was held in trust all these years. It should have been delivered in 1959, a hundred years after it was placed with the bank. They screwed it up due to an acquisition or some such reason. Here it was, with their apologies."

"So, if Signe was in South Africa in 1859, when did she tear these pages out? How did they get to a trust in a Norwegian bank?"

"The banker's letter said Signe's sister placed them there. Signe must have sent them home to Norway."

"So, now you have these pages, but I assume you can't read them. What are you going to do?"

"I scanned and sent them to translation services. Because it's old Norwegian and the scanned documents were hard to read, they told me it would take some time for the translation. We agreed that they would be sending the pages as they translate them, and last night I received the first two. Let me show you." Her excitement was palpable.

She turned her laptop around so Eric could read.

"The screen saver came on," said Eric.

"Shoot, I always set it to just a couple of minutes of inactivity. Wait, let me change that setting." She took the laptop from Eric, quickly typed in her changes, and gave it back. Hanna waited quietly while he read, jiggling her foot with impatience.

Finally, Eric looked up from the screen. "Signe's diary entries connect her to Alistair Tensbury, the other principal of IL&R and the governor in 1859. Fascinating that she met them. Also, I find it interesting that Signe and a young Senegalese woman talk about an Issa who did some 'big' project he was paid a lot of money for, so he and his girlfriend could go to France. All sorts of thoughts come to mind, Hanna."

"Yeah, right?"

Eric took a look at his watch. "We need to leave to catch the ferry. We'll talk about this later."

"Let me run up and put the laptop in my room. I'll be down in a minute."

Hanna went up.

Damn, I forgot to send that contract yesterday.

Hanna opened the contract and made sure the 'Highlight Changes' command was on. She sent the document to the lawyer.

CHAPTER 5

"Hanna is showing something on her laptop to Eric." Jack and Malek were sitting about three tables over from Hanna and Eric. Jack had his back to them. Malek was facing them. "I can see the screen because there's a glass lithograph behind her, and I can see it in the reflection. I can tell it's text but nothing more," said Malek.

"I wonder what that is," said Jack.

Soon enough, Hanna picked up her laptop, and they watched her and Eric get up from their table.

Malek and Jack followed them to the area across the reception. They turned their faces away as if they were discussing something. Hanna stopped at the reception desk and mentioned her room number. She said she was going to Gorée and asked for a late checkout. Jack and Malek saw Hanna get on the elevator while Eric waited.

Hanna came down, dressed in khaki shorts and a short sleaved white blouse. Her hair was up in a ponytail. They left the lobby and descended the stairs to the parking lot. Moussa saw them getting into a large Toyota and drive off.

"So, she's going to Gorée and then leaving for St. Louis. It doesn't make sense for me to follow her. There isn't anything of consequence she might find in Gorée," said

Malek.

"You sure?"

"Yes, it's entirely focused on tourism. However, when she comes back, we will follow her to St. Louis, right?" asked Malek.

"Yes, she's going to be in St. Louis for two days. I wish we could see what she showed Eric."

Malek stuck his hands in his jeans. "You know, there's a way to find out. Did you notice she didn't have her backpack with her when she came down?"

"Yes, I did."

"So, she left her laptop in her room."

"Must have."

Malek took out a little plastic key card and showed it to Jack. It looked like any other hotel key card. Off-white, without any writing on it.

"Oh, no! We aren't doing anything which can get us in trouble," said Jack, flustered

"Trouble? Who said anything about trouble? One of my guides is very tech-savvy. He read online about the way to create a hotel master key card. This is something he came up with."

Malek twisted the card in his hand, laughing.

"It should open any hotel room. He checked it out, and it works – at least in the ones he tried. He isn't a bad kid, and he doesn't use it for anything nefarious. It was just a challenge for him. As long as this little device works and her laptop isn't closed, I could check out what she showed Eric. I know how to get in and out of a computer without disturbing anything."

Jack looked at Malek aghast.

"Absolutely not!" Jack's voice sounded less convincing than his words. "We can't get into illegal activities. What if we are caught?"

"You won't be doing it, Jack. I will. Don't worry. I won't get caught. I'm not taking anything from her. Besides, this is Africa. There's little you can't pay your way out of." Malek grinned.

Jack didn't like it but was beginning to feel as if this might be an opportunity he shouldn't miss. But, if this renders results, he'll have to come up with a good story to tell Tensbury.

He thought for, what felt like, a good minute.

"Alright. Take a napkin and make sure you don't leave your fingerprints anywhere. If you can't open the door with your device, you abort. If you can get in, but the laptop is closed, or the screen saver is on, you abort. If you can get into the laptop, try to find a specific folder on the desktop. I'm betting the folder includes both Scandinavian as well as English documents. Open the docs in English and take photos with your phone. Don't stay any longer than ten minutes. Absolutely no longer. And make sure she can't tell you were there. I'll wait here. Right?"

"Right" Malek went off.

Jack took a seat by the waterfall in the reception. He waited, anxiously checking the news on the election on his cell phone. He wanted to distract his thoughts from what he just agreed to.

It didn't take long before Malek returned.

"I got in. We got lucky. She left her laptop on. No screensaver. Here are the pictures of the two documents I found. I'm sending them to you right now."

"You left everything in the room as it was, right?" Jack was nervous. "Do you think she can tell that someone was in her laptop?"

"Don't worry. She won't notice anything."

"Let's hope so. You know how the saying goes: 'better to be lucky than brilliant because it's more consistent,'" said Jack.

"That's funny. I think one should aim to be both. Just in case." Malek grinned.

"Do you need to get some clothes from your apartment before we leave?" asked Jack.

"I stay in a hotel. I have time to get my things from there. I'll see you back here in an hour or so. They won't be back before that, given the ferry schedule. I'll tell Moussa as well."

After Malek left, Jack went up to his room and packed his bag with a few pieces of clothing for the trip to St. Louis. Then he brought up the pictures of the documents Malek had snapped and read them carefully.

Jack reminded himself that he and Tensbury had assumed that Hanna was here on a Labor project to find out about an event involving Alistair Tensbury. They further assumed that she was following the dairy pages to get this information.

He took out his laptop and pulled the documents up on the screen. He had the pictures of the logbooks, Alistair's letter to Garnier, and now pages from the diary. He started a new document to try to make some sense of it by listing what he knew. Next, Jack put down his suppositions, speculations, and general guessing.

> *First, the owner of Chez Issa most likely relates to the Issa in the diary. In the diary, Issa's business project's date of 1859, immigration to France and the start of the successful business there, say so.*

> *Issa made some serious money to move to France. How does a Senegalese man in 1859 have a project that yields this much? It must have involved a Westerner. Could this Westerner be Alistair? Something like a Gum Arabic trade deal between Alistair and Haddock. It could, but it could be any other Western trader operating in Senegal. If it was Alistair, could it also involve his Cape ship repairing business? How?*

> *Second, the blackmail note says the 'horrible event' happened in the late 1850s, but there is nothing in the two diary pages from the woman in 1859 that points to any bad event connected to*

Issa's business project.

Jack sat for a while, thinking. He then assembled all the documents he had, plus the list he just typed, and emailed them to Tensbury.

He came down a few minutes later and made his way into the restaurant. It would be some time before they served lunch, and it was empty. He found a table in the corner and asked for coffee. He waited for a while, then called Tensbury.

"Sir, I just wanted to chat about what we found so far."

"Lots of information, Jack, but how in the world did you come by these two pages?"

Jack had given this some thought and believed he had a good story to tell Tensbury.

"Well, you know how good I think Malek is, but perhaps his methods are a little unruly."

"What do you mean?"

"This morning, we sat close to Hanna in the restaurant that was serving breakfast. It's located by a large pool. We were around the corner from the kitchen entrance. I excused myself to go to the restroom. When I came back, I saw Malek standing at the table that Hanna had just vacated, with her laptop open in front of him."

"My God, Jack. Did he just open it?"

"No, it was open."

"Oh."

"I froze. I didn't want to draw attention to whatever he was doing. I sat down at our table and waited. I saw him snapping pictures with his phone. He kept looking outside the large windows where the pool was. I looked out and saw Hanna and her companion on the other side of the pool. They were sitting in the sunchairs chatting with someone.

"Malek came back to our table and didn't say anything. Pretty soon afterward, she came in, packed up her laptop into her backpack, and left the breakfast room.

"Did anyone see him?"

"No, I don't believe so."

"You better keep this Malek on a short leash, Jack. We can't risk any word of this reaching our world here."

"I will, Sir."

"Please."

"I know her plans from the itinerary George sent us. We are going to follow her to St. Louis today. Malek is going to stake out her hotel there and see what she's up to."

"As far as your note, your suppositions are very good. I was just thinking what I can add but couldn't come up with anything."

"Sir, I read some things about business deals relating to shipping at that time. It seems that there were many insurance claims about shipwrecks that were later proven to be false. Could that be the nefarious event here?"

"I don't think so. First, from what I know, such things were not in Alistair's character. Second, even if one thinks the worst of him, by that time, he and his partner were quite wealthy. They would not get involved in a false claim for a single Gum Arabic shipment. But third, and the most important point, is Alistair's peerage. By November of 1859, he knew he was granted the title. He wouldn't jeopardize his new status."

"You are right, Sir. We are missing some pieces of this puzzle."

"Yes, but where do we go for these pieces?"

"I don't know, Sir. Hanna may be on track to nail down some more information that isn't in those pages."

CHAPTER 6

Hanna stood in the bow of the small ferry, taking her and Eric out to the Island of Gorée.

"It's good that you are going to see the island. It's very small and known for having been a center for the slave trade, although its actual role isn't really clear. Some say most of the slaves exported from Africa were processed through the island, and others say it was just a fraction of them. It's highly unlikely that a large number of people came through such a place. But it has become a beacon for those who want to visit and learn more about slavery at its source. Mainly because of the 'House of Slaves.' You'll see it. Very impactful. Several US presidents have visited," said Eric.

The ferry arrived in Gorée. Eric and Hanna got off and strolled through the picturesque narrow streets. Old colonial buildings, with bougainvillea here and there, lined the streets. Cars were not permitted on the island. They turned onto Rue Saint-Germain, passed the Statue of Liberation, and reached the House of Slaves.

Hanna saw the small holding cells on the bottom floor and the large colonial rooms on the second. Here, the slaves were shackled to the walls in the dark cells. Men, women, and children were kept in different cells, waiting to be shipped out.

Hanna could feel the misery emanating from the walls of the cells, and it left a tremendous impression on her.

Around noon, Eric and Hanna were back at the hotel. Hanna ran up to collect her luggage.

She finished packing. Her laptop was still out. She sat down on the bed with it in her lap. She checked email. The third translation service had come through and sent Page 2. It would now fit in-between Pages 1 and 3. She read the new page quickly and went down.

"Eric, I got another page! I'll read it to you in the car. Let me check out."

After she paid, they got into Eric's car and took off.

They stopped by Eric's place so he could throw some things together. She stayed in the car. His bungalow was on a nice, quiet street, with flowers spilling over the fence.

They left Dakar on the N2, and very soon, the landscape changed. From a city, the surrounding environment turned into a forlorn road of dust with a few small villages along the way to St. Louis. As they passed villages, she saw shacks of wood, interspersed among half-finished concrete buildings with wall-less rooms, beds, and furniture visible, like dollhouse displays.

Every now and then, a cascade of bougainvillea adorned the landscape like a glorious dab of color on a grey picture. Between the villages, she viewed the arid landscape stretch endlessly into the distance. The land consisted of mostly flat, sandy, red clay. Hanna saw an occasional baobab, its upside-down root-like branches, dark silhouettes against the deep, blue sky. Her mind was drawn to Saint-Exupéry's 'The Little Prince,' and she irrationally wondered if the 'elephants were able to eat the baobabs' here. She enjoyed her memory of the pictures in the diminutive book.

"Now you are seeing rural Senegal," said Eric.

Along the road, Hanna saw fruit shacks with women, baskets on their heads, raising their fists at small, dusty children running circles around their mothers chasing old tires with sticks. Truck tires were scattered along the road. They were stacked, used as decoration, or just lying here and there.

"What's with the men sitting around on their haunches drawing pictures in the sand with sticks. Are they writing?"

"Not sure, but it's typical to see them like this. Maybe Koranic verse. It's much more religious out here than in Dakar."

Curiously, as they came closer to St. Louis, the surroundings became even more desolate than before.

Hanna sat quietly, absorbing the experience.

"I know this sounds crazy, but I think someone was in my laptop while we were gone."

Eric snuck a peek at her. "What do you mean someone was in your laptop?"

"When we returned to the hotel after the trip to Gorée, I checked my email and got the new diary page. It was Page 2. Then I decided to pull up Page 1 to connect Signe's writings. I looked in the recently opened documents. At the top were the documents from Signe's diary, not the contract which I opened before we went to Gorée! Not the contract! I can't imagine how it could happen unless someone was in there taking a look at the diary pages while I was absent. I checked everything in the room, and nothing had been moved." She paused. "Maybe I'm just imagining things."

"You probably are." Eric looked at her sideways to gauge her expression. She had a resolved look on her face.

"Now, in addition to the diary, I'll always have my computer with me."

"Okay, here is Page 2. Let me read it to you. It's short."

Hanna pulled out her laptop and turned it on. She opened the document. "Remember, you saw Pages 1 and 3 this morning in the restaurant. This is Page 2. It didn't come in order."

Page 2.

Dear Diary,

Today I walked down to the port to see Captain Taraldson. I slipped out before anyone was awake. Oh, how upset they were when I came back after having been out alone! To the port no less!!

Well, my walk to the port was uneventful. There were mostly Senegalese people around and they paid me scant attention. When I got to the place where Ingeborg was moored, I saw Captain Taraldson at the pier. He was directing the workers who are now trying to mount a new mast. He was so happy to see me! He inquired how I was doing, and I asked him the same. He said he had found a room in one of the little port hostels and that the work on Ingeborg was going well. He said the sailors had been given some time off and were spending time in port.

He also said I should stay away from the port eating and drinking establishments since they were rough and not a place for a lady. That, of course, got me interested, but I thought better of going there. You should be proud of me!

On my return from the port, I ran into Mr. Tensbury and a man he introduced as Mr. Smith, his assistant. You would not believe the flaming orange hair on that man! Like a peeled and glowing carrot. I thought it was strange that they were out and about so early.

More tomorrow.

"Eric, I thought about what Issa said yesterday about his ancestor talking about the 'Red Headed Devil.' His ancestor left Senegal in 1859, and that's when Signe met this red-headed man. Too much of a coincidence, don't you think? I think it was the same man. The one having done some 'horrific deed.' And Signe writes that he worked for Tensbury."

"Could be."

"Issa's ancestor then built all these halfway houses – maybe he was atoning for this deed he talked about?"

"Yeah, maybe he was," agreed Eric.

"If, and it's a big if, it's the same Issa, and the red-headed devil is Mr. Smith, then Tensbury must be involved as well. In those days, a person being an assistant to a wealthy businessman wouldn't have much money. He wouldn't have a project that would provide Issa and his fiancée with enough money to set up their new life in France. Tensbury must have been the one directing Mr. Smith."

"What kind of project do you think it might be?" asked Eric.

"Could be a Gum Arabic deal. The deal went bad, and one of his competitors could have been hurt, or worse. I didn't mention the second letter I read in the IL&R files. I didn't think it was relevant. It was from Alistair to Garnier. The letter refers to an American cotton trader Alistair met in London. Alistair thought this trader would be able to open a new Gum Arabic market for IL&R in America. It seems that a lot was happening at IL&R in those days. One of these deals could have gone very bad," Hanna repeated.

"Too many presumptions, Hanna." Eric was quiet for a bit. "Or maybe not."

Again, Hanna's thoughts returned to her uncle. "Eric, I think I need to explain why I am so edgy about my laptop now. You know how I told you my uncle died?"

"Yeah."

"When I examined the circumstances of his death, a lot of things didn't point to it being just an accident. I mean, the police don't believe someone caused his death, but they're still looking into the case."

"Really!" Eric took his eyes off the road for a second. "If the police don't believe it, why do you? Do you have any suspects?

"Please bear with me. I'll go through my thought process."

She recounted the conversation with Helen about her uncle's death.

"Do you really think the British political parties, or their affiliate, get into such criminal activities? I think that's a stretch."

"I don't know." Hanna put away her laptop. They rode in silence for a while.

Eric was perturbed. "I don't think it jives. Too many assumptions."

Hanna turned around in her seat. "Just to add to all my assumptions, I think someone is following us. The same car has been behind us since we left Dakar."

Eric took a look in his rearview mirror.

"I don't think so. With this road, it would be natural for a car to be behind us all the way. Not easy to pass here."

Hanna didn't feel convinced. She looked back again. The car was now further behind them, but she could still see it. After suspecting someone looking in her laptop this morning, she felt very uneasy.

She decided to get off this subject.

"I can see why you wanted us to take the company car."

"Yeah, this drive would have been deadly with the Jeep. Now you have an air conditioner and a soft seat." Eric glanced at her with a smile.

"Tell me more about Faidherbe. I read some about him as I was researching IL&R, but I'd like to know more."

"Faidherbe basically put St. Louis on the map. He dreamed of creating a French African empire and had grandiose plans for West Africa. He built a series of forts up and down the Senegal River to prevent the locals from levying tolls on the trade. He didn't completely succeed, as you have seen from the letter you found at IL&R and from the Guardian article, I told you about. As Signe mentions, he set up a system bringing water to the western part of St. Louis. He also built a very long bridge over the Senegal River, connecting the island of St. Louis with the mainland. You'll see it as we drive in. It's pretty impressive."

The land was desolate and barren as they approached St. Louis. They crossed the Senegal River, and the bridge was impressive. The massive steel arches were already lit against the evening sky. After crossing the bridge, they came into a small city with period buildings.

They made their way to Hotel de la Poste, where her uncle had reserved rooms. It was a well-known hotel in St. Louis. Its buildings still held the charm from the French colonial days.

"You know Hanna, the St. Louis Jazz Festival is this weekend. I thought we would go tomorrow night."

"Patrick mentioned it."

"It's pretty well known. On the music scene anyway. Over the past three decades, the city has built a following for jazz enthusiasts. It's the largest such festival in Africa and draws some of the world's best jazz musicians. Do you like jazz?"

"I do. I even play it now and then on the piano. Very poorly, I think, but I enjoy it."

"I'm sure you are just being modest. I always found jazz musicians good since they often improvise."

"I try." Hanna got out of the car, smoothing her shorts.

She insisted on paying for both rooms, and although he argued, Eric was impressed. He liked this independent woman.

Hanna got to her room, and before taking a quick shower, she checked her email – nothing from the translation services. She checked the news online. Every media outlet was talking about the British election. The polls showed that the race was very tight.

She met Eric in the lobby, and they walked over to the restaurant that belonged to their hotel, the Flamingo. They had dinner and agreed to meet tomorrow morning to see the Governor's mansion and the market.

CHAPTER 7

Jack and Malek followed Eric's Toyota at a safe distance.
"Thanks for snapping those pictures."

"Is that some of what you were looking for?"

"Unfortunately, not. They were more personal things of hers, not related to Hanna's work. But still, thanks."

On this two-lane road, there was no way to be inconspicuous to the car in front of them. Jack saw the Toyota swing to the side of the road. It stopped in front of one of the little fruit-stands that littered both sides of the road.

"Bloody hell, they stopped!" Jack made a hand gesture. "Let's park in front of them."

"Let me call Moussa."

Jack listened to Malek speak to his guide in rapid-fire Wolof. Malek drove past the fruit stand and parked.

"I told Moussa to park right behind us."

Sitting there, Jack saw another car pulling up in front of them.

"Who is that? Are they also buying fruit?"

"Doesn't look like it. Those guys are just sitting in their car. Are they following them too?" Jack sounded astonished.

"Don't know. Let's wait and see."

Soon enough, Jack saw the Toyota pass, and the other car

swung out behind it. Malek got back on the road. There was now a car between his car and the Toyota.

"You are right. Those guys might be following them too. Who are they after, Hanna or Eric? Or maybe both?" Malek looked at Jack.

"Competition, I guess." Jack gave a nervous laugh.

Jack saw Malek making sure they stayed behind the Toyota and the other car.

After they had crossed the bridge into St. Louis, they were careful not to lose sight of the Toyota. Jack knew which hotel Hanna and Eric were going to because of the itinerary. It was late, but he wanted to make sure they would not miss any of Hanna's other stops.

The other car also persistently followed.

"I'm serious, Malek. This can't be a coincidence, right?"

Malek didn't answer. Just off a square, the Toyota turned into one of the small streets and parked. The car in front of them also stopped since it couldn't pass on the narrow street. Malek stopped too.

"This is Hotel de la Poste. That's where they're staying, right? What do we do now?" Malek asked.

"It's late, and I assume they'll go about things tomorrow, not tonight. Let's make sure you stake them out tomorrow morning to see what they're up to. We'll also see if those people are following them."

Jack could see Hanna and Eric grab their bags and get out, and it seemed they handed the keys to a valet because the Toyota left. The other car took off in front of them and turned onto another narrow street.

"Yes, let's skip tonight and get to them tomorrow morning. I doubt they could do anything of interest tonight." Malek put the car into gear. The two of them, plus Moussa, headed off to their hotel.

Day 6

CHAPTER 1

Thomas didn't notice that he was sipping tepid tea and gnawing on stale toast.

After his usual scan of all the leading papers in the morning, he was fascinated by an article in the Financial Times. A reporter published a piece he had presumably worked on for a while. It was about an American businessman, Alex Hurt. Mr. Hurt had extensive business interests and was a major contributor to the US Democratic Party. He was especially keen on backing ultra-progressive members and causes. Starting several years ago, Mr. Hurt regularly hired three British business consulting companies. They consulted him concerning his private holdings. He paid them many-fold rates of what was typically charged for these types of services. All three companies went into business in the same year when Mr. Hurt first hired them.

The Hurt business constituted a hundred percent of these companies' annual consulting receipts. This reporter followed the money. He discovered that these three companies were major contributors to the Labor Party and aligned associations in the UK. According to the reporter, this affair smelled of money laundering for illegal, foreign political contributions. The Electoral Commission was going to investigate.

Thomas liked this type of really 'Nice' news in the morning. He hoped the media would expound on the Electoral Commission investigation quickly.

He finished his breakfast and immediately got involved in the morning activities.

First, he needed to attend to Andrew's constituency stop and press-conference. Second, he shouldn't forget that tomorrow was the mock debate rehearsal. He would make sure that all the moving parts were in place.

That evening, Andrew caught up with Thomas at CCHQ. "Have a moment?"

"Yes, I need a break. Let's grab a smoke outside."

Once outside, in Andrew's hiding place, they both lit up.

"How about that Financial Times story about Alex Hurt? Labor is starting to send us presents. It's like Santa Claus in May."

"I love Christmas gifts in the spring. It's better than the crap we got a few days ago." Thomas took a deep drag and thought about Andrew's radicalized ex-girlfriend story.

"Yes, this is great, but we also need to do our own research to keep the momentum going. You and I have both looked at the numbers, and it's too close. We need to modify or change some of our messaging. I know it's late, but we should be able to get a fresh spin out. Not only through our central channels, but also through the MPs. In the case of those candidates, we need to select the important issues locally and back them with everything they need to win. Let's not make the mistake some other campaigns did and neglect those we think are in the bag. We don't have much time."

"I know, Andrew. I'm working very closely with Ian. He's doing a good job making sure all the local efforts, programs, and messaging are coordinated. But what about you? Do you have any other Christmas presents? New ideas for messaging never hurt. I have several, but you first."

"Alright. Here goes one. Labor is lousy with women in their leadership. They only have one woman in the cabinet.

Our shadow government has over 50% women and minorities, which would remain if we are elected. You are next."

"I like this game," said Thomas. Here is mine. "The PM has spoken about euthanasia in Britain. A new leftist issue. Should terminally ill patients be allowed assisted suicide?"

"I would not touch it. Let Labor alienate religious people without us getting into it," said Andrew.

"You are right. Here is another one instead. We need to raise an issue of free and fair exchange of ideas at our universities. We need to cough up a couple of examples where a university effectively prevented conservative speech on campus. Our young conservative followers will appreciate this one," said Thomas.

"Good one. This next one is a biggie. Let's emphasize how far left Labor shifted since the last election. It feels like they want to bring back 'Clause IV' and nationalize some of the industry again. We shouldn't be afraid to force them to answer this question. Maybe they will publicly commit to, what most of us think, is a Marxist way of thinking. And one more thing. Our members don't want us to leave any false Labor sympathizers' media statements unanswered. We need to set up a timely procedure to address those. Also, we need to encourage our most effective MP debaters to challenge their opponents on the issues raised in those media statements. It worked before, and it should work now. We should assign a person to coordinate this effort."

"That wasn't one. Those were three. You are supposed to have only one at a time. Wow. Want my job?" asked Thomas, trying hard not to laugh.

"Only if you take mine."

"I think we better leave it as is."

Thomas' assistant walked over to them. Apparently, she knew where they were taking their breaks.

"I have good news." The young woman crossed her arms over her chest, warding off the evening chill. "Labor numbers are falling in the polls. We think it's because of the Financial

Times article and because the Electoral Commission has started an investigation."

Thomas turned to Andrew. "How is that for Christmas in the spring?" He threw a satisfied look Andrew's way.

"Oh yes, and Seth is looking for you, Thomas."

"I better go in and get some of these ideas moving," said Thomas.

CHAPTER 2

Eric and Hanna met at the Flamingo, where breakfast was being served by the pool.

"I see you brought your laptop. Don't want to leave that behind, do you?" Eric was giving her his usual playful smile.

"Look, I really believe someone was in there, okay?"

"Okay, okay."

"Are we seeing the Governor's Palace first?" asked Hanna.

"No, first we are going to have a wonderful breakfast. And only then, are we going to see the mansion."

When they finished, Eric said, "Now, grab that laptop of yours and let's go." He led her in the direction of the Palace. As she walked, her auburn hair caught a glimpse of a sunray, turning it almost red.

"You already stand out here. And that red hair really completes it," said Eric playfully.

"Yeah, it does that in the sun," said Hanna.

Walking down the street, they passed many wonderful old colonial buildings. They were painted in various sun-bleached colors. Similar to Gorée, many of the buildings had balconies, also painted in bleached colors. Unfortunately, most buildings needed repair.

Now and then, a horse-drawn carriage rolled by, usually

filled with tourists. There were plenty of people on bicycles on the road now that the jazz festival was underway.

"Look, there's a goat eating trash on the sidewalk. What's with the goats wandering free?"

"Yeah, they wander here. Those goats belong to no one. If someone wants to slaughter one for a meal, they're welcome to it. But you can see how skinny they are. Not really appetizing." Eric grimaced.

"You know, Hanna, these goats always bring back Bill the Goat, the US Naval Academy's mascot," laughed Eric.

"A goat?"

"Yeah, a live goat. We keep him on the sidelines during games. It's hilarious, but it's a tradition."

"Did you play?"

"Not at the Academy, but I played all through high-school."

They continued walking on Rue Général de Gaulle and soon ended up at the Faidherbe square, the center of town. With its back to the river, stood the Governor's Palace.

"This square is where St. Louis splits into two parts. The North quarter, the South quarter, and the Governor Mansion in the center."

"It's beautiful. How has the city maintained what looks like its original colonial appearance?" asked Hanna.

"There are apprentice workshops that provide instruction to hundreds of craftsmen in different restoration trades. They use traditional materials to maintain and upgrade the city. The meticulous adherence to the original look of the city makes it a World Heritage property."

"That statue. I suppose that's Faidherbe?"

"Yes, that's him."

All over, people were busy with lights and props for a large stage on the square. Eric and Hanna passed a young man in traditional garb, arranging the microphones for the stage.

"They're setting up for the festival tonight, so we'll have to walk behind the stage. I made a reservation with the curator of the Palace, so he should be waiting for us."

Cables were running everywhere, and they had to walk carefully. They passed behind the stage and saw an older man standing on the side of the gate to the Palace grounds. The Palace was a three-story building, painted white. There were elaborate balconies in the middle of the second and the third floor with the fourth story balcony, extending into a small tower above the building. The man was wearing a light pink shirt, grey suit pants cinched up with a belt on his thin frame, and black loafers without socks. His lined face broke into a wide grin when he saw Eric. The two greeted each other.

"Hanna, this is Monsieur Thiam." He turned to the man. "This is Hanna Arnol. I want to show her this wonderful building."

The man shook her hand and opened the gate. They passed through the front yard and mounted the stairs to the second-floor building entry. Inside there were long corridors with paint flaking off the walls, but it was beautiful. It seems that the walls had been colored turquoise in their heyday, but the colors were faded now. She could see the light turquoise doors leading off the hallways. The windows also had turquoise shutters.

"Come, Madam."

Hanna followed M. Thiam into the building. They slowly followed the man as he took them on a tour around the house, which had many rooms. Two big rooms on the second floor were purportedly a dining room and a dance hall. Smaller rooms on both the upper and lower floors were sleeping rooms.

After touring for quite a while, they said goodbye and thanked Monsieur Thiam. Eric handed him a couple of bills as they left.

Exiting the house, they saw that the preparations for the jazz fest were even more frantic. A man on a ladder was setting up strobe lights, and they avoided walking under the contraption. Throngs of people had stopped to watch, gathering on the street.

"You wanted to see the market too, right?"

"Yes. Remember, that's where Signe went with that girl from the governor's house."

"Okay, let's go. I realize the market Signe went to was close to the square where we are now. That doesn't exist anymore, but there's another one, not far from here. It'll still give you a flavor for what a Senegalese market looks like."

They crossed a short bridge to the area west of the island of St. Louis. It was more impoverished than what she had seen on the island.

After a little while, they came to Avenue Dobbs, where the market was located. The street was made of packed sand. As they walked along the road, they saw a blue pickup truck left haphazardly in the middle of the road. Small stores, doors open to the road, were selling all sorts of things. Colorful plastic chairs, plastic bowls, clothes, and fruit, including watermelons, which spilled out over the sidewalk. She saw a stall selling shoes. Another one selling swaths of colorful cloth.

Clothes hung between all the buildings attached with clothespins. There were not many cars on the small street, but plenty of horse-drawn carriages. Most of the horses looked well cared for. The sidewalks were full of people. Women with baskets on their heads, mostly in brightly colored clothing. Some kids came running up to them, hands held out for a coin. Hanna couldn't help herself but give some money to each kid.

"You shouldn't have done that," said Eric with a droll look on his face. "Now you will be deluged by them."

He was right. Pretty soon, they were swarmed by young faces, looking for a trifling. After a while, the kids stopped.

"I'm sure this doesn't resemble what Signe saw. Based on her description, the market was more complete, with more items then. I only took you here so you could see a Senegalese market. There are markets for tourists with beautiful clothes, masks, and other artisan items. Would you like to go to one?"

"No. As you said, I don't think this is what Signe saw, but it was good for me to experience it anyway."

"Okay, let's head back to the hotel then. Are you up for the walk? Should only take us half an hour or so."

"Absolutely," said Hanna, and they made it back to the hotel easily.

Hanna's phone vibrated and she took a look.

"Eric, I just got an email back from our lawyer regarding a contract we are negotiating. It'll take me a couple of hours to work on it. Can we meet here around seven or so?"

"Of course. We'll have dinner and then hit the jazz fest. I'll see you later."

Just as Hanna got to her room, Helen called.

"Hanna, are you alright? Tell me."

Hanna unstrapped her sandals, and fell back on the bed, tired from all the walking.

"Yes, the pain has sort of let up."

"Good."

"A lot has happened, which helped. I decided to go to Senegal, as my uncle planned for us. So, I am here in St. Louis, in Senegal now."

"What! Are you serious?"

"Yes, and it's very nice here. Now, about my news. Remember how some pages were torn out of Signe's diary? I have received the translation of a couple of them. They cover her stay here in St. Louis. She wrote about staying at the Governor's Palace and going to the market. I wanted to experience what Signe saw here, even if it's over 150 years later. Today I did. I saw the Governor's mansion. It was a little shabby, but it still gave me an idea of where she was staying, you know. The market wasn't where it used to be. Probably didn't look very much like the one she saw. But Helen, I am so glad I did this."

"I'm happy for you, honey. What else?"

"Remember I told you about the research I did for my

uncle and what I found out about Alistair Tensbury? The Tensbury who became the 1st Baron?"

"I remember."

"He met Signe here."

"Wow!"

"Some things about him I can't figure out. There are some unethical business deals he made. That's all over the news. But there are things that the newspapers don't know about. Based on what I found out here and the excerpts from Signe's pages, I think Alistair did something much worse than what is in the newspapers. And it happened around the time Signe was here."

"Do you have any idea of what it was?"

"That's the thing. I can't figure it out. Remember that folder I found about Tensbury in my uncle's office? That was about the election, remember?"

"Yes, I do."

"You suspected there might be a connection between my uncle's research and the British election. You thought that someone looking for the missing pages could have accidentally caused his death."

"I remember."

"Now, I am coming around to your thinking. I am certain, if the Tensburys know about this 1859 event, they would want to keep this dark secret under wraps. Especially now during the election campaign. So, who knows? I am sure the family wouldn't get involved in anything like this, but some rogue operator might."

"Really? So, what are you going to do?"

"I don't know. I have nothing to go on. I'm leaving the day after tomorrow. I didn't get all the pages yet, though. Not sure what else I'll find there."

"This is a hell of a story."

"Yes, it is. Unfortunately, for now, I only know that something definitely happened, but I don't know what. So, stay tuned, as they say." Hanna stopped for a moment.

"I have to go. I'm heading to a jazz fest tonight."

"Alone?"

"No, I have this guy from UNESCO keeping me company."

"Oh, oh!"

"No, he's just taking me around."

"You'll have to tell me about that later."

CHAPTER 3

Hanna worked on the contract and then sent it back to her lawyer for a final review. After taking a shower and putting on a nice, white cotton dress, her strappy sandals, and some makeup, Hanna was ready to have a good time at the Jazz Festival. She met up with Eric in the reception. He had put on a pair of khaki slacks and a light blue shirt. She noticed he still wore his sneakers.

They went over to the Flamingo for dinner. The pool shimmered in turquoise, lit from every side. They had a bottle of wine and sat there chatting.

"So, what do you do when you are not working?" asked Eric.

"I have my horses. Pilar and Taurus. Pilar jumps. I'm good on her, if I may say so myself. About 3 feet. Average really. But I can take her around a full course."

"Do you ever fall?"

"Oh God, have I fallen! Never badly, though. I'm lucky. I never broke anything."

Hanna took a sip of wine. "And what's your day like? Do you look over Heritage sites like St. Louis and Gorée?"

"That's a small part of the job. UNESCO spends a lot of time analyzing the main developmental trends here. We try to ensure that Education, Science, Culture, and Communication are all part of their government development agenda. That means interacting with the government at all levels."

"Is there a lot of corruption?"

"Not like in most other countries in Africa, but there's some. What I focus on is education."

"You mentioned you set up a fund for education."

"With that small fund, I'm not able to contribute much," he smiled. "Senegal, for example, is in dire need of support to improve their educational system. To give you an idea, only about twenty-five percent of age-appropriate kids are in middle school, and it gets worse from there. At UNESCO, we try to do as much as our budgets allow. As part of my job, I get involved with some of our top priorities."

"Must be very gratifying work."

"It is, but it's also sometimes depressing. It'll take a long time for Senegal and the other West African countries to be able to educate kids the way they should."

"Makes my work seem superficial," said Hanna.

"We all have a role, Hanna. Altruism only goes so far. We are lucky to have been born Americans, that's all. Our country works very hard to get what we have. We have a long history of overcoming obstacles. Just think of it, in the second part of the last century, it was America who introduced most of the technology the world uses today."

"Nice speech, Eric. Maybe you should go into politics after UNESCO." Hanna raised her glass.

"No, no, no. I don't think so. Let's drink up and get going. The festivities start late, so we'll be right on time."

They paid and strolled towards Faidherbe's Square. There were few streetlights, but thankfully the moon was almost full, and that helped. Now the sidewalk was full of people all heading the same way.

When they arrived, they first ended up in the back of the crowd but could still see the stage. A woman was singing the blues with a jazzy overtone. She was excellent, and people were dancing in the street.

"There's no alcohol," noted Hanna.

"It's not because alcohol is forbidden. It's just that many Senegalese, over 90%, are observant Muslims, and for the most part, they don't drink."

The woman on stage ended her song to raucous applause, and a guitarist jumped up on stage. The crowd was quiet in anticipation. This was one of the headliners from America. He sat down on a high stool and started picking his guitar. Soon jazz filled the air, and people were swaying to the tune.

"Let's get away from here," said Eric, speaking into Hanna's ear. "This is good, but always a little staged. We can head to the side streets and find smaller performances by Senegalese musicians that are usually really good. I think I remember where one is. If not, we'll ask."

They left the area and started heading up Rue Khalifa Ababacar Sy. After the bright lights down by the main stage, the streets seemed even darker than before.

They were talking when three very large men came up the street facing them on the sidewalk. Eric took Hanna's arm and steered her out into the street to let them pass. When they came alongside Eric, they suddenly grabbed him. It took him completely by surprise, and he didn't have a chance to respond before two of them held both of his arms. The other started punching him in the face. One of the men kicked his legs out from behind. He fell to his knees.

Hanna felt helpless and frightened, but she wanted them to stop hurting Eric. She looked up and down the street. No one. No one to help. With despair she saw how Eric dropped to the ground, and one of the men kicked him hard in his abdomen. Eric moaned but didn't yell.

Hanna did yell, kicked the man on the shin, and threw some punches on his neck. She was about to throw another punch when one of the men shoved her to the side. She fell on her backside, and her first thought was that she hoped her laptop, which was in her backpack, wasn't damaged. Then she saw Eric receive another kick, this one to his kidney and forgot all about the laptop.

"You'll stay out of our government business from now on. Next time we won't go this easy on you," announced one of the attackers.

The men withdrew and quickly walked away.

What government business?

Her butt hurt. She tried to get up and winced as she turned over onto her knees. She finally stood up and then crouched by Eric's head. He was conscious but still moaning. She looked around. The street was dark and still. No one was coming either way.

"Eric, can you sit up?"

His eyes were closed. "Yeah, I think I can." With Hanna's help, Eric pulled himself up to a sitting position.

"Damn, that hurts. They knew what they were doing. I haven't been beaten up like that for a long time." He winced. "Not ever, I think." He sat there for a while, catching his breath.

"Come on. Let's try to get you up, so we can get back to the hotel."

Hanna got up, took Eric's hands, and pulled. With difficulty, she was able to get him up. He stood, bent over at the waist, and couldn't change the position.

"They got me right in the kidneys. And in the gut. Damn, that hurts," he repeated. She saw him cringe as he touched his chin.

He put an arm around Hanna's shoulders, and they started a slow walk back to the hotel.

Did this have anything to do with the people I think are following me? Can't be. These guys were really after Eric. What could he be mixed up in?

As they walked, Eric straightened out, and by the time they entered the hotel, he almost walked upright. They went straight to Eric's room, and Hanna put him on top of his bed. Then she called room service for two buckets of ice and a big bottle of water. She went into the bathroom and brought out some cool, wet towels, and started wiping his face. The eyes were not bruised. She unbuttoned his shirt and slid it off his shoulders. Then she undid his pants and slid them off as well. She looked at his lower back. A big bruise was beginning to form. As she touched it, Eric moaned.

"This one looks bad. We are going to have to ice it really well."

Room service knocked, and she collected the ice and the bottle in the hallway. Hanna poured Eric a glass of water, lifted his head, and made him drink. Then she made a large ice pack out of a towel and the ice and stuck it under his lower back. She made a smaller one for his chin. Satisfied, she poured a glass of water for herself and took a deep gulp. Eric held the icepack on his face in place.

"If you can talk, what's all this about? What government business are they talking about?"

"Long story. I discovered some corruption in the ministry of education through a friend working there. Local contractors were giving bribes to ministry officials while doing shoddy jobs in schools."

"Bribes, huh?"

"Yep. The ministry, of course, looks the other way. I reported this to Paris. They contacted the ministry, which created a scandal." He drank some water, cringing. "The contractors told me to stay out of their business. The construction companies went back to their cozy arrangement with the ministry, but they know I stand in their way. I guess they just sent these goons to rough me up, so I'll get the message, you know."

"It sounds like you have gotten yourself into a real pickle. What do you do in these cases?"

"Go higher up in the ministry, all the way to the President himself, if need be, to get them to act. Yeah, I might be up for some more of this, but it's part of my job. Well, it's not really part of my job, but I feel like it is, so I do it." He managed a little smile.

"I don't think you should. It's not safe. As you said, it's not your business, right? It's true what that monster said. Next time will be worse. Now, all you have are some bruises. Bad ones, but only bruises."

Eric was quiet. "You know you were worried about someone following you?"

Hanna nodded.

"Turns out, someone may have looked into your laptop. But these guys tried to rearrange my face. And you? They only gave you a little pain on your butt."

"Glad you are feeling better, big guy. Let me change those icepacks. I'm going to stay here with you tonight. I'll sleep on the sofa. I want to make sure you get that ice changed regularly. Can't have you in poor form while I'm here, can I?"

She fell asleep, knowing she'd have to get up to change the icepacks soon. At one point during the night, Eric wanted to go to the bathroom. She watched him get out of bed with great difficulty, but he managed.

Late in the evening, Malek called Jack, who was sitting in his hotel bar with a glass of wine.

"Hey. Here's the story. They have been doing touristy things all day. They went to the Governor's Palace, where they stayed a while. I've been to the Palace, and it's quite beautiful, even though it's run down. Then they made their way to the local market. It's Sunday, and I don't think they learned anything that we are looking for. They're probably waiting for tomorrow. They may have met someone that I didn't see, but I doubt it. They returned to the hotel and after a while came out all posh looking. I followed them to the Jazz Fest.

"But Jack, I'm sorry to tell you – I lost them. Makes me feel like shit. There were many tourists, and the place is packed with people. So, I parked myself at their hotel, and I think they have already returned. I doubt they'll go out again. By the way, I didn't see any sinister guys around."

"That's alright, Malik. As you said, they're probably waiting for tomorrow. Why don't you come back to our hotel and get some rest? You'll need it for tomorrow."

Jack took a sip of wine and checked the time.

Shucks, I was supposed to check in with Tensbury. Too late.

Day 7

CHAPTER 1

Andrew Tensbury was having a press conference after visiting a small robotics start-up in his constituency.

"What was your impression of the young company?" asked one reporter.

"They're great. I envy the people here. What a wonderful time in their life. What a great environment to work in. We should have more companies like this. It made me want to tell you about an idea we have. I wasn't planning to, but looking at these young men and women, I think I should.

"You know, we in the UK had an excellent start in software coding education in school. We should build on this success and expand this program. We have listened to software companies on how to improve the program. The result of these consultations are ideas I would like to share with you today. There are many people in the software industry who would love to pass their enthusiasm and experience to our schoolchildren. We believe that one-year sabbatical for computer professionals teaching children is an interesting idea. It would greatly benefit the current coding program in our schools.

"We think that the major UK software companies, together with the government, would be willing to fund such a program. We are also of the opinion that we should include interested computer professionals from other English-speaking countries. If Conservatives form the next government, we'll work with all stakeholders on implementing this program."

Reporters had many questions about the proposal. Andrew's training came in handy. He expanded on what could be involved to realize such a project but stayed away from the idea's exact scope and cost.

One reporter, standing close to the place he was speaking from, asked, "How long do you think it'll take to line up all the stakeholders to get on with the program?"

"I don't know, but I can tell you, it's high on my list of priorities. However, anytime I hear of a project involving coding, it reminds me of a joke we had in college. We called it the 'Software Project Law.' It goes something like this. 'Any software project will take at least twice as long as estimated.'" He paused. "Even after you apply this rule."

"There was laughter in the crowd. The hardest unrestrained burst of laughter came from the young software engineers standing around the back of the room.

Andrew raised his hand. "I think in this case, …we will break this law."

CHAPTER 2

Monday morning, Hanna and Eric checked out of Hotel de la Poste and packed their luggage into Eric's Toyota. Hanna insisted on driving because Eric was still in pretty bad shape. His back hurt. His face looked acceptable, though. It was unbelievable that he didn't have large bruises on his face. Hanna patted herself on the back for insisting on staying in his room and icing it throughout the night.

She found it a little tricky driving because she hadn't driven a stick shift for a long time. After a lot of screeching and stop and go, they were finally on their way. They exited St. Louis island, which the Senegalese call N'Dar, and went back over the Faidherbe bridge. Crossing Sor, a suburb of St. Louis, they continued north-east on N2, and after about seven miles, exited and turned left. They reached a large entrance with a sign that said L'Université Gaston Berger.

Hanna drove into the university grounds, a vast complex of buildings. Straight ahead was a tall building that looked like it might hold the administration of the university, so they parked there.

Hanna took her backpack with the laptop and got out to help Eric. He winced as he swung his legs out the door of the car and stood up.

"Are you hurting badly?"

"Don't worry about it." His face looked like he was in pain.

She resolved to find a place for him to rest soon. They entered the building and found themselves in a large hall with a desk in front of the library entrance.

"Perfect, the library. Exactly what we are looking for," said Hanna.

They entered the library. It was completely different from the one at the university in Dakar. This one was modern, with good lighting and a lot of space. Students were spread out, with laptops in front of them.

Hanna and Eric stood there looking forlorn, not sure where to begin.

"Bonjour. My name is Josephine Fall. I am the head librarian here. May I help you?"

Before them was a tall woman with the high cheekbones of the Senegalese. She was dressed in a traditional outfit with bright patterns in orange and yellow.

"Yes, please," answered Hanna.

Hanna explained why they came to the library and what they were hoping to find.

"Let me see if I can help you." Josephine started walking towards the back of the large expansive space, and Hanna and Eric followed.

"We have a lot of old documents that were not transferred to Dakar. Unfortunately, they're not all digitized."

Eric and Hanna sat down at one of the tables, while Josephine spent some time at one of the many workstations located around the area. She took some notes and moved to the bookshelves. After they had waited a while, she came back with a couple of books and binders. The books looked old and didn't have proper book covers.

Josephine sat down beside Hanna.

"Here is a port log from 1859. You said you visited the Dakar University and found an entry in a log about a ship named *Ingeborg* in the port in November. You also said that you are interested in the ship named *Adelia*."

"Yes, I am."

Josephine carefully went through one of the binders. She found the page she was looking for. Her finger ran down the handwritten lines.

"Here. Yes, here is the entry about your ancestor's ship, the *Ingeborg*. It was flying a Norwegian flag, the captain's name is Taraldson and she had only one passenger, Signe Olsen. It was in port for a week or so, having the mast repaired."

Josephine turned to Hanna, "This was your ancestor? Correct?"

"Yes," Hanna said proudly. "She travelled alone, and she was very young!"

Eric smiled.

"And here is a British ship named Adelia. She was from Cape Town, sailing to England."

Eric and Hanna looked at each other. That was the ship that brought Alistair Tensbury to St. Louis.

"Were there other ships in port during that time?"

"Seems like there were many ships in port while the *Ingeborg* and *Adelia* were here. I see mostly trading ships originating from France."

"Very interesting. Is there other information about these ships?" said Hanna, hopeful.

Josephine looked at the pages in the port logbook for the dates prior to the Ingeborg's arrival.

"There were also an American and another British ship in port for a while, but they left before the Ingeborg came in. That's all I have about the ships. Let me look at this other volume. It seems that someone has accumulated French newspaper clippings where Senegal is mentioned."

"Also, I am interested in any information about Gum Arabic deals involving a company called IL&R. Especially one that was unusual."

Josephine sat bent over the volume for quite a while.

Meanwhile, Hanna took a look around. Here the students looked somewhat older than what she had seen in the Dakar library. Hanna guessed there were more graduate students here. Reference workstations like the one Josephine had used stood empty, and all the furniture seemed new. There were fabric-covered chairs and seating areas in strategically placed locations. One area had a rack of newspapers.

"In those days, it would take a long time, sometimes months, before an event in a colony would get written about in a French paper."

"Months?"

"Yes, sometimes."

"Right."

"I can't see anything particularly interesting after November till the end of the next year. Mostly articles about military movements, small wars with the locals, and acquisitions of new territory inland. There's also a mention of a storm that November. Sorry, but that's all I have." Josephine closed the volumes.

"Where else do you think I can look for more information?"

"Since you have been to the library at the University of Dakar, I can't recommend any other place."

"That's okay. We appreciate your help."

Hanna thought of something. "Madam Fall, I am just curious if sometimes there are people like us who come to look for different historical information about St. Louis?"

"Not often. Actually, several days ago, a British gentleman was looking for information during the same period. But it happens very seldom. I wish you luck." Josephine shook their hands.

"How do you like that, Eric? Again. A British gentleman, the other day, ha?! Just what I was thinking about. Someone else is looking," said Hanna decisively.

"You are right."

"I want to go over those volumes again."

Hanna reviewed the two binders. She was looking for a large commercial deal to be mentioned in the newspaper clippings. There were articles about commodity shipments, but nothing that appeared out of the ordinary.

"I think we are done here." Hanna picked up her backpack, and they left.

They got to the car.

"I'll drive now," said Eric."

"You sure?"

"Those aspirins you gave me are working. I'm tired of your dismal driving," he said lightly.

"I am getting really good with a stick-shift!"

"You are, dear," he laughed. "But let me drive now."

In all reality, she was thankful he would be driving again. Much less stress. Besides, he seemed a whole a lot better.

They drove back onto the N2.

A couple of miles before St. Louis, they heard loud gunshots. Hanna jumped with fright and reached out for Eric's arm. "What is that?"

"Nothing to worry about. There's a military complex here, the Prytanée Militaire de St. Louis school, and they probably have target practice today."

They approached St. Louis and turned south towards Dakar. There was a lot more traffic today than when they came up two days ago. Hanna turned around and looked over her shoulder. There was a string of cars behind them on the two-way road. Cars were not passing yet moving along at a good clip.

"We'll arrive in Dakar late afternoon, early evening. We could go to the American Club after dinner and watch a movie." Eric stopped.

"What about tomorrow? You told me you were leaving tomorrow, right?" He had a glum look on his face.

"Yes, I leave tomorrow. I have to be at the airport two hours in advance. With the long drive, I have to be up pretty early."

"I'll take you to the airport. We'll meet for breakfast, okay?"

"Thanks so much, Eric! It bothers me that I haven't found out anything of substance." She couldn't let the subject go.

"Why was my uncle so insistent we travel to Senegal right now?"

"You didn't get all the translated pages yet, did you?"

"No." She shook her head.

"Maybe they hold the key to that question." Eric kept his eyes on the road.

When they got to the hotel, it was evening. The traffic to Dakar had been terrible and slowed them down.

"Let's grab a quick bite and then head to the American Club. I think you'll enjoy it. They're playing my favorite movie tonight. It starts at nine. You'll love watching 'Casablanca' under the stars. It's really something."

CHAPTER 3

Jack, Malek and Moussa were tracking Hanna and Eric to the Gaston Berger University. When Hanna and Eric went into the library, Jack remained in the car. Malek followed them to the library to retrace their steps and check on what they had been looking at.

After a couple of hours, Jack saw Hanna and Eric leave. Moussa followed them. In a short while, Malek was back.

"The librarian was very helpful. They looked over some old books again – the port logs from November 1859. I snapped some pictures of the pages, so you can sort them out. I'm sending them right now."

"Do you have them in sight?" Jack heard Malek ask Moussa as he drove out of the university compound.

"Moussa is with them. They're on their way back to Dakar," said Malek.

"I guess we are going back to Dakar."

Jack looked at the pictures Malek sent. He saw Alistair's ship Adelia.

He turned to Malek. "You know, the information about the ship logs you got at both libraries may be useful. The company involved has its beginning in the 1800s. So, those two pages from her laptop may not be a personal story, after all."

243

"I'm glad we are getting somewhere."

When Jack and Malek got to Hanna's hotel, they went to the reception area and took a seat in the corner away from where Eric was sitting. Then Jack saw Hanna. She had changed clothes from this morning. She had on a flowing white skirt, with a sleeveless blouse on her tanned shoulders.

Eric got up and walked with Hanna to the receptionist counter. Jack heard Hanna say she was leaving tomorrow.

She's keeping to her itinerary.

Jack saw them walk towards the hotel exit. Hanna had her backpack. Moussa called Malek. He was following them.

"Let's see if she left her laptop in her room again."

"Malek, don't you think the laptop is in her backpack?"

"I'll find out," said Malek.

"I heard her telling the receptionist her new room number."

Malek went up to Hanna's room but was back soon. "No go. Housekeeping was in the room and I didn't see the laptop on the table. She must have taken it."

They waited for Moussa's call. Jack had to decide if Malek should join him.

A call came in from Moussa, and Malek conversed with him quietly.

"Jack, they have gone to a place called the 'American Club.' It's for expatriates to get together, eat, drink, play tennis and watch movies," said Malek.

"Well, it's late, and it sounds like Hanna is just out socializing. We are done for the day, and tomorrow she leaves. I think we have done all we could. I have some data from the pages and the libraries. Let's see what my employer can put together from that."

"I understand. Sorry I didn't find much."

"We tried Malek. In any event, you have been a great partner. Can you send your bill to me in London?"

"I will. It has been good knowing you, Jack. It has been fun."

"Thanks. I enjoyed your company, Malek." They both got

244

up and shook hands.

Jack went up to his room.

Tomorrow he was going back, and Hanna was leaving too. Did she see or pay attention to the Adelia, Alistair's ship? He was sure she did. It was in the diary pages.

He emailed Tensbury the pictures Malek had snapped today.

Jack confirmed his flight. Then he called Tensbury.

"Good evening, Sir."

"Hi, Jack."

"Not much today, Sir. Just confirmation that a Norwegian ship, Ingeborg, with a Captain Taraldson, was in for a mast repair and that it had only one passenger, Signe Olsen. So, this is the woman who wrote the diary, who, I assume, is Hanna's ancestor."

"Did it say that there are as many Olsens as there are fjords in Norway?"

Jack laughed. "I am sure many more, Sir."

Then, Jack said seriously, "Hanna either figured things out from the diary or is going back as empty-handed as we are. In the first case, the Labor project is complete, and they're ready to go after Andrew."

"We can only hope that she doesn't have any more than we do. All I know is, you did an excellent job under challenging circumstances. Thank you. Thank you very much."

"Too bad we didn't find out more."

"Tomorrow evening is the debate, Jack. Please come to my flat after your flight. We'll see if Labor has any surprises then."

"I'll be there, Sir."

CHAPTER 4

Thomas' office door was wide open. He was standing by the window looking out at a bleak London morning.

"Have a minute?" Seth looked in.

"Absolutely. What's new?"

Seth entered Thomas' office.

"I wanted to let you know about the latest bunch of answers from the media outlets we contacted. As before, some politely declined to commit calling us before publication, citing their policy. Others said they would make an effort, if at all possible, whatever that means. This was a good idea. My group has already gotten several calls on minor pieces, and I provided favorable color to the media reports. Nothing major. If that comes up, I'll consult you first."

"Excellent work, Seth. Let's hope we only get good coverage." Thomas gave Seth an enthusiastic pat on the shoulder.

Thomas then walked to the room where they were doing the mock debate. It was time to start the session. Most of the participants were already there.

"Good, Thomas is here, let's start," announced Andrew.

Lord Tensbury sat at the back of the room. Thomas' team had set up a podium and arranged for the session to be recorded. Thomas had invited a select group of MPs, each with specific expertise, and encouraged candid advice. Tensbury knew that after this, Thomas and Andrew would agree on a particular strategy for the debate. Then they would select sound bites from the recording. These sentences or paragraphs Andrew would memorize. This is what needed to be repeated over and over. If he does it well, the sound bites will be in the minds of the electorate when they make their decision.

They would also rehearse, edit and rehearse again opening and closing statements.

Tensbury was listening, and the rehearsal sounded tense at times. Thomas had been through this before and was very exacting. During a break, Andrew made it over to his father.

"Hi, dad. What do you think? I'm pretty stoked. I'll knock his pants off. It's late in the game, but it should make a difference."

"Andrew, the reason I wanted to chat is because I thought of something. Remember that article that came out in The Guardian about Alistair's affairs with the tolls in Senegal?"

Andrew nodded.

"It's unlikely, but there could be more there. You need to be prepared. Maybe I'm paranoid, but I'm worried that Labor might have unearthed something else about Alistair's business. They might be waiting to spring it on you during the debate. Maybe this is why they finally agreed to the debate."

Andrew sat quietly, looking at his dad. "What is this all about? You are deflating my balloon. Now I'm worried."

"No need to be. Remember, your namesake, Intel's Andrew Grove, who you like to talk about. His famous quote is 'Only the paranoid survive.'"

"Anything else?" Andrew sounded terse.

"No, that's it. It's most likely nothing, and I'm reaching. I thought it should be in the back of your mind if something comes up. But it doesn't mean to be afraid. You and I know you are the right person to lead the government. So be ready to win this debate."

"Alright, Dad. Thomas is calling me. I have to get back up there."

Tensbury saw Thomas and Andrew fist-bump and Andrew returned to the podium.

Tensbury continued listening to Andrew practice. Thomas had set up a good cast of MPs for Andrew during this mock event. Everything proceeded well.

Andrew came over when it was finished. He looked tired.

"Do you need a ride to your flat?"

"No, Henry is waiting for me. You did very well. You'll blow him out of the water."

They walked to the exit.

"I'll see you after the debate." Andrew gave his father a hug. "I'm looking forward to it. I really am."

Tensbury wondered if Andrew was trying to convince himself or if he truly felt that way. He hoped it was the latter.

CHAPTER 5

From the car, Hanna gave her guide Mustafa a call.

"Hi, Mustafa. It turns out I won't need your services tonight or tomorrow. I'll pay you for the week tomorrow morning. It would need to be early. Please come at 7:30."

"I'll be there, Madam."

They arrived at the Club and sat down for a beer at the bar. Everyone was speaking English, although Hanna heard some accents. The lights over the tennis courts went out, and the Club gained a cozier feel to it.

Hanna looked out over the pool. The lights came on, illuminating the water below in bright, turquoise tones.

"Amazing. Birds are swooping in over the pool. At night! How strange."

"Those are not birds. They're bats. At night they come out and pick off the bugs from the surface of the pool."

"I had no idea bats did that. Right among people, no less."

"Just one of Africa's wonderful mysteries, my dear," Eric beamed proudly.

Chairs were set out in rows for the movie, and a white screen was rolled down. Hanna could see one of the Senegalese employees fiddling with an old-style projector. A huge movie reel was loaded. She realized it was a very old copy of the film.

Eric took her by the arm. "Come on. Let's sit down."

They sat towards the back, and the other chairs filled up. As soon as the movie started, Hanna was transported to a different world. Casablanca was a favorite of Hanna's too. Although she has seen it many times, 'Here's looking at you, kid,' got to her every time. She wasn't usually a sentimental person, and movies rarely made her cry. But no matter how many times she watched Casablanca, she shed some tears when Bogart sacrifices his love for Ingrid Bergman and makes her leave with her husband. Heartbreaking.

She looked up into the inky black sky, with its dusting of stars, and realized for the first time since her uncle died that she felt happy. Eric took her hand in his, and she didn't withdraw it.

After the movie, they went back to the hotel.

"Let me look at your back again. Come on to my room."

They took the elevator and stood there, not looking at one another.

Hanna opened her door and waved Eric in. He stood in the middle of the room, and she pulled his t-shirt up. They both felt a little tipsy after several beers at the Club.

"Ouch, looks nasty."

"It's not so bad." Eric turned her around and put his hands on her shoulders. He looked into her eyes.

"Hanna, I've been wanting to kiss you ever since we met." He drew her towards him slowly and bent over her face. Ever so softly, he touched his lips to hers. She drew him closer and put her arms around his neck.

They kissed again, now more passionately.

She pulled back.

"Maybe this is a really bad idea." She left his arms and went to stand by the window. She could see the hotel gardens brightly lit down below and glimpsed the waves rolling in on the beach.

"Maybe. But maybe not." Eric's voice was hoarse.

"I don't think we should begin something that can't go anywhere. I'm sorry. I didn't mean to lead you on."

Eric stood quietly in the middle of the room where she had left him. He didn't say anything for what seemed like an eternity.

"Hanna. I understand. I do understand."

Much as she wanted him, she couldn't get tangled up with a man she would most likely never see again after tomorrow. Hanna heard her door close. She took a deep sigh.

Day 8

CHAPTER 1

Hanna woke up refreshed. She had slept well. First thing she did, was check email – nothing. She got her luggage together, rolled it to the elevator, and down into the lobby. She passed by the singing birds, again wondering how they kept live birds in the top of the trees. Their song was beautiful.

She entered the restaurant where breakfast was being served and sat down.

"Hello there, sunshine," said Eric as he came up behind her and touched her shoulder. She turned her face up for a kiss, and he sat down across from her.

He ordered coffee and an American breakfast with eggs and bacon. She was eating her croissant.

"Thanks for coming so early, and thanks for taking me to the airport."

"No problem. Get any more pages?"

"No. I looked before coming down."

"I'm very curious what you will find out. You have my email."

"I'll let you know."

They finished their breakfast.

"I need to pay Mustafa. He's probably in the lobby already. Then we can go." She felt sad and melancholy. She could see that he felt the same.

"It has been a fun couple of days. Maybe being beaten up wasn't, but the rest was." Eric paused.

"Let's go."

Hanna paid Mustafa and thanked him for his service. She checked out, and Eric helped her down the long stairs with her luggage.

He drove her to the airport. They didn't talk much during the drive. Leaving was awkward. They had only been together for several days, but it felt longer. She thought they had developed an intimacy which they both know they would have carried further if they would have been together longer. Eric had been with her while she learned new things about Signe, Tensbury, and Africa.

Yes, Africa. It's a special, beautiful place.

"I'll miss you. My days will become awfully boring without you around. But I have this whole government scandal to work through, so maybe it's better you're not here."

"I'll miss you too. But, as I told you, you should stop trying to be involved in Senegalese politics. After what I saw, you would be putting yourself in serious danger. And this time, I won't be around to rescue you," she smirked.

Eric parked, and they entered the departure terminal. She had already checked in, and as she was ready to get past security, Eric pulled her into a tight hug. They held on to each other for a long time. She felt tears threaten to spill over, but she held back. He broke the hug and kept her in his arms, looking into her eyes.

"Hanna, it wasn't to be. Not this time. But who knows what will happen in the future? Let's stay in touch, okay?"

"Okay," she said.

"I'll go now." She picked up the handle of her rollaboard. As she passed through security, she saw Eric leave with a wave. She waved back and then willed herself not to look again.

CHAPTER 2

Hanna sank down in one of the chairs in the lounge at the airport.

Her phone rang.

"Hanna, I've been thinking about you. Haven't heard from you. Are you alright?"

"Helen let's get on Skype. Hang up. I'll call you." Hanna opened Skype and dialed Helen.

"That's better. You look great, actually. Where are you?"

"On my way back to London from Africa, then onto Sweden to take care of my uncle's affairs. I do feel better. It's been an interesting couple of days. How are you? Back from India?"

"Yes, I am. I'm rested. Those first-class flights my company springs for are wonderful! Real bed to sleep in. Foie Gras for dinner and other luxuries. Wonderful."

"I'm waiting for my flight to board. Five hours to Paris, then another 1 or 2 to London. Yuck. You know, I was thinking about my uncle and all the trips we took together when I was young. Didn't have any problem flying then! I told you about the trip to Paris we took that summer when I was thirteen. How beautiful it was walking along Champs-Elysée first time! Visiting the Louvre with the Mona Lisa. I didn't understand what the big hoopla was about. Just a little painting behind tons of glass."

"You sound much better. What happened in Africa?"

"Helen, they say you either hate or love Africa. I love it, and I know I'll be back one day. Too much to tell you now. Later."

"What about your uncle?"

"Didn't find out anything that might relate to his death. Nothing." Hanna stopped.

"Met a guy, though."

"That guy from UNESCO you mentioned?"

"Yes. One of those things where I wish he was close to where I live, not in Africa. I finally found someone compatible, who meets my rather high, I have to admit, expectations."

"You said it!"

"It's such a shame that he's so far away. The relationship was a bust, even before it truly began. But who knows what the future will bring? I can always dream. I'll have to tell you more about it later."

"Can't wait."

"Honey, they're boarding my flight. Have to go. I'll call you in a few days. Bye."

Hanna boarded.

As soon as they reached the altitude where the captain said it was okay to use Wi-Fi, she pulled out her laptop and logged into email.

Excellent! Here are the remaining pages from the translation services.

She started reading. As she progressed through the pages, her pace slowed. Some places, she had to read twice. Many times, she had imagined the contents of these torn-out pages, but not this. It was just too much to digest.

Hanna collected herself. She remembered her grandmother saying, 'Some things you take with you to your grave.'

Yet, some people seemed to have this need to tell all.

She reclined her chair and closed her eyes. She put what she had read out of her mind and dreamed of being with her horses, getting ready for a long ride in Portola Valley. But that would have to wait. She sighed.

She finally landed at Heathrow.

Damn, this airport is large.

She felt like an ant on an anthill scurrying off to find the next morsel. In this case, an exit from the terminal.

Where is the stupid exit?

Finally exiting the arrival terminal, she grabbed one of the taxis. She dialed Lord Tensbury's number.

She got voicemail and decided to leave a message.

"Hello Sir. My name is Hanna Arnol. I found some information about our ancestors that might interest you. I'm only in London till tomorrow. I hope we can meet. Would you please give me a call?" She left her number.

How often does he check his work voice mail?

It was probably forwarded to his cell phone. She hoped so. She felt almost in awe in addressing herself to this man, a Lord after all. She needed to meet Lord Tensbury in person with the information she learned from the diary. Provided she could meet him tomorrow, she would leave London in the evening. Back to Sweden to arrange Uncle Noah's effects and see to his will.

Hanna arrived at Hilton in Westminster on John Islip Street.

She loved this Hilton. This time her admin had booked a room on the 10th floor. She checked in, made it to her floor, and opened the door to her room. The view was dazzling.

She slipped out of her travel clothes and stepped into the shower. What a pleasure. This hotel had American style walk-in showers, and she stood under the hot downpour for a long time. She got out, toweled off, and fell into bed, bone tired.

Forget about dinner.

After a while, she realized that tired as she was, she couldn't sleep. What she had read in the translated pages changed her view of some things. The view she had growing up.

She was too exhausted to think about it now, so she clicked on her cell phone, pulled up her book, and read until she could sleep.

CHAPTER 3

Lillian was seated in the office of her boss, James Miller. She wished she had something interesting to spring on Tensbury for the debate tonight. She had really tried.

"So, what do you think, Lillian. Will our man do a good job tonight?" Miller asked.

She knew how much work had gone into preparing Nithercott for the debate.

"I think he'll do a fine job. You prepared him well." But she knew what a poor debater he was and hoped they had succeeded.

"So, what can I help you with?"

"I'm a little concerned about this campaign contribution story. Can you tell me anything about that?"

"I know, that is untimely. We dropped the ball on that one. We should have monitored the donations more closely."

"Right, it was unfortunate."

"The PM will be speaking about this tomorrow during the press conference. The Electoral Commission has yet to mount an investigation, so it shouldn't get a lot of news coverage. I can tell you that we are, on our own accord, taking immediate action. We returned these funds to the respective parties today. We also asked all associations aligned with the Party to review their donation lists."

"This calms my concern somewhat. I have been worried it would make a difference in the polls. The numbers haven't changed too much even though it has been two days since the media reported it, so I guess I shouldn't fret."

"Lillian, you are doing a fine job, and I don't think you need to worry about this.

"Thank you, Sir."

"Do you think you'll have something new in the works for us? Something that might change the dynamics of the election?"

"We are running at full steam, and I have a very intriguing long shot that may come through."

"Good, we still have today and tomorrow. I appreciate your group's energy."

"Thanks, Sir."

Lillian rose and left Miller's office. She stopped outside and drew a deep breath. She prayed she could find something about this elusive 'heinous deed.' She still had tomorrow, and she hoped that Harry with Irina Consulting had something to contribute.

She remembered the conversation with Harry this morning.

"Is this Lillian Perry?"

"Yes. Who is calling?"

"This is Harry MacDuff with Irina Consulting. 10 Downing Street has retained us to support our Party during the election process. I understand you run the Labor campaign's research group?"

"Yes, I do. What can I do for you?"

"Lillian, we only have today and tomorrow to drive up our standing with the electorate. On our side, we don't have anything actionable to release now. I'm not sure, but you may not have anything major either. Am I right?"

"That is correct."

"We have seen a couple of excellent stories that surely

originated from you. Good stuff."

"Thank you."

"I think it might be a good time to get together. Combining some of the dead-end leads we worked on separately may lead to something workable. It might make a difference at this late stage."

"It might," said Lillian cautiously.

"How about we meet tomorrow morning and discuss any avenues we could take together?"

"Makes sense. You can join us here at Labor HQ at eight in the morning. Does that work?"

"Sounds good."

Lillian hated the fact that her Tensbury work wasn't panning out. She would have liked to avoid this meeting. But this wasn't a time for grudges. No matter how irritated she was with Downing Street about retaining a consulting group to parallel her work, she had to take this meeting.

CHAPTER 4

Jack was sitting on the sofa in Tensbury's living room. He had come straight from the airport and was there to watch the debate.

"I wonder why they agreed to a debate?" asked Tensbury. "Why did they have such a sudden change of heart so late in the game?"

Jack didn't answer. It was a rhetorical question because they both knew what it might indicate.

"Here, have a drink," said Tensbury, handing a snifter with good cognac to Jack.

The TV was on with the sound muted. BBC was hosting the event, and the panel was having a pre-debate discussion. Tensbury and Jack were very anxious, anticipating what might be a ruinous debate for Andrew.

"You know televised debates have become more and more important to the electorate. A majority of voters are expected to tune in tonight." Tensbury was filling a void in the conversation.

"Imagine, we only began this recently. The Americans have been doing televised debates since the 1960s. It's still such a novelty for the Brits."

"I just hope they don't spring something on him, Sir."

"Let's keep our fingers crossed. Let me turn the sound on, so we can listen to what these clowns have to say."

Tensbury took a seat in a large armchair.

Soon they were inundated with opinions from all the 'experts' on the panel. Boring for the most part, but the debate was just about to begin. Then they heard the BBC host introduce Andrew and the PM as they walked on the stage. The debaters each took turns giving their introductory speeches, and Andrew's was excellent. He hit home on all the significant points and looked straight into the camera as he spoke. The PM looked left and right into the audience.

"The PM didn't mention anything negative in his introduction. So that is good for us." Jack was sipping his cognac.

The debate began on the topic of immigration, something that was top on everyone's mind.

"There are currently too many immigrants entering our country for the immigration system we have in place. The system is overwhelmed. And, the number of cross-channel illegals keeps rising," said Andrew. He went on to expound on his argument. "With Labor having been in power for almost five years, immigration had skyrocketed, and nothing is being done to manage it."

The PM had a lame response of only letting in individuals that were more desirable than others. Tensbury and Jack knew that the polls showed that the electorate wanted a more drastic change to the immigration policy.

"That was strong, I think," said Tensbury. He was sitting upright in his chair, staring intently at the TV.

The two continued to debate support for schools. Andrew said that each teacher receives uncountable numbers of documents from the government each year, and they have to continuously complete all the required forms. How could anyone pay attention to students and teaching under those circumstances? The Tories wanted to eliminate much of the red tape, which Labor had put in place.

When the need to curb crime came up, Andrew made a proposal. Although the Tories were all for cutting cost, this was one area that they didn't want to touch. He suggested adding another three thousand police, men and women, to patrol neighborhoods and fight terrorism.

After about fifteen minutes, Tensbury reasoned, "Perhaps the PM is waiting to bring something up at the end for more effect."

"I don't know, Sir. I think Nithercott would have said something already if he had anything up his sleeve."

They continued watching as the two debated energy policy, the trade deficit, and foreign affairs.

"You know, in America, even though they're told not to, the audience claps when the contestants make good points. Not here. This is much better, I think," said Jack.

The debate was nearing its end, and the PM had yet to say anything of consequence to Andrew.

"It seems they don't have anything. Or they're avoiding a direct attack and are keeping it for tomorrow's media." Tensbury felt there was no reason to relax yet.

They watched until the two contestants shook hands, and it was over.

"So, as of now, no surprises. I hope it stays that way. I also hope that our worst fears were wrong. This is one place where I want us to be very wrong about Labor. Of course, there's always the possibility that they have been looking for more information on Alistair's 'deed,' thought Hanna. And not found it."

"Just as we haven't," said Tensbury.

"We have one more day, and the enigma of the blackmailer, to be sure."

"Who do you think won, Jack?"

"I think Andrew did, Sir. Andrew definitely did. I look forward to listening to the results tomorrow morning. Are you coming in tomorrow?"

"I have an early doctor's appointment tomorrow. I don't

know if I'll swing by the office before I meet the blackmailer. I would have liked you to join me, but whoever it is, he or she told me to come alone, and we need to adhere to that."

Then, Tensbury concluded, "It has been several days since we started. We learned some things. Nothing to upend the decision tree I drew earlier, though. It's still the same. We still don't know who the blackmailer is or his or her connection to Labor. Remember, the decision tree from my systems course?"

"Yes, I do. I hope the tree has strong roots, and it helps." Jack had an uneasy smile.

Jack got up to leave, and Tensbury led him to the door.

Tensbury was setting the water to boil for the tea in his kitchen.

What if I go to the meeting tomorrow, and it's all a ruse? And Labor is ready to spring something on Andrew. I need to do everything I can to warn him. To find out what truly happened in Senegal in 1859.

What other rock did we not look under?

My family. If someone in the family would have papers pointing to a bad event involving Alistair, why would he or she keep them? Why not just destroy them? I once read an answer to that question. Besides some sort of pathological behavior, there was only one reason why people would keep such things. They kept it to deflect a second source of damaging information if it ever comes to light.

So, let's say my grandfather had something. He could give it to my father or Aunt Sally. If it were to my father, I would eventually know. So, he gave it to Aunt Sally. The way she talked to me...I don't know...I have a feeling she is not telling me something. If it was explosive, but grandfather still wanted to give it to her after he was gone, how would he do it? It would be in his will. The copy of the will is at Kent. I do not have time to go there.

He wrinkled his brow and considered the idea further.

Elisabeth and I looked over some of the family wills a couple of years ago when we worked on our will for the boys. I do not remember anything special about it. There was the usual large gift to charity, in support of the family's favorite causes. The family estate went to the one bearing the title. Otherwise, everything was to be divided equally between my father and Aunt Sally. He created a trust for me much earlier.

Wait a minute. There was one item spelled out separately. Yes, the family bible. It was to go to Aunt Sally. The description of the book was something like, 'It is a book which looks like a box. Inside the box is the Family Bible.' Of course! She has this beautiful old book in her library. I remember seeing it in the old glass-faced bookcase, next to the windows.

So, in an outside chance that the information existed, it should be in that book. God, why haven't I thought of that earlier. Why? It's a very long shot but at this point, I need to take it. As much as I hate to lie about my reasons, I need to call her again tomorrow morning.

Day 9

CHAPTER 1

For the Labor HQ meeting the next morning, Lillian brought biscuits, tea, and coffee to the conference room. She came with Ethan since he was the person most familiar with the Senegal pursuit.

Harry MacDuff from Irina Consulting and a couple of people from his group were already there.

"Thank you for suggesting this meeting. It's a good idea to pool any and all leads we have. If we get creative, we might be able to get something out before tomorrow." She looked at Harry.

He was pouring coffee at the table where Lillian had arranged the drinks and food and had a biscuit on a plate at his seat already. It irritated her that he didn't seem very attentive.

"Ethan, why don't you start us off?"

Ethan proceeded to tell Harry and his colleagues about the Vicar's letter he found. Ethan recounted how he had gone to Senegal to find out any information about Alistair Tensbury's dealings that might correspond to the note. He explained that he hadn't been successful.

Harry, now seated, said, "Interesting. We were also looking for some event Alistair Tensbury was involved in. Our information came from a person who worked with him in

Africa. We ran into something that started out looking very promising."

Harry took a bite out of his biscuit.

"About two weeks ago, a Ph.D. student named Otis Benson, from the Cambridge English Literature department, called the MP in his constituency. Otis told him that he might have something that would help Labor in this election. The MP directed him to us.

"Otis Benson's dissertation subject is 19th century writers, who are not well known today. He has access to boxes and boxes of books and manuscripts in the archives at Cambridge. He found a novel written by a Geoffrey Smith, called 'The Lonely End.' In one scene of this novel, the writer describes a conversation between a father and his twenty-year-old son.

"Based on his research, Otis assumes Geoffrey, the writer, had derived the story from his relationship with his own father. Otis called Geoffrey's father, Smith Sr."

Harry picked up a notebook.

"I have my notes here. One pertinent advice Smith Sr. relates to his son reads something to the effect of,

> There may come a time in your life when loyalty, or the desire to advance in your career, will go against your beliefs or better judgment. Don't agree to do anything you believe is morally wrong. If you do, you'll regret it all your life, and it will always be on your mind.

> I was once employed by a good, wealthy person who was generous to me. I was very devoted to him.

> However, one time, when his pride was challenged, he decided to do an illegal and immoral thing. He had an American acquaintance who was also involved in that project. My employer asked me to help him in this affair. Although I wasn't the one who conceived

of it or profited from it in any way, I did not refuse to help him when asked. The result was even worse than he or I could possibly imagine.

All my life, I carry enormous anguish and remorse over my actions."

Harry brought his eyes up from the note and looked at Lillian. "A lot of what constituted the plot of the novel had to do with the subject of remorse, which Otis thought would be a substantial part of his thesis."

Lillian was listening intently, thinking that the whole 'bad deed' story was about to come together.

Harry continued, "Otis looked further into the manuscript draft and other notes that were in the box. He went through a lot of interesting material related to this novel. Geoffrey Smith, the author, relied quite a bit on the background of his father, who had a full and eventful life and achieved financial success. This, apparently, allowed Geoffrey to get a great literary education from Cambridge. Geoffrey also became a professor of English literature at Cambridge before he wrote the novel."

Harry stopped and drank some coffee.

He referred again to his notebook. "Here, I have one of Geoffrey Smith's notes that were attached to the manuscript,

Father spent most of his working years in Africa, and I think there is more to an event that happened there than he let on. I was lightly prodding him to add color to the story. It appeared as if he kind of wanted to talk about it but was reluctant.

That is what the note said."

Lillian was waiting for Harry to get to the crux of the matter, but he took his time. He bit another piece of his biscuit and washed it down with coffee.

"There were more notes expounding on the novel theme.

273

One of the other people mentioned was an American called John Haddock. He was mentioned in several notes. Here is one of them,

> *Today father's old friend and his wife came over for dinner. Sitting at the fireplace after our meal, they had a long conversation about hunting. It was mostly about the duck hunt. Then the father said to his friend, 'Those duck hunts were great Sam, but they were nothing like the big game hunt in South Africa. I didn't do much of it, but the man I worked for hunted quite a bit. He invited many people to join him and not only Brits. One of his guests was especially impressed by the hunt – an American cotton trader from Mobile, Alabama, named John Haddock.*

Again, Harry lifted his eyes from his notes. "So now we got a name," he said and continued. "A little further in the box, in a different bundle, Otis found another note. This one also related to the manuscript's theme. It was dated a couple of weeks before the others. It reads,

> *I had a great conversation with father today. We discussed his association with a wealthy businessman when father worked in South Africa. He didn't mention the name, but from other notes I had read, I knew who it was – the 1ˢᵗ Baron Tensbury.*

That's the ancestor of Andrew Tensbury," continued Harry. "Then the note says,

> *My father's assistance to this businessman, in what turned out to be a 'heinous deed' is one he regrets all his life.*

This is the end of the note."

"That sounds very promising. Where did you take it next?" Lillian was feeling upbeat.

"So, we have Alistair Tensbury, John Haddock, and Smith Sr. all involved in this 'heinous deed.' From the notes Otis found and from Alistair's note to the Vicar that Ethan found, we now know that at least two of the people involved were very remorseful. I have a hunch that John Haddock felt the same. Assuming that John Haddock was involved, we tried but couldn't find any additional information about this event either in the open sources or in Otis's notes. And, of course, we couldn't ask the Tensbury family."

People around the table smiled.

"Oh, by the way, I am not sure anyone in that family knows about this. It has been so many years, and I don't think Alistair wanted anyone to know about it," Harry added.

"We thought it was a dead-end street. The only person who may have known something about this affair is this guy Haddock. His descendants could have some letters or other papers describing John Haddock's interactions with Alistair Tensbury. But we wondered how in the world does one find and interview, what we figured was, over a hundred descendants of a John Haddock, a hundred fifty years later? And do it in a very short period of time. I thought we had shut down the lead."

Lillian was on pins and needles, whishing he would get to the point.

Harry continued, "However, one of our associates, Shelly Anderson, got very creative. She used the online service called 'BeenVerified.' She ran: 'John Haddock', 'Alabama', 'Mobile', '1800s' plus 'cotton trader.' The result – over a hundred people who could potentially be a progeny of John Haddock. She came to me with a plan to locate a descendant with some of the information we needed.

"She suggested we call the people on the list and run a script by them. Something like: 'I'm working on a book on English and American cotton trade in the mid-1800s. In my research, I ran across a John Haddock, a cotton trader from Mobile, Alabama. Is he your ancestor? Do you know anything interesting about how he built his business?' Depending on the answer, we would take it from there. I told her to go ahead to see if she could track someone down. It was a long shot, but this late in the game, I figured we might as well try.

"She hit pay-dirt finding a Ray Haddock in Atlanta. He claimed his ancestor, John Haddock, had a cotton trading business in Mobile in the mid-1800s. They chatted, but as soon as Shelley mentioned Alistair Tensbury's name, he started to clam up. He said he only had one letter draft thanking Tensbury for introducing Haddock to some buyers in England. That was it. Shelley decided to get a little more aggressive. She asked if he knew of any business deal or some other interaction between Tensbury and Haddock that was unusual or interesting. As soon as she did, he told her he didn't have any more information and shut down the conversation."

Harry picked up another biscuit.

"So, where did it go from there?"

"Nowhere," Harry said. "Dead end. We couldn't take it any further. Although we still suspected Ray Haddock had some information he didn't want to divulge, we just hit a wall. Given time and resources, one could infiltrate Haddock's environment and succeed. But we didn't have either."

"Too bad. Do you have anything else?"

"No."

Harry had finished his biscuit and was wiping his fingers on a napkin.

"I guess we both did our best, Lillian. This was a last-ditch attempt anyway. What I do know, after hearing your story, is that something was going on at that time in Africa. Something big that included both Alistair, Smith Sr., and probably Haddock as well. But it seems we have exhausted our leads. We certainly tried, though."

"Damn it, both of us had a good lead to the same event. We shouldn't kick ourselves for this not working out. We supplied plenty of good material during the election, and I'm sure it helped our Party. But I absolutely wanted to get this one!" said Lillian resolutely.

After exchanging their views on Labor's chances tomorrow, they were done. Lillian led Harry to the door and shook his hand.

"Maybe we should have worked more closely together during the entire time leading up to this election," said Lillian, thoughtfully.

"Right. But this is how 10 Downing Street wanted it. I believe they were thinking we would be more productive working each on our own. Hope to work with you sometime in the future, Lillian."

CHAPTER 2

Tensbury woke up with a start. It was the day when he would meet the blackmailer at the hotel and hopefully put this whole affair behind him.

Who could it be? Was Labor involved or not? The blackmailer could be Hanna or someone else.

His wife called.

"Hello dear," he said. "How are you, Elisabeth?"

"Hi, darling. I'm well. Missing you."

"Well, it's a short week. I'll be home tomorrow for the vote, and Friday, the office is closed. I look forward to a long weekend with you."

He thought, that with the resolution of the situation with the blackmailer, he would feel much better at home.

"Is Jack back from his vacation? It was rather abrupt."

"He's back. I'll see him today in the office. Remember, I have to see the doctor for the physical this morning, so I won't have a chance to work much today."

In the back of his mind was the large amount he withdrew from one of their accounts. It was an account they didn't usually use. He prayed she wouldn't notice. At least for a while. There was something else that bothered him. What was the tax law impact on this sort of thing? He should have looked it up to make sure he was making the withdrawal from the appropriate account, but he had been too scatterbrained this past week.

"Hope the visit with the doctor goes well. I'm worried about all the stress you are under."

"Oh, I'll be fine. See you tomorrow, dear."

He put a hot water pot to boil his tea, cut a slice of bread, and put it in the toaster. He wished it was a fresh croissant but would have to wait till he was home for that.

Oh, yes, I need to call the hospital.

Tensbury dialed his aunt's hospital and asked for Dr. Ahur's nurse.

"Lord Tensbury?"

"Yes, may a speak to Sally Tensbury?"

"Sir, Dr. Ahur asked me to transfer your calls to her. Please wait a minute."

Then, "Hello."

"Hello, doctor."

"Unfortunately, the treatment isn't working as well as we hoped. The medicine makes her very drowsy. She mostly sleeps. She doesn't talk much and doesn't take any calls. If it changes, I'll ask her to call you. Sorry, I don't have better news. We are still hopeful."

"Thank you, doctor. I'll wait for her call."

There was only one day left for Labor to spring something on Andrew. He needed to find a way to see this bible now.

Tensbury called Fred.

"Fred? This is Simon Tensbury."

"Hello, My Lord."

"Fred, I just spoke to Aunt Sally's doctor. She says my aunt has taken a turn for the worse and doesn't take calls. It seems it'll take longer for her to recover."

"I know. I am sorry, Sir."

The uncomfortable feeling was back. Now he had to lie to Fred.

"A while ago, she told me that I should get the family bible she got from my grandfather. There's something from him there. Something she wanted me to see. I think I should do it now."

"Of course, Sir."

"Shall I come over this morning, say, at eight?"

"Yes, Sir, I'll be waiting."

"Thank you, Fred."

Tensbury picked up his briefcase and headed towards his car.

"Good morning, Henry."

"Good morning, My Lord." Henry eased the car out into the heavy morning traffic.

"Let's head to my Aunt Sally's place, and then we'll have to go to my doctor. Do you remember her address?"

"No, Sir, I don't."

Tensbury gave Henry his aunt's address.

The traffic was at a standstill for a long time and then crept along slowly. He finally arrived at his aunt's large townhouse in Knightsbridge.

Tensbury rang the bell. Fred opened the door, solemn expression on his face. "I am sorry, My Lord, about your aunt. I hope she'll get better soon."

Tensbury knew the man was attached to his aunt. He had been helping her for the last fifteen years.

"Yes, they can do miracles these days. She'll get better. It'll just take some time."

"I hope so."

"Fred, I remember seeing the bible in the library. Is it still there?"

"I think so, Sir." He led Tensbury to the library. The bookcase was locked.

"I think the key is in the desk, Sir."

Tensbury opened a couple of drawers and found a set of keys. One of them opened the case, and Tensbury carefully removed the box.

He opened the engraved box, which held the bible. In the

bible, there were two envelopes.

Could I have been right? Are these two what I need?

He picked up one envelope. It had his grandfather's handwriting on the top, 'To my Sally." Inside was a single page with his characteristic, carefully written script. The other envelope was yellow and fragile and didn't have any writing on it. It wasn't postmarked. He opened it and looked at the handwriting. It was a style with distinctly formed consonants but challenging to read. He recognized the script from the documents he had read in his library. The papers were in Alistair's writing.

He took a look at his watch. He had to leave. He wanted to be sure he made it to the doctor's office on time. With the traffic so heavy, he worried that he might be late if he stayed to read the letters.

He placed the envelopes in his briefcase and took the box with the bible. He thanked Fred and left.

Back in the car, he asked Henry to take him to his doctor's office.

The waiting room was full, and although he was burning to read the letters he had fetched, he didn't want to do it there. Once he was called and saw the doctor, they told him he had to have some tests done, which further delayed him. He checked the time. He would have to go directly to the hotel after this visit.

When he arrived at the hotel, he told Henry to find a parking place for the car and get himself something to eat. Tensbury knew he wouldn't be ready to leave until that afternoon.

As he entered the lobby, Jack called.

"Hi. Didn't see you here in the office this morning, Sir. Are you at the hotel already?"

"Yes, I am. I plan on going to the office later, so I'll see you right after the meeting."

Tensbury was a little early and continued towards the restaurant. There, he waited to be seated. He sat down in the restaurant where lunch was in full swing. He figured he had time to take a look at the envelopes he had just picked up.

"Would you like some coffee? The buffet is open now, Sir," said the waitress. Tensbury looked up. She was a slim girl of no more than twenty. They must be hiring university students, he thought.

"Some tea, please. I will not be having lunch." He was too nervous to think about food.

The girl ran off and soon came back with hot water and a tray of teabags. Tensbury choose Earl Grey, put it in his cup, and let the girl pour hot water over it. He took a sip.

He then pushed his teacup to the side and pulled out the two envelopes he had collected from his aunt. First, he opened the one from his grandfather.

My Dearest Sally,

When you were born, God gave your mother and me the greatest gift one can receive. We love you, unconditionally. We always hoped that the warmth of our love will have made you a good and happy person. It did. And that all your life, that warmth will follow you wherever you are.

Your Dad.

P.S.

I have to ask you to do one task for our family.

Nowadays, and probably in the future, our ancestors' deeds play a significant part in one's standing in the society. Our family carries the title and is a member of the House of Lords. So, this is important.

Alistair Tensbury, who, as you know, was the 1st Baron Tensbury, did many brave and useful things for our country. Unfortunately, he also did one awful, ghastly thing. As a result, he was *trying to atone for this deed his entire life but couldn't wash the stain off his soul. The note in the second envelope, included here, will tell the story.*

I have no way of knowing if the information in the note also exists somewhere else. It might exist as a recollection of some other person who was part of this dreadful event. If it does, it may come to light one day.

I do not want any man, called Lord Tensbury to ever know of this event. I would like you to <u>make sure</u> that no one in our family ever exalts Alistair.

When you get older, as we all do, eventually, you should pass on this information. Pass it to the younger sibling or close relative of the future Lord Tensbury to carry on this task.

Thank you.

Tensbury removed two sets of papers from the second envelope. One consisted of several papers folded together and the other just one page. He picked up the short note first. It began, 'Dear Vicar Jones' and wasn't signed. The note had a lot of strikethroughs and additions in the margins. The paper was brittle and yellow, and it appeared to be a draft that had never been sent.

His phone vibrated, and he took a look at it. He saw a number he didn't recognize, so he let it go to voicemail. Then he turned his attention to the paper in front of him.

Dear Vicar Jones,

As I mentioned after service last Sunday, I don't expect to be forgiven for what I have done. Maybe I can pass through the end of my days a little easier, and with less weight on my shoulders, if I reveal to you what torments me. I have perpetrated a heinous deed in Africa, which I can't describe here. I'll have to find some time alone with you. The weight of this event has burdened me gravely over many years. I have told no one, but now, I feel the need to do so at this later stage in my life. I'm tortured each day, and it's getting worse as time goes by. I have built schools and hospitals and shared my wealth to the greatest extent in the hopes that I could atone for my sins. But my mind never settles.

As we discussed last Sunday, I'll come to see you this week.

Thank you for being here for me.

What sins was he referring to?

Tensbury's heart started beating faster. This was probably the information they had been looking for all this time. Tensbury quickly unfolded the other set of papers.

It was a note, several pages long, written in the same practically illegible handwriting as the short note he had just read. In addition to the dismal handwriting, many sections were stricken, and notes were written in the margin. This was also some form of a draft. It wasn't addressed to anyone, but as he started reading, he realized it had to be to the same vicar as the note he just read.

A person does not send letters like this to a parish vicar, thought Tensbury. It could be a draft of the story about the 'horrible affair' the blackmailer mentioned in his note. Tensbury continued reading. The further he got into the document, the more perspiration he felt building. If this is close to the information the blackmailer has somehow acquired, Tensbury knew how close this might be to derailing Andrew's campaign. It would also tarnish his family's good name.

God don't let any of this show up in the media.

He reached the end of the papers, looked up, and stared

into the distance. He could see the waitress heading for his table and waved her off.

His stomach was in knots. He had lost what little color he had in his face, and his throat felt parched and constricted. Tensbury took a sip of his tea, careful not to drip on the letters.

Now I understand what Alistair meant by 'my sins.'

That is why Aunt Sally told him not to pay much attention to Alistair. My grandfather's letter is probably why she wanted to talk to Andrew. She wanted to advise him not to dwell on Alistair. The noises around him melted away, and all he could hear was a hissing sound in his ears.

CHAPTER 3

Hanna woke as Mans called.

"Ms. Arnol?"

"Sorry, I just woke up, so I'm a little groggy. Inspector Mans?"

"Yes. I wanted to tell you that the coroner's results came in, and your uncle died from that fall on the stairs. As I said before, there was no sign of foul play, and you should know that this was a tragic accident, nothing else."

He fell. No struggle. Probably nothing. Could have been pushed, unexpectedly, of course.

"Thank you, inspector."

"How have you been?"

"Not so good, as you can imagine. He was an amazing man, Inspector Mans." Even though she didn't really know the Inspector, she had observed his kindness already.

"Well, I hope you'll be doing better. Where are you? Back in Stockholm?"

"No, but I will be in a day or so."

"If you need anything, call me, alright?"

She remembered how thoughtful he was in the cafeteria after she had identified her uncle. It was good to know that there were policemen like him around.

Tensbury looked up and saw a woman approach. She was dressed in a white blouse tucked into jeans and white sneakers. Her brown hair flowed around her shoulders. As she came closer, he saw it shining with reddish highlights. She had an expectant look on her face.

"Lord Tensbury," the woman said breathlessly. "It's so nice to see you here. I left a voice mail last night hoping you would call me, and I tried reaching you again this morning."

Tensbury pushed the letter to the side.

Then she said, "I'm sure you have been busy since I haven't heard back." She stopped and took a breath.

"Pardon me. I didn't introduce myself. I'm Hanna Arnol. I have been trying to contact you because I have some information for you regarding our ancestors."

She proffered her hand. Tensbury half rose and reached for it. She had a firm handshake.

"Arnol? Please." He motioned for her to sit.

Hanna pulled out a chair and sat down across from Tensbury.

She had soft wrinkles around her eyes that belied her youthful figure. Deep green eyes sparkled with excitement. Mid-thirties. A little older than what Tensbury and Jack assumed as they were looking into her background.

"A gentleman named Arnol contacted me some time ago. He said the same thing. That he had information for me."

"That must have been my uncle. I wasn't aware he called you."

Coincidence. This is the Hanna Arnol we followed in Senegal. She isn't carrying anything, and she isn't mentioning the extortion. It's too early for the meeting in the lounge. She isn't the blackmailer. Now, I am sure. But what information does she have?

He drew a ragged breath. This week had tired him, and he

was glad it was coming to an end.

"I don't know if this is a good time, but there are some things I want to share with you," she repeated.

"Forgive me, Ms. Arnol. Actually, it's not a good time." Tensbury checked his watch.

"Ms. Arnol, I'm afraid I need to leave. I have some business to attend to. Don't get me wrong. I'm very interested in speaking with you. Could we meet for coffee? Right here at the hotel in the lounge? Say at five?"

"That's fine. I'll be in the lounge at five."

He laid a ten-pound note on the table, rose, took his briefcase, said goodbye, and left.

CHAPTER 4

It was close to 1:30 when Tensbury entered the lounge. The bar with its high barstools was empty this early in the day. A bartender, polishing glasses, was there, nonetheless.

Tensbury looked around. A man sitting at one of the low tables stood up when he saw Tensbury.

"Lord Tensbury?"

Tensbury walked towards him.

"Yes."

"My name is Ray Haddock," The man reached for Tensbury's hand. "Please sit. An ale perhaps?"

Tensbury sat down.

"It's a little early for me to drink, I'm afraid," Tensbury declared with a smile.

"I understand."

"Yes, I still have some business I need to take care of. Please, go ahead. I would like us to address our issue as soon as possible."

He felt nervous and impatient, worried he would say the wrong words and have the whole thing fall apart.

"Oh, I hope we can chat for a minute, Sir. Or do I say Lord Tensbury each time I address you?" asked Ray, a lopsided grin on his round face.

Tensbury didn't answer. The skin on his face was drawn tight over his cheekbones. He could hardly contain his worry about what was coming. After what he had read in the vicar's letter this morning, he dreaded to hear more.

Ray launched into what he had to say.

"See, I hate to ask for money. The only reason I got into this affair is because my daughter has an unusual form of cancer. She needs treatments only available in Germany, which I can't afford. I don't have insurance that will cover it, you see. I love that child more than anything in this world and will do anything to keep her safe and healthy."

"I can understand that. I have two boys myself."

"I found a letter my ancestor wrote that has been locked up for over a century in my cellar. He met Alistair Tensbury in the mid-1800s. I traced the name to you."

Tensbury tensed.

"Now things have changed, and I don't need the money for the treatment. Just got a call yesterday. The doctors say the medical device company that's involved, is footing the bill for everything. That company will pay for the hospital, the doctors, and the treatments – everything. Now the doctors say they can operate."

He stopped and took a long swig from his mug.

Tensbury could tell the man had consumed a few already. He was ruddy and happy. Tensbury was cautiously pleased.

Is there some catch to this situation? Will I still get the papers the man had committed to bring?

Right on cue, Ray said, "I have the material I mentioned. It's yours. I don't want it. I don't want my daughter ever to find it. This isn't an inheritance I'm proud of." Ray sobered up as he said it. "Then again, I'm sure you'll feel the same way."

He pulled out a manila folder from a rucksack on the floor and opened the folder.

"Here is a letter my ancestor John Haddock wrote to his brother after his trip to South Africa where he spent time with

290

Alistair Tensbury. It was returned to him when his brother died."

Ray slid the envelope over to Tensbury. "Here you go. Do whatever you want with it, but please remember I never want to hear or see anything related to this nasty business again."

He abruptly stood up.

"The only reason I'm here is because I thought I was going to collect the money and give you the papers. Now that I don't need the money, I still want to make sure you get the papers. I'm sorry you had to go through this."

He shook Tensbury's hand, and without saying another word, he walked out.

It had all passed so quickly, and Tensbury sat there, stunned. The implications dawned on him. That he wouldn't have to pay was a relief. But, more importantly, Tensbury was convinced that the Labor Party or its affiliate must have indeed been involved. Ray Haddock, apparently, did refused to divulge anything to the person who contacted him. Tensbury picked up the envelope. It was addressed to an Edwin Haddock, and the return address was for a John Haddock.

He put on his glasses and started reading.

After a while, Tensbury stopped and looked up. Having read the vicar's letter this morning, it all fell together. He understood what Ray just said. Tensbury resolved to destroy these papers.

He decided not to follow his grandfather's approach. These papers should not exist. He didn't want his sons to know anything about this!

How could he have bragged about Alistair all these years? The truth was that Alistair had been capable of engaging in this sort of endeavor.

Tensbury had been reading for quite a while. Finally, he replaced the letter in the envelope and placed it in his briefcase.

He thought of Hanna Arnol. There was still her 'some

information for you regarding our ancestors.'

What was that all about?

But at this point, he didn't think he should talk to Andrew about anything.

He planned to pass by his office before seeing Hanna – he wanted to see Jack. He thought about calling Henry for the car but decided it would be better to walk. The sun was out, and for the first time in a week, he felt like he could fill his lungs with air.

After Tensbury arrived at his office, he knocked on Jack's door. He was in a lighter frame of mind after the walk back from the hotel.

"Come in," said Jack. "Oh, it's you, Sir. I have been on edge this all-morning thinking about your meeting with the blackmailer. Did you get the papers?"

"I did."

Jack saw that Tensbury wasn't carrying any papers. He half rose, expecting Tensbury to ask him to join him in his own office and show them to him. Instead, Tensbury walked in, shut the door, and sat down in one of Jack's guest chairs.

Tensbury started, "Alistair and this Haddock, whose letter we read at my home in Kent, didn't only meet but contrived an abhorrent plan. The affair ended up even worse than they planned." He searched for words.

"Jack, this action of theirs ended up in the 'terrible affair' the blackmailer was writing about. I have been contemplating this as I walked to the office. I thought of how to handle it and not put you in a difficult position."

He stopped again.

"Let me explain. Obviously, we don't want what I found ever to get out. In addition, I don't want you to be in a position in the future where you have to lie and perjure yourself. It's very probable, Andrew will become PM. Who knows, you may be working somewhere else when someone approaches you with questions about the Tensbury heritage."

"I see."

"It very well might happen, you know. So, I'm thinking, it's better if I just tell you that what those two men contrived ended up so badly that they were trying to redeem themselves for it all their lives. I want you to be able tell whoever is asking that you truly don't know anything about it. For the same reason, I have decided not to say anything about this event to my sons nor my wife. Beyond that, I do want to tell you about the meeting with the man who wrote the blackmailer note."

Tensbury recounted his meeting with Ray Haddock without describing the content of the papers he read.

"Sir, how do you know this descendant of Haddock doesn't release these same letters tonight?"

"I don't. He could have copied everything. If he does release it, it'll ruin Andrew's chances tomorrow. But having met the guy, I don't think he will. It isn't in his best interest. Then again, it's not probable but possible, there were other people who knew about that event in Africa, and that information could still become public. On my part, I will shred everything related to this event."

Then he thought of the ramification of his conclusion. "Also, I now believe that Labor or their affiliate did contact Ray Haddock. They apparently assumed that there was, or could have been, shady business deals in Alistair's time in Africa. They probably found the same letter from Alistair to Garnier about opening the American market as we did. They then traced the American cotton trader in the letter to Ray Haddock, but he refused to collaborate."

"And what about Hanna Arnol? I understand that she wasn't a lead we should have followed. But there's still that call from her uncle before he died."

"Oh, yes, let me tell you. This is fascinating. When I was at lunch waiting to see Haddock, she walked into the restaurant and introduced herself."

"Oh!"

"Yes. It turns out she left two voicemails trying to reach me. It seems she just has some information about two of our ancestors. As I understood from her demeanor, her story has nothing to do with the horrible event. We agreed to meet this afternoon. I just hope there are no more surprises. Tomorrow is the election day."

"I hope so, Sir."

Jack drew a deep breath. He was happy the whole thing was over. He looked forward to going back to his regular job, pulling research and strategizing on bills with Tensbury. Earlier, he took a look at what they had missed this past week at the House of Lords. The work was building up, and they had to attend to it.

"Jack, I can't begin to tell you how grateful I am for all the support you gave me this week. I couldn't have faced this situation without you! Your offer to go to Senegal, arranging things with Malek, and being on the lookout for what Hanna was doing, was beyond anything I could have asked for."

"I'm glad it all worked out, Sir, even though it sounds as if it has been a difficult ending for you," Jack looked at Tensbury. He didn't seem as tranquil as Jack would have expected at the culmination of this affair.

"Is there something else that troubles you, Sir?" Jack knew him well enough to see he had other things on his mind.

"No, nothing. I'm just worn out after what we have been through."

He got up from his chair, and so did Jack.

"We have a lot to talk about when we are back next week. It'll be good to get back to normal, don't you think, Sir?"

"Yes, it sure will. I'm glad it's over."

"Agreed."

Tensbury looked at his watch.

"I need to head over to the hotel and meet Hanna. And thanks again for all your support! Let's say we put this behind us, hey, Jack."

"Yes, Sir."

Jack heard Tensbury carefully close his door. He started packing up to leave. This past week had left him exhausted.

The blackmail ordeal was over, and Jack was pleased to see the familiar sparkle in his boss' blue eyes again.

Could I have done better? No!

Questions still remained, though. Tensbury had appeared convinced Haddock wouldn't release any information.

What if Labor was up to some mischief? And they already know the same info from a different source. We won't learn that until tomorrow.

It would have been interesting to read the information Haddock brought. It must have been explosive, since Tensbury said he wouldn't even share it with his family.

Jack realized he had to put this whirlwind to sleep, and hope that anything like it would not happen again.

CHAPTER 5

Hanna's foot jiggled impatiently under the table. Bad habit, she thought. She knew she did it when she was nervous and even during business meetings. It was distracting and looked unprofessional. She willed herself to stop. It was after five, and he was late.

Lord Tensbury made her uncomfortable earlier today. She expected him to be more interested in what she had to say. Now she was indecisive as to what to tell him – how to tell him!

How much should she say about things that led to the events? Or should she just launch into the story?

She looked around. The Hilton had a typical hotel lounge, but nicer than most she has seen. It was modern, though. Not her style. It was close to Westminster, and she imagined it wasn't just Lord Tensbury who frequented the place. Hanna looked around to see if she could spot anyone who looked like they might be from the House of Commons or Lords. The lounge was rather full. Everyone seemed to be wearing suits. Some with colorful shirts and ties. She saw a couple of women here and there in nice-looking skirts or pants and jackets. Many people were older – over fifty.

Frustrated, she checked the time again.

I hope he comes.

A waiter came over, and she told him she was waiting on someone else before ordering.

She picked up the phone again and texted her boss to call her. She needed to tell him about the call she had received earlier. It was from Tom, the CEO of the company they were acquiring. It was negative, and she hated to have to relay the information via voicemail. She thought the deal was done when she left the meeting in London before going to Dakar. And now the investors were getting cold feet. Without their support, her company wouldn't be able to acquire the new entity.

She looked up and saw Lord Tensbury.

"Ms. Arnol, I apologize for my tardiness."

He folded his tall frame into the rather low lounge chair.

"No worries."

The lights were dim, but she thought he looked much more rested than he had this morning.

"Did your business go well earlier today, Sir?"

"Indeed, it did. I'm very much relieved. And hungry. Are you?"

"Yes, I am."

She wasn't hungry at all. The large lunch she had earlier filled her up.

Tensbury grimaced from the loud noise around them.

"I thought it would be better to talk somewhere more private. At this time, half of Westminster is here. I don't know if you would agree, but we could take a walk over to my office. It's right down the road on Cowley Street, not far from here. We can speak more privately in the office." He quickly added. "My assistant is there. She can order in some Chinese for us. Do you like Chinese?"

Hanna looked around. The commotion in the room made it difficult to hear what he was saying. Ordinarily, she would feel very uncomfortable joining a man she just met in his office in the evening. But he said his admin would be there.

Besides, she felt like she knew the man, even though only from her research.

"Okay. I love Chinese."

Leaving the lounge into the lobby, Tensbury took his phone out of his pocket and called his office. Hanna heard him ask his admin to order Chinese. He also let her know they were on their way.

They exited onto John Islip Street and started walking. The sidewalks were busy with people leaving work and hurrying to restaurants, pubs, or home by the tube. They passed St. John's Smith Square.

"Do you often walk to your office?" Hanna tried to keep up with Tensbury's long gait.

"I try to walk whenever I can. Westminster isn't far from the Hilton, where I often have lunch. When the weather is good, I try to walk there too. How about you? Do you live far from where you work?"

"Well, I often work from home, which is typical in Silicon Valley. When I need to go to the office for a face-to-face meeting, the drive is about twenty minutes. Our company is pretty much digital now. We mostly meet over the web."

Using Lord North street, they crossed Great Peter street and entered a typical old London street called Cowley. Three- and four-story brick buildings lined the street. The face of the buildings gleamed with bright white window-frames.

They continued to chat about their work. After five minutes, Tensbury turned left, and they entered a building. He pushed the number one button. The elevator rose, and the doors swooshed open. She found herself facing a large, double-doored suite, with the name Arrowstood on a bronze door plaque.

Tensbury opened the door. She entered a pleasant anteroom where crown molding adorned the high ceiling. Facing the door stood a desk with a large computer screen, and behind it sat an attractive woman. She greeted them with a wave.

In one corner was a couple of chairs around a low table with magazines stacked on top of it. Hanna could see a hallway off to one side. The décor was of a muted sage scheme, which she found soothing. Tensbury introduced his admin and then showed her through the hallway into a small conference room.

"We can talk in here," he said in his modulated voice.

Hanna picked a middle chair and sat down.

Just then, a young man in his twenties walked in with a food delivery pack over his shoulder.

"Hallo," he said. "Can I put it here?" Tensbury nodded, and the young man proceeded to withdraw several Chinese dishes, rice, and a host of soft drinks. Putting a wad of napkins and chopsticks on the table, he said, "cheers," and left.

"This is a bit simple, but I hope you don't mind. I just thought it would be better for us to be alone when we talk. Sounds like you have something important to tell me."

"I think it was a fabulous idea." She chose a box of Kung Pau Chicken and a Diet Pepsi. They began eating. She noticed Tensbury was very deft with the chopsticks. She thought that Chinese must be a favorite of his. Maybe because of working late at the office.

"You mentioned my uncle contacted you a week ago." Hanna took a sip of her Pepsi. "Tragically he died falling down the stairs in his home in Stockholm shortly after that."

"I'm so sorry to hear that."

"Thank you. Yesterday, I realized why he was contacting you and that's why I called. You see, our ancestors' paths crossed a hundred-fifty years ago in St. Louis, Senegal."

"How so?"

"My ancestor Signe, in 1859, when she was a girl of eighteen, sailed from Norway to South Africa and stopped in St. Louis. She wrote a diary every year of her life. My uncle had all the diaries, but the pages that describe her being in St. Louis were missing from the 1859 diary.

"They were missing. How?"

"I wasn't sure. But about a week ago my uncle called, and said he found them. They were in Norwegian, and he was going to translate them. He spoke Norwegian and was, of course, able to read them himself and called you right away. When I found them at the house after his death, I had to send them in for translation since I can't read the language."

"Right."

"Before he died and the missing pages came to light, I helped my uncle with his 19th century nautical blog, which was his hobby after he retired. Because of my knowledge of French, he asked me to help him research Alistair Tensbury's IL&R work in Senegal."

Tensbury was listening intently.

"When my uncle died unexpectedly, and in a manner that didn't jibe with him being a healthy, sporty man, I got suspicious. I wondered if he had asked me to do the Tensbury research because he was helping his friend at the Cornelian Society, which supports Labor causes. Perhaps he was looking for some negative information about Alistair Tensbury, since that was the ancestor, your son was speaking about. You see, my uncle had leftist leanings. And, as distraught as I was, I started thinking that maybe some conservative group supporting Tories had a hand in my uncle's death."

Tensbury threw up his hands.

"No, that could never happen."

"I feel terribly guilty that I didn't spend more time with my uncle. He was the most important person in my life. He raised me since I was twelve when my parents died in an accident. There was no one else. We were supposed to finally spend time together, going to Senegal for a week, to retrace Signe's steps. Since he had just received the diary pages, I thought that there might be a link between the pages and his death. So, even though I didn't have the translated pages yet, I decided to go on this trip as he planned."

"Let me get this straight. You went to Senegal thinking

someone, or some group, might have killed your uncle?"

"In part."

Tensbury scooted his chair back a bit. Briefly, she realized how uncomfortable he was. He was used to sitting at the head of the table.

"As the days went by, the combination of the bad press in the Guardian, and some of the documents I found, pointed to Alistair's minor business transgressions, nothing more. Nothing that could have affected the British electorate and definitely nothing that could have caused my uncle's death.

"But then I received the first three translated pages. From them, I learned that Signe met Alistair Tensbury in St. Louis in 1859. Also, from these pages and a story I heard in Dakar, I deduced that an awful event did occur around that time in Senegal."

"What led you to think so?" said Tensbury.

Hanna recounted the facts she learned, pointing to this event. An event involving Issa, Alistair, and his assistant Smith.

"It all just fell together from a timing perspective," she stated. "I know an awful event happened. I just don't know what it was."

"That's some kind of story."

"I know. You're probably thinking that if the press gets a hold of a story like this, it could alter the Conservatives' and your son's chances in the election, right?"

"I know it would."

"It probably would, but the point is, it shouldn't! It shouldn't have any effect. No matter what it is. What happened over a hundred-fifty years ago isn't relevant to who Andrew Tensbury is. Not as a person nor as a politician. From what I know, Andrew has proven himself to be a fine legislator and having been the leader of the Shadow Cabinet, he must have the trust of his peers. I don't know that much about British politics, but I think you call your political platform a Manifesto, right?"

"Yes, the Manifesto is where we commit our beliefs and plans to the electorate."

"Well, I think a politician should be judged based on his character and the Manifesto he stands by. He shouldn't be judged by something his far-removed ancestor may have been involved in. This country is one day from the election. I'm sure you know more than I do, but I don't think anyone has brought forth any negative information about Andrew. Nothing that would question Andrew's character or what he has done in his life. That is all which should count."

"I agree," said Tensbury.

"As I said, I don't know what Issa, Smith, and Alistair were involved in. But whatever it was, it's a reflection of their life and character and has nothing to do with Andrew. Moreover, if I would have found out what they did in 1859, I would never have let the political dirt diggers know about it." Hanna took a breath. "I think your son will win tomorrow. You must be so proud of him."

"I am."

Then he asked, "What happened to your search for the reason your uncle died?"

"I didn't find anything. I don't regret going. It was a great experience. I got to see the things Signe wrote about in her diary. I got to experience Africa. I know I'll go back. It's special. The smells, the sounds, the heat. But to your question, I guess, I'll never really know the reason."

CHAPTER 6

Tensbury's thoughts wandered. He felt this uncanny need to confess everything he had learned today. Confess wasn't the right word and not what he needed to do. More like share it. His only fault was being boastful and believing in the infallibility of the man who brought the peerage into his family. He didn't know the man. He remembered the family stories of his ancestors and the medals they earned, lining the library walls in his home. He may not have known Alistair, but he knew his father and grandfather very well. Good and kind men, always eager to help the less fortunate. Both bravely served their country in two world wars.

This young woman, with her easy smile endeared him in more ways than one. First, she had already figured out that Alistair was involved in something deplorable back in 1859. And second, she firmly stated that she would never share anything that happened over a century ago with the media. It meant a lot!

"I'm sure you still have a lot of affairs to set right in Stockholm."

"I do, and I leave tomorrow."

"Tomorrow is a crucial day for our country. It looks like we will win. It's important not only because of my Party and my son's efforts and beliefs but also for the country's direction. If Labor wins, we'll head deeper into socialism."

As they spoke, Tensbury thought,

What a burden.

He felt like the two letters from the family bible and the letter from Ray were glowing through his briefcase at the end of the table.

Tensbury drew a deep breath. He didn't realize Hanna was sitting quietly waiting, for him to say something.

"Hanna." He paused. "There's something that relates to the story you shared with me, which I feel I should tell you. This morning, I saw old papers from which I learned about this horrible thing Alistair and Smith did. Although I have only known you for one day, I somehow feel I can trust you. You have told me that you would never share any negative information you might find out. Now, I would still like to remind you that if what I'll tell you ever becomes known, it would damage this election and future efforts of my son."

She said without hesitation, "I understand, Sir."

"This isn't a pretty tale, so prepare yourself."

Tensbury set his soda aside.

"I don't know where to start. You know so much about Alistair already."

Tensbury had been looking down at the carpet but now looked up. She saw in his face that he was hesitating.

"Sir, if this isn't a subject you feel comfortable with, I understand completely. Like I said earlier, I have something to tell you that I think you'll be interested in."

Tensbury didn't appear to listen and launched into his narrative.

"In 1858, in London, Alistair met John Haddock, an American cotton trader from Mobile Alabama. They were introduced through a mutual banker."

Tensbury continued to tell Hanna about how the two traveled to South Africa together and became friends.

He pulled at his collar and loosened his tie. He explained

how on the trip, Alistair and Haddock shared their business experiences.

"They discussed slavery in Africa and around the world. It was 1858, and slavery was outlawed in most countries, but not in America. However, the US didn't import slaves from Africa anymore. Haddock told Alistair that he didn't use slaves in his business. His father willed him many slaves, but he freed them all, except several who helped around the house."

"Yes, it was right before the Civil War," said Hanna quietly.

"Correct, it was. Alistair told Haddock that the end of the cross-Atlantic slave trade had been a long and bloody one. The British Royal Navy constituted the West Africa Squadron in 1807. Its function was to protect Africa from cross-Atlantic slave traders. This Squadron largely ended this slave trade to the West. From 1807 till then, the Squadron captured many slave ships and freed hundreds of thousands of Africans. Unfortunately, he said, this didn't exactly reduce the number of African deaths. Slave ship captains would throw slaves overboard, still shackled, to avoid detection if they were chased by a squadron vessel. Most of those people drowned.

"Alistair mentioned that in 1848 France liberated slaves in four areas of Senegal, called 'quatre communes,' and made them French citizens."

Tensbury stopped and took a sip of his soda. "Although discouraged by the French, the African Kings and chieftains still traded slaves between themselves. That would never stop, in Alistair's opinion. Alistair also told Haddock about Article VII of the French emancipation decree. The article held that any slave that entered the quatre communes in Senegal was automatically deemed a French citizen.

"Because of this, runaway slaves from all over flocked to these areas. There was a fear that the inland slave owners, losing their slaves, would no longer trade goods with the French. Eventually, Article VII was relaxed so that the slaves who tried to enter these areas could be turned back. The arrangement made it very difficult to transport slaves to coastal regions of Senegal for an illegal slave trade across the Atlantic.

"The Africans living in the quatre communes, who used to aid the slave trade in the past, were now facilitating commodity deals between Western traders and the tribal chieftains. None of them wanted to risk their somewhat lucrative business to illegally bring slaves to the coast. If they got caught, they would go to jail and lose their French citizenship."

Tensbury ended his tale, got up, and went to the end of the large table. On the chair, the one where he usually sat, he reached down into his briefcase and pulled out a manila folder. He returned to his seat across from Hanna and opened the folder. Inside were papers that looked like pages from very old letters.

"Apparently, when they arrived in South Africa, Alistair invited Haddock on a hunt. It appears hunting was a passion of both men. Alistair had proximity to some of the most exciting hunting grounds in the world, where large wild animals roamed. Haddock was limited to hunting alligators around Mobile in Alabama. This is Haddock's letter to his brother describing the hunting expedition with Alistair."

Tensbury reached for his reading glasses in his pocket, put them on.

"Let me read them to you,

Dear Brother, my adventures in Europe and South Africa have been great. I know we'll meet soon, and I can tell you about that in person. But there is one account I have to share with you now. I'm ashamed to have participated in this affair. It was, in fact, I who put it all in motion.

Of course, I have forgotten the exact conversations I had with Alistair Tensbury, the man who invited me to hunt in South Africa, but I wanted to capture the story, nonetheless. It isn't one I'm proud of, dear brother.

During our hunt, I had just seen my host shoot and kill an enormous wild boar just before it was about to ram one of his local hunting aids. He rescued him in the nick of time. Soon, the pig laid within a couple of yards of the skinny, black man, who had sunk to the ground with his head between his knees, thankful to be alive. 'Get up, you old pansy. I just saved your arse. You should thank me.' Alistair turned to me. 'How about that, my old chap? That's what I love about this sport – it's so damn unpredictable.'

Haddock was obviously impressed by Alistair."
Tensbury stopped his reading and picked up the next page. "Let me continue,

The vigor with which he had led the hunt that day, starting at dawn, left me bone tired. But I have to tell you, I felt deliciously alive in a way I had not in a long time.

We returned to our camp, and I went to my tent and rested. After a while, I took a seat by the fire. Alistair had not shown up yet. As I waited for him to join me, I reflected on our week together hunting. I thought I had gotten to know him pretty well during our time sailing down the African coast. What I had seen this week told me deep in my bones that I was in the presence of an almost unsurpassable fellow.

I knew that although my host had seemed to enjoy showing off his prowess and his surroundings all week, the great man was getting bored. He probably considered me only a simple, if wealthy,

> *cotton trader from the Americas, without any lasting value in terms of friendship. Yet, my wealth far exceeded his, and I knew he didn't have a title, which is so impressive on the continent. But wealth aside, Alistair was ready for me to leave soon. I knew that much.*

Haddock was frustrated with Alistair boasting."

Butterflies flew in his stomach as he was second-guessing himself with every word.

Is it truly a good idea to share this with a woman I hardly know?

"This was 1858, and Alistair hadn't been awarded peerage yet." Tensbury completely loosened his tie and removed it. He hung it over the back of the chair next to him.

He resumed reading, his voice rumbling.

"Here begins the disturbing part.

> *Dear Brother, you know my competitive nature. It has gotten me into trouble more than once. My thoughts were now focused on the fact that I didn't want to leave this man with the impression that I was only a weak-hearted, simpleton from America.*
>
> *With all the stunts Alistair staged that week, my own prostrations seemed feeble. All I demonstrated was strong horsemanship and a keen eye. Hunting those slithering, surprisingly quick alligators around my home has honed my skills. So, I was quick to react when I identified my mark during our hunt.*
>
> *You know, I have always considered myself rather fearless, but after the feat with the boar today, I knew Alistair bested me. Much as I respected the man, his lack of humility made my competitive bile rise and threatened to make me*

cough. I needed to find a way to impress him before I left. To beat him at his own game of one-upmanship in some way.

I tried to envision some 'what-if' scenario that could impress him. Could I find a bait that Alistair would swallow where certain failure would bring him to his arrogant knees? Slowly an insidious thought wormed its way into my consciousness.

This started the events you have spoken of," said Tensbury.

"Wait," said Hanna softly. "You said you received this today? Why has it been hidden for so long?"

"Haddock's descendant, slightly older than you, found this letter in his cellar while clearing out old boxes. He recognized my name and looked me up. I was very confused when both he and your uncle contacted me around the same time, saying virtually the same thing. That they had information about my family. Haddock's descendant handed me these papers today."

"I see."

Tensbury focused on Haddock's letter again.

"Let me continue,

After a while, Alistair joined me at the fire. We had a good dinner – a stew made from the boar he killed that day. We also enjoyed some of the fine cognac Alistair brought from his home.

Now comes the part that I have hesitated to put in writing, but I have to share it with someone, and the only person I trust is you, my Big Brother! You have always been there to guide me, and I wish you were there that damning day. You would have prevented me from entering into a situation I couldn't get out of, and which ended in tragedy.

This is when the awful story begins."

Tensbury knew that at this point he had committed himself to tell her this awful tale.

CHAPTER 7

After a while, Tensbury continued, as if attacking the content in the letter.

"Let me go on,

> *Alistair bragged about the cognac we were enjoying - from the Grande Champagne Cognac region in France. He gave me a bottle before I returned home, and I believe it's probably worth a lot of money. I'll save it for the day when you visit me!*
>
> *I remembered he told me about the laws in Senegal and slaves being free in certain parts of the country. The chieftains were trading amongst themselves inland. He thought it had become impossible for any Westerner to engage in the slave trade because of the antislavery laws. Yet, I prodded him to see if he knew of anyone who had attempted to buy slaves and bring them to the coast. He said he didn't, but it would be of no use anyway because no captain would be senseless enough to try to run the British Squadron.*

I told him I thought I knew some slave ship captains who would be crazy enough to make that run. 'Are you sure?' he asked. 'You mean, they will risk the ship and the cost of the transatlantic voyage to do it?' I said they might. 'Hard to believe,' said Alistair. He then sat quietly, looking at the fire. At this point, he took the bait.

'Tell you what, my dear fellow. If you can get a ship to the shores of Senegal with a captain who can run the Squadron, I'll supply the slaves.' I could hear the firewood crackling.

It was time to decide, and I went along.

So, we agreed on a double wager. Alistair bet he could procure the slaves from the inland tribes and deliver them to the coast near St. Louis. I bet that I could equip a ship and find a fearless, daring captain. For the right amount of money, the captain, would find a crew and get the ship to Senegal to pick up the slaves. He would then successfully run the blockade on the way back to America.

We firmed up the possible wager outcomes. If both of us fulfilled our part – nobody wins, nobody loses. If Alistair could not deliver slaves to the shore of St. Louis – I win. If Alistair successfully brought the slaves to the coast, and I fail to bring the ship and take the slaves to America – Alistair wins.

You see what I was talking about? Alistair wasn't only involved in the toll antics, but he was also arrogant and dangerous.

"You must understand that all my life, I have been told that Alistair was an upstanding man. The one we all admired. He was the one to whom Queen Victoria awarded peerage, giving him the title of Baron. He bravely fought during the First Afghan War. He built the businesses in Africa, leaving our family with significant wealth."

Now, Tensbury saw that Hanna was beginning to understand why he was so distraught.

He continued his story, now describing the events in his own words. "They shook hands and settled that this gentleman's bet would have a token £500 wager. The rest was just details. They agreed on the number of one hundred slaves. They also agreed that the ship would arrive in St. Louis around the middle of November of the next year when the weather was most agreeable. It would fly the American flag and, as such, be identifiable to Alistair's representative. They confirmed a code word. The roundtrip's expense was substantial. If Alistair failed to deliver the slaves, he would buy a Gum Arabic cargo for the ship's return voyage."

Tensbury raised his voice with distain and anger. "These two arrogant men, in the heat of trying to impress one another, committed themselves to perpetuate the evil of slavery trading. Something neither of them approved of!

"Also, from what I read in these papers, neither Alistair nor Haddock, had any experience in this type of enterprise. How were they planning to overcome the hurdles and 'succeed' in this wager, as they called it? Alright, maybe Haddock had ships, and for a lot of money, he would find a captain and a crew to do this awful bidding, but why would Alistair agree to deliver the slaves? He had no experience in such things. According to his own description, delivering slaves to the coast of Senegal was impossible to do."

Hanna wiped off the ring her drink had left on the table.

"Then, how did he do it?"

"I got my answer today. By incredible coincidence, this morning, I got Alistair's written account of this event. You see, Alistair, just as the ancestor of the restaurant owner Issa, you described, was trying to atone for this evil deed all his life. So, he wrote a draft of a kind of confession to a clergyman at the end of his days, where he described his thought process. He reasoned that, yes, it would be difficult to get slaves, but he remembered what his assistant Smith had told him recently. This assistant was the man in the translated pages you mentioned."

"Yes, the one with the 'flaming orange hair,'" said Hanna.

"Smith met a Senegalese man named Issa when he was in St. Louis looking over the IL&R books. Smith didn't tell Issa who he worked for. This was customary at that time. Over time Smith and Issa had become friendly, and Issa told him that he desperately wanted to leave St. Louis with his fiancée and get married in France. Issa's business was helping chieftains trade products, like Gum Arabic, with the Westerners. He was making money and had been saving for a long time, but it wasn't enough to settle in France.

"He was looking for a well-paid project so that he could fulfill his dream. Issa once told Smith that it didn't make much sense to stop the transatlantic slave trade since slavery was still widely practiced within Africa. He didn't know how slaves were treated in the West but thought it couldn't be worse than in Africa. Their life here was awful, he said. Within tribes, they called their slaves 'cattle slaves.' They were used as currency between the kingdoms."

"That is terrible!" exclaimed Hanna.

"Because of Issa's desire for a well-paid job, Alistair thought he could use him to obtain the slaves for the bet. Issa had the contacts, the experience, and was audacious enough to do such a project."

"And what about Haddock?" asked Hanna.

"Haddock wrote to his brother that he figured the investment would be workable. He didn't believe Alistair would be able to get the slaves to the coast, so he wouldn't need to transport them to America.

"He would use a trusted person to act as an intermediary who would arrange the trip in his own name. He had just such a person in mind. This person would ostensibly rent a ship from Haddock and arrange to pay for the crew and the supplies. He would then retrofit the vessel to hold the slaves. And he would do it so the ship could also be able to take on the cargo of Gum Arabic from Senegal. This person would have to do the retrofitting secretively, but Haddock knew it was possible.

"In the highly improbable event that Alistair would deliver on his side of the bargain, the ship would be ready. After preparing the ship, this person would get ahold of a captain in Mobile who used to run slaves in the Caribbean. Haddock was sure this captain could be persuaded to make this trip for a handsome fee.

"The crew and the captain would be expensive, given the dangerous journey. On the other hand, Haddock reasoned he could make a considerable profit off the proceeds of the cargo sale, be it Gum Arabic or slaves."

Tensbury got up, "Hanna, I need to walk around for a minute. Do you mind?"

"Of course not. I need a break too."

His lanky frame seemed a little stiff as he approached the door and left the room. She looked around the conference room. It was styled in the same hues as the anteroom, except here, the colors were more pronounced. There was an occasional dark red detail here and there. Very tasteful, she thought.

She felt sorry for this man. What a shock it must have been to find out your ancestor, who brought the all-important title to the family, wasn't who you thought he was. She understood him.

Soon enough, the door opened, and Tensbury returned.

"Thanks for waiting. I had to stretch my legs."

"I was just looking around here at the décor, and I think it's lovely."

"It's cliché, but it's my wife's doing. She's good at those things." Tensbury sat down.

"Now, let me tell you the worst part, and the final reason, I know, Alistair lived his life in constant search for some form of absolution."

"What could be worse than agreeing to purchase, transport, and sell a hundred people!" Hanna exclaimed.

Then she softened her voice. "What happened to the wager?"

"Yes, what happened to the wager." Tensbury pulled the other document in front of him but then put it back. "This part, I don't need to read. It's etched in my mind."

Tensbury resumed telling Hanna about the events.

"Alistair managed to procure the slaves with Smith's and Issa's help. Smith hired Issa to meet the captain of the American ship. Issa told Smith that he knew just the route to bring the slaves to the coast and the place to load them without being detected. When Issa met the captain, he conveyed the location, date, and time to load the slaves.

"Then Issa went to one of the tribal chieftains with whom he had an agreement to buy one hundred slaves. He led the slaves to the point of the rendezvous.

"Alistair writes, Smith arranged with Issa that he would only give him the remaining three-quarters of the money once he saw the slaves loaded.

"If anything went wrong, he would not acknowledge the deal."

"Smith watched the process, sitting on a hill overlooking the loading of slaves. As planned, the slaves were delivered on time. No-one stopped them. They were loaded onto the ship, and money changed hands. Issa and Smith returned to St. Louis together. If anyone asked, Issa was to say he took Smith on a sightseeing tour south of St. Louis."

"Was Alistair in St. Louis while this was happening?"

"No. Several days later, Alistair was on his way north from the Cape to London to receive his peerage. Alistair's ship barely missed the storm. Near the Senegal coast, he saw a wrecked ship and African bodies in the water, shackled to beams of wood. They didn't find any survivors. Alistair knew immediately that this must have been the tragedy he and Haddock had set in motion."

Hanna sat quietly in shock.

After almost two thousand years, when most people in the pagan world didn't fret much about the lives of slaves, these two men of high social standing got into a pissing match that killed over a hundred people.

How could this happen? If it was today, could something remotely similar occur? Does it? Not here in the Western world but elsewhere. Yes, it very well can!

"Alistair had to live with this horror haunting him for the rest of his life. From the draft of a letter to his vicar, I know that at the end, he hoped God would somehow absolve him of this sin. He tried to redeem himself by engaging in multiple philanthropic activities for Africans, both in Africa and at home."

Tensbury looked haggard. He had deep dark circles around his eyes, and his face was grey.

"What about Haddock? How did he learn about the end of this horrible affair?"

"Alistair sent him a message which arrived in 1860. He said that he, Alistair, fulfilled his part of the wager. However, he recognized Haddock couldn't perform his part because of the storm and the issuing disaster. Therefore, nobody wins – everyone loses."

"And Haddock?"

"Haddock, as you can imagine, was also distraught about the whole affair, and was deeply aware of what he had done. He was responsible for the death of over a hundred people. The next year, he wanted to do something to atone for his role in all of this. I know from the notes his descendant found, that right before the civil war he got involved with financing the runaway slaves to get from the South to the Northern cities in

America."

They both sat quietly for a while, each immersed in their own thoughts.

"I plan to shred these documents the minute I get home tonight. I don't want my sons to be tainted by this tragedy."

"I can understand that Sir."

"But thank you for listening to me."

Hanna turned around and looked through the window. It was getting dark outside.

Her thoughts flew to Signe's diary and Uncle Noah. She saw nothing in the diary pages that could point to who or what might have caused his death. Uncle Noah must truly only have wanted them to walk in Signe's footsteps, as they had planned all along.

She though, that judging by the fact that the British men appeared everywhere she went, and the fact that someone was in her computer, meant that some Tory or Labor affiliate, or both, were looking for something in the diary pages and in Africa.

In the diary – it's not there, in Africa – I couldn't find it. Mans said Uncle Noah died of natural causes. But some rogue Tory affiliate, while searching for the pages in his home, to preempt Labor, could have stumbled on him, and inadvertently killed him. I suppose I'll never know who.

And what about the Signe story? Would Tensbury want to hear it tonight, or would it be too much? I'm leaving tomorrow, so it must be tonight.

CHAPTER 8

Hanna turned back to face Tensbury. "As I mentioned," she started. "Our ancestors crossed paths in 1859. I have the translated pages from Signe's diary here on my laptop." Hanna pulled out her laptop. "I put them in one document. Here are the relevant pages. I am going to read from the diary, Sir.,

Dear Diary,

It's wonderful to be back on the Ingeborg! Although I enjoyed St. Louis, there is nothing like the seas. It worries me if I will ever be happy on land again. But that is truly silly. I can't become a sailor, can I!? I laugh as I write this. The trip on the Ingeborg has been exhilarating, and other than the storm, beautiful. To watch the ocean as the sun sets, sinking into the horizon, is something I can't describe and will never forget. Now I'm on my way to a whole new life. I already experienced so much of Africa in St. Louis and can't wait to see South Africa! I know it will be very different.

Dear Diary,

There is now another passenger on board. His name is Leo Tensbury, and he's the son of the gentleman I met at the governor's dinner party when I first arrived.

He approached me on deck the first day just as we were leaving the Senegal River delta. He has the good looks of his father but seems very shy. He told me he is twenty-three years old. He is traveling from England to South Africa, where his father has a ship repairs business. His father has asked him to come and work with him since he plans to expand the business.

On his way, he stopped in St. Louis to see his father's other business, the Gum Arabic export company, IL&R. To his surprise, his father was in St. Louis as well, on his way to London.

Ingeborg was sailing to the Cape sooner than the ship Leo was waiting for. His father was leaving for London within days and procured a passage for Leo on the Ingeborg.

It's incredible how much faster you become friendly here on the seas! We have begun an exciting conversation. He is very knowledgeable. We have talked about everything. The fact that there has been a rapprochement between Britain and France, and that they together declared war on China.

We talked about the fact that there is now a woman in the General Medical Council's Register in London.

This is interesting to me since I believe women should have equal rights to men in all areas of life. We share a love of horses. I told him how I like to hunt on my dear horse Norsk, and he told me about the British hunts he participated in. They are so different from my experiences.

He has a strong voice despite his shyness, which seems almost to have disappeared. Perhaps it was just that he was uncomfortable being alone with a young woman on a ship for such a long voyage.

Dear Diary,

I have not applied myself to my English studies. That's not very smart. I want to be able to speak English well when we arrive. I have been so committed to the books throughout the voyage. But I do like to socialize, and it's lovely to have someone interesting to talk to.

You know the old Signe isn't one to talk about feelings, but I have shared a lot with Leo. I've spoken about my happy childhood and how it hurt me to leave Pappa. I told him how I insisted on taking this trip despite all the opposition at home. I described my fiancé Lars and told Leo how I have been waiting for him the whole year he has been away. Now we will get married in South Africa.

Leo's life is fascinating! He is the oldest son and spent his younger years at a school called Eton. He explained how boys live there and go home on holidays. I can't imagine living away from Pappa during my school years, but he explained it is common for many in Britain. Then he went to Oxford University. Of course, I have heard of Oxford. There he graduated with a degree. He studied mathematics, history, and natural science.

To prepare himself for his father's ship repairs business, he has spent time studying the trade in different Port of London wharves. He speaks very respectfully of his father.

Those are the first entries." Hanna halted but didn't look up. "And here are the next,

Dear Diary,

It's been a long time since I wrote. I have been too busy. I'm a different person from the old Signe who sailed from Kristiansand. You better believe it. I think differently. I believe I speak differently, and I know I'm prepared to live a different life.

Spending all these days with Leo, exploring various subjects, has given me more education than any old textbook at home could give me. His knowledge of history, for example, is deep and I am so interested!

I have to say, I am feeling an attachment to Leo that I never felt to anyone else. Leo and I have stayed away from the others. Even from Captain Taraldson,

That was at the beginning of their relationship." Hanna scrolled forward in her document.
"And another entry,

Dear Diary,

From the moment I wake up until I go to sleep, I think of him. Of him! How can this be? What is happening? I even dream of him. All I know is that I want to be with him every minute of the day, and I know he feels the same. I'm not sure what

is going on, but it doesn't matter to me.

I'm out here in the middle of the Atlantic, and that's a fact. There is no one to look over my shoulder to tell me what is acceptable and what isn't. Oh, by the way, Captain Taraldson ignores us completely.

You can tell she's falling in love."

Tensbury pulled himself up in his chair. Just then, Hanna's phone rang. She fished it out of her pocket and checked who was calling.

"I'm sorry, Sir, this is my boss. Have to take it." Hanna stood up and left the room.

CHAPTER 9

"Deepak," said Hanna. "Thanks for calling. I wanted to let you know that John called last night."

"Anything special?"

"He told me the investors might be pulling out."

She could hear Deepak breathing.

"If they do, the deal goes south, Hanna."

"I know. I wanted to catch you ASAP, so you could give them a call. Find out what's going on and hopefully turn this thing around."

"Ok, I'll stay up late and call them first thing tomorrow morning their time. How are things otherwise? Or maybe I shouldn't ask."

"No, it's ok. Still need to button up my uncle's things. I plan on coming home next week."

She knew she would be taking more time off than initially planned, but she didn't care to explain. She snuck into the restroom and then returned to the conference room.

"Sorry." She sat down at the table. "Please let me continue, Sir. Here is the next entry,

Dear Diary,

I knew it would happen, and it did. Leo kissed me

today in my cabin.

Kissing Leo is so different from kissing Lars or any other boy when I was growing up. When he kisses me, I feel 'taken.' Yes, 'taken' is the best word I can think of. I feel exposed to the world, and I love it. You know how strong I am. I have always been in control. These feelings I have for Leo are like a shock to me. I'm not afraid of what will happen. I'll take each day as it comes, and I won't think about tomorrow.

Leo and I spend all our time together. We walk on deck and watch the sunsets. It's my favorite time of the day. They are glorious and seeing them with him beside me makes them even more so. He holds me tight, and I feel like I have entered heaven. We continue to talk, although less now since we are kissing so much. I love to kiss him. He has the most wonderful mouth. His lips are soft, and his mouth strokes my cheeks as he caresses my ears. I never thought there was such delight in having another person near me. After dinner, we retire to my cabin. It's larger than his.

I'll have to skip the next entry. Too personal."

Hanna appeared to have reached a culminating point. It was uncomfortable reading this in the presence of Lord Tensbury.

"So, they had an affair on board."

"Yes, they did, Sir." Hanna looked at Tensbury across the desk.

Tensbury crossed his arms over his chest. "Go on."

"This next page is too intimate for me to read, she repeated herself." Her cheeks were burning. "I'll go to the one right after,

Dear Diary,

Leo and I and have discussed the future. He has asked me to marry him, and, of course, I said yes. I want nothing more than to live my life with this man and to bear his children. I fantasize about how we will arrange our home. How many children we will have. How they will mature with us. How we will grow old together! It aches inside me every time I see him, thinking that this secluded bliss will soon be over. But I know it is only the beginning of our journey together! Of course, I'm breaking my betrothal with Lars. I will have to tell him as soon as I arrive.

Yesterday was Leo's birthday, and I didn't have a gift for him. He says it doesn't matter. That I'm his gift!

Let's say she was very much in love," Hanna paused.

She moved past a few pages. "The next entries are very relevant,

Dear Diary,

Leo's father gave him a letter. He was supposed to open it on his birthday. He just came to my cabin to read it. In it, his father explained that he believes his contribution to the country, both militarily and economically, has impressed the Queen. Therefore, he is to present himself in London so she can grant him the title of Baron. He had not expected this and is very proud.

Leo's father said that as Baron, he becomes a member of the House of Lords. This is a very important and prestigious role in the government. He said that he must adhere to all appropriate social conventions and will be highly scrutinized

by others. So, all family activities must be aboveboard - social as well as business. His father told him that Leo should not speak about this matter until he returned to South Africa. Now, Leo told me, but he knows he can depend on me to keep it secret.

Dear Diary,

Now comes the scary part. In the letter, his father asked two things of Leo.

First, he is to learn the ship-repairs business in depth. And second, he must maintain and improve his father's relationship with the Dankworth family in Cape Town. Mr. Dankworth owns a firm with ties to a medium-sized bank in London. His firm is one of the very few that provides some limited banking services in Cape Town. This firm could lend his father money to expand his business.

Leo's father wants to buy out his competitor, as well as begin to provide ship maintenance supplies and some dry goods to the ships in the port.

According to Leo's father, the Dankworth family is expecting Leo's visit. They have a nineteen-year-old daughter, and his father wants him to befriend this girl so that the two families can get close. Only for three or four months – till he is back, he said.

His father said she is pretty, but Leo is free to do whatever he wants when he comes back. Through her, Leo should build a strong relationship with Mr. Dankworth and talk to him about what he learned about the banking business at Oxford.

Leo must impress him. His father reminds him that the tasks he is asking of Leo are critical. He ends by saying that he trusts Leo will do a good job.

So that's it. That's what his father asks of him. To court another girl for four months! I know that Leo does not refuse his father's strong requests.

It is not an unreasonable request, but his father doesn't know about us. So, yes, I'm scared. How will this impact our future? I am too shocked tonight to go on any longer. I have to sleep and hope things look better in the morning.

Here their lives changed," said Hanna.

CHAPTER 10

"This was obviously a bitter moment for them." Hanna stopped, feeling awkward.

Tensbury was listening attentively.

After a moment, she said, "I'll continue,

Dear Diary,

I'm confused. We have talked about our situation and decided that I will return to Norway for half a year and then Leo will send for me and we will get married. Doing this will allow him to uphold his obligations to his father. Learn the business and befriend that girl.

I hate the idea of him seeing another girl. What if he falls in love with her? Well, I don't believe so. We are too much in love. But this is not so easy. I must say I tremble inside. It has added a painful disruption to our plans.

What will we do apart from each other for six months? The idea of returning to Norway alone is awful. How will I explain the feelings that have caused me to make such a life change?

Everything was set for me to marry Lars, and now I have decided to shift my entire life to a destiny with Leo. I look at him and know that he is worried about me. I know he feels guilty, putting me through this ordeal. What about when he finally asks for me to come? Will his father object? Will he have to disregard the wishes of his father, whom he respects so much?

Leo, of course, says his father will let him make his own decisions. That he's a just and respectable man and would not cause his son to suffer in the important decision of choosing a wife. This situation is constantly on my mind. It has interrupted the joy I was experiencing before.

Sir, the following entries are principally the reason why I wanted to meet you." Hanna took a sip of her lukewarm drink. "I'll go on,

Dear Diary,

I am scared. My bleeding has not come. It has now been ten days since the day it should have started. I'm always regular to the day, so I'm afraid of what it means. Also, my breasts have changed. They are more sensitive now and feel heavier.

You know, I never had much, to begin with, so I certainly notice it.

Yes, I'm scared. I'm tired of being scared. Remember when Frida became pregnant? As her best friend, I know everything that occurred throughout her pregnancy. Every little sign.

Captain Taraldson says we'll arrive in three days. Oh, what should I do? I <u>know</u> I'm pregnant. I just feel it.

Dear Diary,

We will arrive in two days. I have thought about the situation deeply. I absolutely can't face a pregnancy out of wedlock, and Leo can't marry me right now. It would violate his father's request. He needs to court that girl. As part of the Tensbury family, Leo is to be held to the highest standard, as his father says in the letter.

Staying in Cape Town, pregnant, and alone is crazy. I even considered that maybe we could marry in secret and I could go home to have the baby. But that is nonsense. We could never keep something like that hidden. I know Cape Town is very small.

No, I have thought about it and thought about it, and there is only one thing to do, and it breaks my heart. I'm going to sever my relationship with Leo and marry Lars. Lars and I have known each other since school, and we have always been very close. I'll tell Leo my conscience won't let me break my engagement to him.

Leo won't believe me, but I have to say something. I'll have to stay strong! Maybe I am wrong, but I can't take the chance. I love him so much, that I'll never tell him the true story. That's how much I love him!

Now, there are many things I must do. I must convince Lars to marry me right away. I'm pretty sure I can insist since we have been away from each other for over a year. I shudder at thinking about what I'm going to have to go through. My only peace of mind now is thinking that I will be able to look at Leo's and my dear child every day and remember our love.

Dear Diary,

Writing these pages about Leo and me has been a wonderful way for me to put down these amazing times and experiences. But they can't remain in my book. I thought hard about what I must do. I'm going to tear all this out, package it up and send it to Agnes. I'll ask her to put the package in a trust with a bank with instructions to deliver it to the oldest person in the Arnol family in one hundred years.

My experiences are so wonderful, I can't bury them. Besides, it is only fair to tell my descendants who their real ancestor was.

After one hundred years, Lars and I, and Leo's and my child will be no more, so there will be no one left to hurt. These will be my last words here.

Sir, that's where these diary pages end," said Hanna.

"I was in awe of Signe all my life, and the stories about her adventures were always alive in my family. She was heralded as this brave, ambitious woman. Finding these pages from her diary, describing this love affair, disappointed me in a way. On the other hand, I am happy that she was able to experience love for the first time in her life. I was just surprised. Astounded is a better word."

Tensbury sighed. "Then what happens? The story doesn't end there, does it?"

"No. From her diary for the following year, I know that she gave birth to a child about seven or eight months after her wedding. Everyone thought the baby was premature when it was born, but she knew it was born to term. People marveled at the boy being so well developed and healthy." Hanna stopped for a minute.

"That child is my ancestor. So, we are, in fact, related," she said, with a guarded smile. She didn't know how he was going to react to this information.

She reached down into her computer bag, extracted something, and gave it to him.

"Please take a look at this picture. It's a photo of my father and my uncle. It was taken some time ago. I think there's an uncanny resemblance between my father and your son, Andrew, don't you think?"

Tensbury studied the photo for a long time. He looked up, nodded, and gave it back to her. What a day it must have been for him. He looked vulnerable, and she almost wanted to reach out and stroke his hand.

That would not be appropriate. Europe isn't like the US. At home, we can be much freer with our emotions.

Tensbury stared at the wall over her shoulder. After a while, he said, "Hanna, it's been quite a night. The story I have told you threatens my son's bid for PM. So does this, in a way. The election is tomorrow, and it would be terrible if any of this information got out. Have you told anyone else?"

"No, I haven't. My uncle read it, but he's dead."

"But you had it translated into English?"

"Yes, but I sent the pages to three different translation services. I split the pages up, so no one service has coherent information."

It unlikely, but some curious translator could have put something together. Especially considering it was somewhat salacious in the end. Alistair Tensbury's name was mentioned, and Andrew Tensbury is in the news. I don't want to bring that up.

"Where is this diary now?"

"It's in my room."

"May I have a copy?"

For some reason, she hadn't foreseen this request, so she took time to respond. The diary contained Signe's personal feelings and descriptions of her love for Leo. It also held her subsequent experiences with Lars.

"No, Sir," she said resolutely. "This diary is written by

Signe and must stay in the family. And the family means me. There's no one else. At least for now. At some point, these diaries may pass on to my child, but I expect that won't be for quite some time." A little smile touched her mouth.

"I will not repeat any of this to anyone. I don't think my progeny would want to bring it to light either."

He nodded his head. "So, we are related," he mused. "I have to introduce you to my boys. But after the election. I hope you'll be back here in London soon?"

"Yes, I believe I will." Hanna thought about the deal that might fall through. She might not return to London for a long time.

Tensbury stood up, shrugged into his jacket, and put the letters and his tie in his briefcase.

"I'll have my driver take you back to the hotel, and I'll walk to my flat. It'll feel good after this evening."

She picked up her backpack and joined him at the head of the table by the door. He gave her a warm hug and then escorted her into the anteroom. He instructed his admin to arrange for his driver to take her back to her hotel.

Then he walked out the door to the elevator, waved goodbye, and was gone.

Two Months Later

"Andrew, over here." Lord Tensbury waved at Andrew. Tensbury and his oldest son Samuel had been waiting for half an hour, and he was late, but that could be understood. The Tories had taken the majority of the seats in Parliament, and he was now the PM. Protection officers had already combed the place and now situated themselves around the area and where Andrew took a seat.

"Thanks for setting this up, Dad. I really needed a break. And it's nice to see you, big brother." Andrew gave his brother a hug. He sat down next to Samuel. They were in the booth furthest to the back of a little non-descript pub not far from Westminster.

Tensbury put his hand over Andrew's and squeezed it.

"It's wonderful to have both of you here. What has it been? A couple of months at least, since your campaign, Andrew." Tensbury smiled at both of them.

"So, how is 10 Downing Street?" asked Samuel.

"This minute, it's pretty quiet, and Jessica is waiting for me to get home, so this will be a short one."

The waitress came over, and Andrew joined his dad and brother in a pint.

"How are you, Samuel? How's it going with those undergrad girls throwing themselves at you?" He grinned. Samuel was the least likely professor in the world to look outside his marriage, and his brother knew it. A rather shy, plain man, he was tall like his father and his brother. Otherwise, he was different in many ways. Andrew had the looks and the passionate personality of his father, and he was always the one who dominated a conversation.

Andrew didn't get a response. Samuel just blushed. Andrew turned his attention back to his dad, who was reveling in seeing his two boys together. Tensbury loved them both, and this sort of bantering had gone on throughout their childhoods.

"And Dad. Busy with the business and House of Lords?" asked Andrew.

"Very busy. There's an uptick in demand on the business side, and there's never a dull moment in the House. Sitting on the Science and Technology Committee gives me a unique view of the technological advancements and challenges taking place. You would love this kind of thing."

"Well," Andrew sighed. "Right now, I have a different type of 'thing' cut out for me."

"After one month, you must be pretty used to the life over there. Is it as challenging as they say, son? I'm not going to ask about specific policy issues. Thought we would leave that out for tonight."

"Thanks. But yes, it's challenging. There never seems to be enough time in the day. It's a blessing that I got Thomas to join me as Chief of Staff."

"Well, that's excellent. How did you manage to get him to leave his consulting firm?"

"His second in command runs it for now" Andrew drank his brew.

"Honestly, without Thomas' support, I'm not sure how I'd make it. He keeps Downing Street moving smoothly." Andrew stopped.

Then he asked, "How's mum? I can't believe I haven't seen you two these past months. You have to tell her how much I miss her and that I'll make a point of getting out to

Kent."

He looked at Samuel. "And when did you see mum last? Been a while, right?"

"I have an idea, sons. I'll have her come stay here at the flat, and we can all have dinner. She'd love to cook for your families."

"We'll have to do it before my trip to Geneva. I leave next week Tuesday."

"Sounds like you have a lot to prepare for. I'll have her come down this weekend and call you two."

Tensbury looked at Andrew. He was proud of his son. He looked tired, though.

"Do you get enough sleep, son? Sorry, now it's the dad talking."

"No, I don't, but that's how life is going to be, and I better get used to it. Don't worry. I'm young. As they all say in the press."

Samuel turned to his dad. "Sorry for Aunt Sally. She was so good to us."

Andrew added. "A wonderful human being. So sorry to lose her."

"Yes, she loved you."

They were quiet.

Tensbury thought for a while. He looked at both of them.

"Sons, I have something to tell you."

"Don't make it sound so ominous, Dad," said Andrew.

"I didn't mean to, but it's kind of on the serious side."

"Alright, what is it?" said Samuel.

"Right before the election, I was approached by this woman named Hanna Arnol. She had the most interesting story that involves our family and hers."

"Yes...?" they both said at the same time.

"She had found an old diary written by her ancestor in the 1800s. The diary shows her and us related. So, she's a new member of our extended family and a very interesting one, I must add."

"What is the diary story?"

"Don't be impatient, Andrew. I'll tell you when she comes to visit us." Tensbury took a sip from his glass.

"Very mysterious. When do we get to meet this woman? Would be fun," said Samuel.

"She's American and only comes to London on business. Her company has offices here, so I assume she'll be here in the not-too-distant future. She promised to call me. I think she's as interested in meeting you as you are meeting her."

"Sorry to cut you short, Dad. I have to leave. Jessica is waiting for me, probably with dinner ready. I miss you and mum. This job just doesn't give me a lot of time for private life."

"I'll set up dinner for this weekend. You can both get away, right?"

They both nodded.

"We'll spend some quality time together then," Tensbury continued.

Andrew squeezed his brother's shoulder as he got up. Simon Tensbury got out of his chair and hugged Andrew. They watched him walk away with the guards surrounding him.

Tensbury's new glass came, and he stared blindly over Samuel's shoulder. He remembered the tumultuous week before the election. He could not be sure there was not another source of the tale, and that it would not be brought to light in the future.

The End

Thanks for Reading

Follow Kate Backford

 Facebook.com/KateBackford

 Twitter.com/KateBackford

About the Author

Kate Backford grew up living in many places around the world and speaks several languages. After an MBA and a rewarding career in Silicon Valley, Kate now focuses on writing. At other times, she enjoys swimming and hiking with her husband along the Gulf of Mexico on the West Coast of Florida. She is working on a series with Hanna Arnol, a Silicon Valley executive, traveling on business, solving mysteries in different parts of the world. She aspires to combine real-world experience and knowledge to create inspiring characters within interesting, intricate mysteries.

Made in the USA
Middletown, DE
04 February 2022

60165537R00213